CYANIDE
IN THE SUN

*And Other Stories of
Summertime Crime*

CYANIDE IN THE SUN

And Other Stories of Summertime Crime

edited by

MARTIN EDWARDS

This collection first published in 2025 by
The British Library
96 Euston Road
London NW1 2DB
bl.uk

CONTENTS

INTRODUCTION

We all enjoy taking a break every now and then, but sometimes getting away from it all can be murder. This book gathers vintage short mystery fiction with a holiday theme. The sheer variety of stories in this collection illustrates the fact that detective writers relish writing holiday mysteries (as I do myself) just as much as crime fans enjoy reading them. In this branch of the genre, authors have the freedom to place their characters in unfamiliar settings, where they may soon find themselves disconcerted by troubling events, far from the comfortable security of their home life. The potential for conflict and mystification is enormous.

Ten years have passed since the publication of my first holiday-related anthology for the British Library's Crime Classics series, *Resorting to Murder*. When introducing that book, I discussed various examples of this sub-genre of crime writing, but there are many more that deserve to be remembered. Space allows me to talk about just a few of them.

A very early example that has stood the test of time was written by Wilkie Collins at the age of twenty-eight. In 1852, his friend Charles Dickens published a story by Collins in the magazine *Household Words*, in which the narrator recounts a terrifying experience during a visit to Paris: "We were both young men then, and lived, I am afraid, rather a wild life in the delightful city of our sojourn." This story, "A Terribly Strange Bed", later included in Collins' collection *After Dark*, may have been an apprentice work in some respects, but it was gripping and memorable enough to achieve enduring popularity. Much-anthologised, it has been adapted for film (in Poland) and television, as an episode of *Orson Welles' Great Mysteries* in 1973.

Collins knew and loved Paris, and many notable holiday mysteries have been written by authors who were extremely well-travelled. Their experiences overseas have often formed the backdrop to mysterious tales. Arthur Conan Doyle was a prime example. His early story "J. Habbakuk Jephson's Statement", published in 1884, pre-dates the creation of Sherlock Holmes and offers a fictional explanation of a famous real-life mystery in the form of an account by Jephson of what happened when, hoping to recuperate from a severe cough, he took a trip to Europe. Deciding to sail to Lisbon, he has the misfortune to book a passage on the ill-fated *Mary Celeste*.

In the twentieth century, opportunities for holidays in Britain and overseas were no longer confined to the privileged few. As it usually does, crime fiction reflected this development. Let me give a few illustrations of mysteries inspired by the evolution of the hotel industry and the development of walking, coach, and sea tours, and trips in which holiday-makers have the chance to visit a variety of locations.

A hotel may aspire to be a "home from home", but the rapidly shifting populations to be found in hotels offer rich possibilities for unexpected encounters and criminal shenanigans. However luxuriously appointed they may be, they provide an essentially unstable environment. Can we be *absolutely* sure that we haven't booked in to the room next door to a murderer? If British crime writers needed any encouragement to explore the criminal potential of hotel life, they received it in the form of two sensational murder cases of the 1920s.

In July 1923, the socialite Marguerite Marie Alibert and her husband Ali Fahmy Bey arrived in London on holiday. They stayed at the Savoy Hotel, along with their entourage, and after watching (ironically) a performance of the operetta *The Merry Widow*, they returned to the hotel and had an argument, which ended when Alibert shot her husband. She was tried for murder but "the Great Defender", Edward Marshall Hall, secured her acquittal, and she lived to a ripe old age.

Less fortunate was Sidney Harry Fox, who was hanged for murdering his mother. Her body was found in the Hotel Metropole at Margate in October 1929. There had been a fierce blaze in room 66, where Rosalie Fox and her son had been staying together. The initial ruling was death by misadventure, but when Sidney tried to cash in her insurance policy (which was due to expire imminently) the police became suspicious.

Leading crime novelists from "the Golden Age of Murder" between the wars wrote a wide variety of mysteries which made good use of a hotel setting. J. J. Connington's *Mystery at Lynden Sands* (1928) is an ingenious whodunit in the traditional style, whereas J. Jefferson Farjeon's *The Z Murders* (1932), which has been republished as a British Library Crime Classic, is a thriller about a crazy serial killer who shoots his first victim at a railway hotel—where the rapid movement of people enables the villain to commit his crime without being observed.

Murder Mars the Tour (1936) is an early example of the murder-on-tour story and was the first crime novel published by the classicist Kathleen Freeman under the name Mary Fitt. The narrator is encouraged by his brother to go on a walking tour of Europe with several members of the same club. The trip is described atmospherically, even if the plot is a little thin. The British-born Hugh Wheeler, who emigrated to the United States, and wrote under the names Q. Patrick and Patrick Quentin (initially with Richard Webb and later solo) was responsible for a novella, *Passport to Murder* aka *Mrs. B.'s Black Sheep* (1950), which follows Mrs. Black's Tour for Girls from Paris to Italy. It's a characteristically snappy and ingeniously constructed mystery, and the same is true of the Julian Symons story which is included as the final story in the collection you're holding.

The most renowned murder-during-a-coach-trip novel is Agatha Christie's *Nemesis* (1967), which sees Miss Marple given the task of joining a tour around stately homes and gardens with a view to tracking down a killer. Christie set several of her novels and short stories around holidays, with examples ranging from superb full-length mysteries such as *Peril at End House* (1932) and *Evil Under the Sun* (1941), to the excellent short story "Triangle at Rhodes" and the rather less well-known "Problem at Pollensa Bay".

Sea cruises also provide the "closed circle" of suspects that bring out the best in many detective novelists. *S.S. Murder* (1933) by Q. Patrick is an enjoyable puzzle told in epistolary form, while Freeman Wills Crofts' love of cruising is reflected in *Found Floating* (1937), in which a family party goes on a trip to the Mediterranean. Inevitably, the most famous cruise mystery came from Christie's pen. *Death on the Nile* (also from 1937) is one of the masterpieces of Golden Age detective fiction; the story has been adapted for stage, radio, television, film (twice), graphic novel, and video game.

The possibilities are almost endless. After the Second World War, travel overseas became increasingly popular and affordable, resulting in a number of good holiday mysteries, such as *Crossed Skis* (1952) by Carol Carnac aka E. C. R. Lorac, which was dedicated to members of a group with whom the author went skiing herself, *Tour de Force* (1955) by Christianna Brand, and *A Telegram from Le Touquet* (1956) by John Bude, all of which have appeared in the Crime Classics series.

This collection serves, I hope, to show the wide range of opportunities for murderous misdemeanours during the holiday season. We have contributions from authors such as Christianna Brand, Celia Fremlin, and Michael Gilbert, who are far from forgotten, as well as from such truly obscure names as the mysterious Christopher Bobbett, whose entertaining story was first anthologised almost a century ago.

The stories offer a wide range of settings and they are also varied in length. The Julian Symons' contribution, for instance, might almost count as a novella. Conversely, there are quite a few "short-shorts", which generally depend on a single plot point. This form enjoyed particular popularity in the 1950s when the *Evening Standard*, an excellent market at the time, published scores of brief mysteries. Five of the stories in this book—those by Andrew Garve, Victor Canning, Nicolas Bentley, Anthony Gilbert, and Michael Innes—were presented as part of a group under the general title "Murder on Holiday" in the *Evening Standard* in July 1956.

As ever, I'd like to thank those who worked on this book at the British Library, as well as the friends who made suggestions about the contents, notably Jamie Sturgeon (who supplied me with copies of one or two particularly hard-to-find stories), Nigel Moss, and John Cooper.

If you're reading this collection on holiday, I hope you enjoy it—but keep your eyes peeled for sinister strangers prowling around your resort or hotel corridors, and if you're travelling in a group, do watch out for your fellow passengers. They might not be all they seem...

MARTIN EDWARDS
www.martinedwardsbooks.com

A NOTE FROM THE PUBLISHER

The original short stories reprinted in the British Library classic fiction series were written and published in a period ranging across the nineteenth and twentieth centuries. There are many elements of these stories which continue to entertain modern readers; however, in some cases there are also uses of language, instances of stereotyping and some attitudes expressed by narrators or characters which may not be endorsed by the publishing standards of today. We acknowledge therefore that some elements in the stories selected for reprinting may continue to make uncomfortable reading for some of our audience. With this series British Library Publishing aims to offer a new readership a chance to read some of the rare material of the British Library's collections in an affordable format, to enjoy their merits and to look back into the worlds of the past two centuries as portrayed by their writers. It is not possible to separate these stories from the history of their writing and as such the following stories are presented as they were originally published with only minor edits made for consistency of style and sense. We welcome feedback from our readers, which can be sent to the following address:

British Library Publishing
The British Library
96 Euston Road
London, NW1 2DB
United Kingdom

KILL AND CURE

Guy Cullingford

Guy Cullingford was the pseudonym of Constance Lindsay Taylor, the married name of Alice Constance Dowdy, who was born in Dovercourt, Essex, in 1907. She was educated at Malvern College and worked as a librarian in Ipswich prior to marrying a solicitor, Maurice Lindsay Taylor, in 1930. The couple moved to Chester, where Maurice was deputy town clerk; a fictionalised version of the cathedral city is the location of Cullingford's historical mystery *Framed for Hanging* (1956). Subsequently, they lived in London and in Bognor Regis. Her enjoyable first novel, *Murder with Relish*, was published in 1948 as by C. Lindsay Taylor. However, her subsequent fiction appeared under the name Guy Cullingford; her publishers preferred her to use a male name, although in later years she couldn't recall how or why she chose that particular pseudonym. After a lengthy period living in an old farmhouse near Colchester, she spent some time living in a flat in the Barbican (the setting of her final novel, *Bother at the Barbican*, in 1991), before settling in Scotland.

Her most famous novel is *Post Mortem* (1953), in which the ghost of an author investigates his own murder. She was by no means a prolific novelist, and although she was elected to membership of the Detection Club in 1961 (her particular friends among the members including H. R. F. Keating and Michael Underwood), several of her books have long been out of print. This is a pity, for novels such as *Brink of Disaster* (1964) and *The Stylist* (1968) are interesting and unusual. Her determination as a novelist to avoid formula militated against commercial success—which

no doubt explains why she spent most of the 1970s mining the more
lucrative ground of television scriptwriting, with one of her TV plays,
Sarah, winning an award at a Monte Carlo festival—but it means that
readers interested in originality of approach will find much to enjoy in
her novels. The same is true of her short stories; this one first appeared
in a Crime Writers' Association anthology, *Planned Departures*, in 1958.

"**A**S I SEE IT, WE SHALL HAVE PLENTY OF TIME TO KILL," SAID A prim female voice.

A pair of masculine hands twitched convulsively upon the papery edges of *The Times* outspread for cover.

"Then I suggest," said the second female voice, "a brisk walk to the end of the esplanade and back. After that perhaps we might buy a few little souvenirs before taking our letter of introduction to the vicar."

The hands relaxed.

Just what the doctor ordered, thought Rex Burnham with a wry grin.

Although an acknowledged master of the cliché, even he sometimes thought literally. Two days ago he had been huddling on his clothes in the doctor's consulting room with that sheepish yet relieved feeling which accompanies a thorough medical examination.

Nervously he had asked: "Well?"

The doctor, who was also a personal friend, was scribbling away merrily at a small pad. He tore off a sheet and replied with an absent air:

"Eh? Oh! There's nothing wrong organically. As sound as a bell, my dear fellow! As to these other symptoms… these nightmares and—um—hallucinations, hah! In my opinion"—he looked extremely grave—"you are being slowly and systematically poisoned."

To say that the patient was thoroughly alarmed at this verdict is putting it mildly. He wouldn't have looked out of place on one of his own book-jackets.

"Yes," said the doctor with a wicked gleam, "you're suffering from an overdose of sensationalism, self-administered. How many of these shockers have you written during the last six months?"

"I prefer to call them crime novels," remarked Rex, cut to the quick.

"I don't care what you call the darned things. I want to know how many."

"Five or six, I suppose."

"Ye gods, man! You're turning yourself into a murder factory."

"I have to live," Rex reminded him sulkily.

"I see no signs of malnutrition. In my considered opinion yours is a fairly advanced case of an enlarged imagination—not necessarily fatal. Mind you, it won't do to neglect it. Could develop into a nervous breakdown. We don't want to rob the public of one of its favourite authors even in the interests of mental health. Well, I've written you out a prescription. Here you are, but for heaven's sake don't take it to a chemist!"

He passed the prescription form, folded in half, across the top of the desk. Rex opened it. He read the name of a private hotel at Bunmouth. *"Dose: One fortnight."*

Rex glared at him.

"You're joking."

"Indeed I'm not! Never been more serious in my life."

"I thought you'd give me a course of tablets—some sort of sedative."

"Maybe I'm old-fashioned. I'm not so keen on experiment, not on friends, anyway. I've never stayed in a dump like that for years."

"That's half the trouble."

"How on earth did you come by the address?"

"I stayed there myself. I ran down to Bunmouth in the car for a breath of sea air and couldn't get into the Royal Bun. There was a golf tournament on, and I had to take what I could get. I made a mental note of it. I've just been waiting for the right patient to send there."

"There may not be a tournament on now," said Rex, brightening up. "I wouldn't mind the Royal Bun so much."

"I dare say you wouldn't! That's not the cure. You want somewhere unlicensed, with a well-balanced diet. Just teetering on the edge of starvation."

"You think this would put me right?"

"I'll bet you my next salary increase."

"It will be most inconvenient for me to get away."

"It will be most inconvenient for you to spend three months in a nursing-home. But you needn't take my advice. I'm used to people who don't."

"I always take advice—when I have to pay for it," admitted Rex.

So here he was in the private hotel, his first morning, after a breakfast more smell than substance, sitting in a room called the lounge on a chair which had the appearance of comfort, but felt like something out of a geometry book.

He was not reading *The Times*, as he normally did, but was listening unashamedly to the conversation around him, a natural defect in those who strive after realistic dialogue. Although Rex couldn't exactly imagine Larry the Eye saying to Slasher Green: "Another lovely morning! We must make the most of it while it lasts!", doubtless he would have shared the sentiment—perhaps even Larry the Eye had a maiden aunt who could, at a pinch, be used as padding.

It is a marvellous thing to come out of one world and discover the co-existence of others as round, as compact and exclusive as one's own. To name a few: the horse world, the yacht world, the golf professionals' world. This obviously was the maiden ladies' world. Apart from the casual coming and going of middle-aged couples, pottering over the countryside in their tiny cars before the seasonal high prices drove them back to their own gardens, anyone else who booked at Baxter's had got in by mistake.

These dear souls mostly went about in pairs; yet, as Mr. Burnham's shrewd eye observed, each twin had a distinct personality and was as often bound by animosity as love.

These two must be Miss Meadows and Miss Faraday; he could detect London suburban in their voices under the gentility, and he had tracked them down in the register. Nosey Parker was Mr. Burnham, it was part of his stock-in-trade, and he was a dab hand at remembering names. He risked a glance over the top of his newspaper. Caught in the act by Miss Meadows, the lean and stringy one, he gave her a smile of disarming simplicity, which she returned with caution.

Rex was feeling a lot better already and even in a strange bed had slept tolerably well with only one bad dream, which he put down to the curry at dinner rather than to the state of his nerves. From his bedroom window he had an unlimited view of the ocean, the sound of it sucking upon stones had lulled him to sleep.

He put down *The Times* and frankly stared about him. Now, that was an interesting old dame—sorry, lady—sitting there in the corner. Stiff with character; he must find out all about her. Later, he would establish relations with the Meadows-Faraday combine and pump them for information; he could see that it wouldn't do to approach her direct and invite a snub. She had the unmistakable aura of breeding and he christened her Lady Rag-Bag. Her dress deserved it. She was also, he decided, deaf; her voice at table, when complaining of stewed figs, was authoritative and harsh. You might have thought from what she said to her companion that the pips had been put in personally to spite her.

Presently, the companion came bustling into the room and hurried over to close the window.

"Oh, Miss Ives, you shouldn't be sitting there in a draught. You know how susceptible you are to colds."

That placed her—the paid attendant—the dogsbody.

Miss Ives lifted her patrician but repulsive head and said harshly: "Open the window again, Bates. At once. Can't you see that I'm enjoying the fresh air?"

Bates cast a despairing glance around the assembled company and said weakly, "Oh, but—Miss Ives—"

"Open the window, Bates!"

The unfortunate Bates did as she was told, then said in as firm a tone as she could muster, "I shall fetch your shawl. Yes, whatever you say, I shall fetch your shawl!"

She hurried out again, face taut and anxious. Rex felt an instinctive sympathy; she looked like he had been feeling latterly. He thought he recognised the end of a tether when he saw it.

"The old Tartar," he thought. "Now there's a ripe subject for murder. I daresay there's a little legacy attached to it as well. It's not much in my line but perhaps if I jerked it up a bit—holy smoke, there I go again! I'm not fit for polite society. No wonder Doc advised me to get right away!"

Conscience-smitten, he marched out of the lounge, past the dining-room door, the letter-rack and the consistently unattended reception counter and found himself on the esplanade.

He helped himself to a lungful of the health-giving ozone and set off at a brisk pace in the direction of the cliffs. The pace soon slackened to a stroll and when he reached the bottom of the cliffs he decided to put off the ascent until tomorrow. He sank down on a slatted seat in the sun.

Maybe I am a little out of condition, he admitted with reluctance, Glancing down, he was aware of a switchback contour starting from his waistline which he hurriedly corrected. Perhaps a few exercises? Meanwhile, how pleasant it was to sit without a typewriter in front of him; he had quite forgotten the sensation.

He was still sitting there when the redoubtable Miss Ives passed him, shepherded by her companion. Miss Ives had on a straw hat which was obviously brought out every year to confront the summer. She also carried what she no doubt called a parasol, whether to protect the garden in her hat or her leathery cheeks was open to question. As the two passed without acknowledgment of his presence, the companion was saying: "But I really don't think you should tax your strength with the climb this warm weather."

In answer to which the harsh voice was borne gratingly back to him: "Allow me to know best, Bates. There is always a good breeze at the top."

Two days later, Rex had ingratiated himself sufficiently with Miss Meadows and Miss Faraday to learn all he wanted to know about Miss Ives. These ladies knew all about everybody and he, too, had not been absent from their innocent speculations.

"I should put him down as something scholastic," hazarded Miss Meadows. "Did you notice how quickly he did the *Telegraph* crossword? The big one, you know, not the little one."

"Schoolteachers are not on holiday now," pointed out Miss Faraday. "He is not quite—*quite*"—she hesitated—"I think he might be someone rather important in a big store. He has the figure for it."

Neither of these guesses would have pleased Mr. Burnham, although he had long passed the stage where he wanted to tell everyone he met that he was an author.

"She comes from an extremely old family," explained Miss Meadows in a carefully lowered voice. "Miss Bates tells me that the Ives have been established in this part of the country for eight hundred years at least."

"I shouldn't have put her age down as quite as much as that," said Rex solemnly. "But then I suppose that she's what you ladies would describe as well-preserved?"

"Oh, Mr. Burnham, you will have your joke! But, of course, it is because of her great age that she is here with Bates—Miss Bates—to look after her. Her own beautiful home is sold up. She couldn't keep it up, you know, partly through lack of staff and partly"—her voice was dropped to the pitch suitable for a cathedral—"through lack of money."

"In a way you disappoint me," commented Rex. "I thought that at least she would have had some sort of title. At least an 'hon'."

"Oh dear me no! She wouldn't like that idea at all. To be Miss Ives—that is really something."

"And to be Miss Bates is to be a feudal retainer. I wonder how she sticks it!"

"There is not much opening for the post of paid companion in these democratic days, is there, Mr. Burnham? Who else would employ her?"

Who else, thought Mr. Burnham at dinner, searching for the one edible mouthful in his cutlet. Yet he was beginning to feel marvellously fit. A low diet and no work were doing wonders to his constitution. He had promised the doctor not to write a word, but the truth was that, in this atmosphere, he couldn't have done so if he had wished. The place was far too quiet; he simply couldn't concentrate.

But his imagination still roved. He couldn't contemplate the spectacle of Miss Ives and her companion for long without thinking how dead easy it would be for Miss Bates to cut her bonds and come into her inheritance. He barely stopped himself from giving her a hint. Strive as he might to repress his professional enthusiasm, at least a dozen gallows-proof ways of dealing with female dragons suggested themselves to his fertile mind. Miss Ives' chief sport was to send that wretched woman scampering up to their joint room to fetch small articles. No sooner did Miss Bates show her face in the lounge with the required object than she was despatched again on another errand.

"And their bedroom is right at the top," breathed Miss Meadows into his ear. "For reasons of economy, you understand. Of course, I know why she does it—" But a belated discretion sealed her mouth.

"And I know why she does it, too," said Mr. Burnham grimly. The old devil, he thought, must have someone to boss around. Her lot had been doing it for generations.

That night he had a return of his old trouble. Miss Bates was impaling her employer on a long sword and he wanted to help her but couldn't move an inch. Luckily, this was an isolated instance.

He was becoming more mobile. Twice he had been half way up the cliffs. At last, one day, he made the top. Miss Ives had been right—that was the devil of it, she often was—and on that exposed height there was quite a stiffish breeze. But he found a sheltered nook a good way back from the cliff edge and sat there at peace with himself and this new curious world. It was deserted. The sun shone in a cloudless sky. He was quite alone. But was he?

A hat he knew rose above the steep, a hat he readily recognised.

Miss Ives and her companion breasted the top, rising like two resurrected ghosts from churchyard mould. Miss Ives was on the side nearest to him; but if she hadn't learned to recognise him across the width of the dining-room she was not likely to recognise him at this distance. Besides, he was hidden by two bushes rampant.

Then something totally unexpected happened—at least to him.

The hat, the celebrated hat, was caught by a gust of wind. It sailed off its owner's head and was borne past Miss Bates right over the unprotected edge. Both ladies started after it, Miss Bates in the lead and, as her agitation took her to a point beyond caution, the redoubtable Miss Ives put forth her parasol and, with its long, pointed ferrule in the small of her companion's back, firmly propelled her over the top. It was all over in the twinkling of a second.

The despairing cry dissolved into the original quiet in which nothing obtruded but the song of a lark. Rex Burnham sat pinned to his seat; no nightmare had ever held him so secure.

Miss Ives turned and without further ado, without a glance either backwards or roundabout, disappeared in the same manner as she had arisen. In the instantaneous glimpse Rex had of her face he could detect no change of expression; she had looked neither pleased nor sorry.

As for Rex himself, he was in a state of shock. The sun still shone but not for him. He was in an arctic region where no sun could penetrate.

For a time he sat entirely motionless except for the trembling of his limbs. A drop of eighty feet terminated by rocks did not suggest to him that he wanted to make reacquaintance with Miss Bates. But what to do—that was the problem.

Had he seen it? He was sure that he had seen Miss Bates go over the top; there wasn't the shadow of a doubt about that. But had he really seen Miss Ives send her over with the tip of that incredibly ancient sunshade? Was it only one more of his—well—his hallucinations?

How could he prove it, even if he wanted to do so? It would be simply Miss Ives' word against his—and who was he? If the police ever came to inquire into his antecedents, he was a thriller-writer suffering from mental strain. And Miss Ives was—Miss Ives. There was absolutely nothing for him to do but to get back to the town, if his legs would take him there.

He staggered to his feet, and went tottering down the path like an old man. He didn't catch up with Miss Ives, not he! Thank God, there was no sign of her! All Lombard Street to a China orange she had gone to report the matter at the police station.

He went straight to the Royal Bun, where he drank three double whiskies and finally returned to something like normal. Nor did he return for his luncheon to the private hotel, not even though they liked to be notified of absences well in advance. Anyone was welcome to his share of the cold ham and salad. It would remind him too much of a funeral feast.

But he had to go back, in the end. He must not draw attention to himself in too obvious a manner. He crept in to the sound of the dinner gong, smelling furiously of strong drink.

He was relieved to find that Miss Ives was taking her evening meal in her room.

He ate with his eyes fixed glumly on his plate. He chewed away morosely and he couldn't have told anyone what he was eating—which was not altogether a dead loss as the chef had been experimenting with corned beef.

He couldn't hope to escape altogether. For the sake of appearances he had to drink his coffee in the lounge, where Miss Meadows and Miss Faraday pounced upon him with the tale of disaster. They didn't mean to be unkind, but they couldn't help enjoying it. The body of poor Miss Bates had been recovered, also the hat, both battered beyond recognition.

"And the funeral is to be held as soon as the inquest is over," said Miss Faraday. "Do you think we should all go as a sign of respect, Mr. Burnham? We should so like your advice."

"I shan't be here," said Mr. Burnham gruffly. "I'm leaving tomorrow morning—by the first train."

"Oh now, what a pity! I though you were staying for the full fortnight. Is it a sudden decision? I do hope that this tragedy hasn't caused you to alter your plans!"

"He had been drinking—he wasn't at all himself," Miss Meadows informed her friend afterwards.

"Business reasons," mumbled Mr. Burnham.

"What did I tell you?" said Miss Faraday later. "I knew he was something in a shop!"

"Who knows?" she went on. "Perhaps it is all for the best. Miss Ives was nearly desperate. Poor Miss Bates fussed so, you know. Miss Ives told me the other day that she would have to get rid of her. But she has such a kind heart under that somewhat forbidding exterior. She couldn't bear the idea of giving her notice."

Rex didn't feel safe until he was settled in his first-class compartment, rattling away to London.

Then and then only was he able to relax.

Oh, what bliss to be going back to the company of Spike O'Harrigan, Larry the Eye, Slasher Green and all those violent characters who sprang to life at the touch of his typewriter.

Never again would any of that fraternity be capable of giving him a nightmare. Now, if he ever saw something which shouldn't be there out of the corner of his eye, he would invite it to join him in a drink.

He was cured, all right.

And if he met a fellow-author in a similar plight, over-writing himself in a vain attempt to keep body and soul together, he would willingly hand on the address.

Miss Ives would still be there for the next hundred years.

DAY EXCURSION

Wilfred Fienburgh

Wilfred Fienburgh (1919–58) was born in Romford, Essex, but brought up in Bradford. He left school aged fifteen and worked as an office boy and as a mill-hand in a woollen mill, before joining the Rifle Brigade in 1940; four years later, he took part in the D-Day invasion of Normandy. After the war, he became a civil servant, but his priority was to pursue his interest in politics and he soon joined the Labour Party's research department. In 1951 he was elected to Parliament as MP for Islington North. His highly promising career was cut short by a fatal car crash.

Writing came easily to Fienburgh, and he wrote regularly for the *Sunday Express* as well as producing books such as *Steel is Power: The Case for Nationalisation*, and a history of the *Daily Herald*. His novel *No Love for Johnnie* was filmed starring Peter Finch, but his detective fiction is much less well-known, probably because he concentrated on writing short mysteries rather than full-length whodunits or police procedurals. His twenty-five short stories about Sergeant Pockle were all published in the London *Evening Standard*; this one, drawn to my attention by Jamie Sturgeon, appeared on 13 July 1954 and seems never to have been reprinted.

S ERGEANT POCKLE, DCM, MM, CHELSEA PENSIONER, NODDED TO the rhythm of the train wheels.

Then his head shot up with a jerk as the close-fastened collar of his tunic nipped his Adam's apple. He looked cautiously round the compartment—would anyone notice if he were unsoldierly enough to unfasten his collar?

The day trippers returning home from Seagate were drowsy with the rare sun. In the corner beside Sergeant Pockle a thin wisp of a man was sleeping with his mouth open. "He's caught the perishin' sun all right," thought Sergeant Pockle, comparing the flaming crimson of the man's cheeks with the dead parchment white of his phenomenally bald head.

Opposite Sergeant Pockle and the bald man sprawled a couple of children. They were sleeping. Their fingers were loosely curled round their Seagate rock, grains of sand clung to the down of their cheeks, their sandalled toes swung limply over the edge of the seat.

Next to them sat their mother. She was also asleep, but restlessly. From time to time a thin sigh shook her 16 stones and her fingers closed round the strap of her enormous handbag.

All clear, thought Sergeant Pockle. He began to fumble with the hook and eye at the collar. Then he pulled his hand away sharply as though it had been caught sliding into somebody else's pocket. Two blue eyes in a brown infant's face had opened and were staring at him unblinkingly.

Sergeant Pockle stared back fiercely, but the two clear eyes looked back unperturbed. Then the lids began to close again.

Sergeant Pockle's hand slid up to his collar, then nipped back to the handle of his cane as a train, blazing with light, snarled and chattered past them. That's torn it, thought Sergeant Pockle. The blue eyes had widened in alarm. When the train had passed they stayed open, alive this time and wide awake. They looked at Sergeant Pockle again, slid over his row of medals to the bald man by his side, then focussed sharply. The limbs gathered themselves into an urgent knot. The boy nudged his mother sharply.

"Ma!" he whispered.

His mother awoke. One minute she had been inert, the next moment she had closed her hands over her handbag and become alert. "What's up, Billy?" she asked.

The blue eyes of the boy were fixed on the little bald man. "That's the bloke, Ma!" he whispered. "That's the bloke I saw pick up your purse."

His mother sighed and turned to Sergeant Pockle. "'E's fair taken it to 'eart," she said. "Lost my purse on the beach with the week's housekeepin' in it. But Billy 'ere swears 'e saw a bloke clearing litter off the beach nip it out of my open handbag with one of them tong things for pickin' up paper. 'E popped it in 'is litter sack, Billy says. Six times already 'e's swore 'e's recognised the bloke. 'E's been readin' too many comics, 'aven't you, Billy?"

Billy writhed. "I'm sure it's 'im, Ma. I'm sure this time."

Ma's voice rose sharply. "Now stop it. Billy. It's bad enough losin' the week's money without 'avin' you carry on." But she looked across at the bald man.

Sergeant Pockle looked, too. The boy looked. Under the concentration of their eyes the bald man snapped his mouth closed and awoke. They looked away, but not quickly enough.

The bald man jerked to attention and smiled. "Can I help, madam?" he asked.

"Oh, take no notice," she laughed, embarrassed. "My Billy says 'e saw a litter collector nick my purse on the beach. Says you look like 'im. 'E's dreaming. I lost it. That's all there is about it."

The bald man grinned. "Well I have a guilty conscience, as a matter of fact," he said. "Truth is I'm a salesman for a soft drinks firm. I went down to Seagate to do my rounds. But I was tempted. Oh yes, I succumbed to temptation. Not a stroke of work did I do. I slipped into my bathing trunks and spent the day in rapturous languor imbibing the solar rays and exposing my epidermis to the breezes, my bag of samples untouched." He nodded to the leather case under the seat.

"That's right. I'm sure," said the mother. "Now go to sleep again, Billy."

Billy sulked. The bald man composed himself for sleep. The train rattled through an outlying suburban station. But Sergeant Pockle did not sleep. He waited a while. Then, with painful care he hooked the handle of his cane round the bag of samples. Slowly he inched it towards him. Every few minutes he looked up.

The carriage load was asleep again. Inch by inch the bag came nearer. Beads of sweat stood out on Sergeant Pockle's face and ran uncomfortably down his cheeks. The bag was now almost within reach. He bent down to open the catch and the high collar of his tunic nipped his Adam's apple.

"Ma!" yelled a small voice. "The funny old soldier's stealin' the man's bag." The carriage jerked awake and the second child began to wail. Sergeant Pockle looked firmly out of the window at the row of back tenements flashing past. The bald man cleared his throat. "Are you interested in my bag, Sir?" he intoned.

Sergeant Pockle cleared *his* throat in reply. "Sorry, mate," he said, "just felt like a soft drink. Hot in 'ere, ain't it."

The bald man looked at him suspiciously. Sergeant Pockle cleared his throat again, and with the air of a man anxious to change the conversation he said, "Epidermis—that means skin, don't it."

"It does," said the bald man, puzzled.

"And when you're sunbathin' 'ow much of the epi-whatsername do you expose?"

"All of it, my man, all of it. From my crown to my toes, save the coverage which modesty dictates as prudent," said the bald man, still puzzled.

"Then you're a perishin' liar," shouted Sergeant Pockle in a voice that had made squadrons of horse tremble, and with a final stoop he opened the catch of the case. The lid sprang open. Inside was as fine a collection of wallets, watches and purses as had been seen outside a lost property office.

The bald man sprang for the corridor door. But Billy's ma stood up, too. The bald man flickered a glance at her enormous expanse of muscle and flesh and sat down again, promptly.

"Your story was too perishin' good," cackled Sergeant Pockle. "If you exposed all your epi-whatsername how come the top of your big bald head is dead white while your ugly perishin' mug is flaming crimson? And the answer is you were wearin' a uniform cap when you was on the beach wanderin' round with your pair of paper-tongs pickin' up wot took your wicked fancy."

"You know," he added, "sometimes the eyes of little children and old men sees clearer than other folk's." He nodded gravely. His high tunic collar nipped his Adam's apple. "Drat it," he said. Defiantly he unfastened it.

THE SECRET OF THE MOUNTAIN

C. Bobbett

By a distance, Christopher Bobbett is the most obscure contributor to this anthology. I am only aware of him because this story appeared in *The Best Detective Stories of 1928*, edited by Ronald Knox and H. Harrington, which is a landmark anthology in the history of detective fiction. Knox's fascinating preface set out the most famous version of his Decalogue, or Ten Commandments, for writers of detective fiction, but showed a lamentable lack of foresight in suggesting that the detective "game is getting played out; before long, it is to be feared, all the possible combinations will have been used up".

Bobbett's story appeared alongside mysteries written by such luminaries as Agatha Christie, Maurice Leblanc, and Baroness Orczy, but his literary career was rather less notable. My understanding is that he was born in 1889 (or the following year; internet sources disagree) and came from Bristol. I imagine that he wrote a few stories for magazines, but where this appealing tale first appeared remains unclear.

"DID YOU EVER GET A MAN HANGED?" JOHNSON ASKED. "Several, I'm afraid, but the details are not very interesting." Travers paused and thought, then he continued. "There was once an occasion when I ought to have done so, but failed, yet I knew perfectly well who the guilty party was."

There was a general chorus of—"Go ahead".

It happened (began Travers) long enough ago to be safe to pass it on; before the War, as a matter of fact. If it had been last year I couldn't very well have told you.

I was spending a well-earned holiday after a particularly long and wearying case at the Yard. Those of you who know me, will need no telling where I was. Somewhere, of course, where there are mountains. This time I was in the Lake District. I was really set on North Scotland, but at the last moment I fought shy of the long journey and popped off to Keswick. I suppose I had been there a week, and was beginning to feel rested and generally toned up.

I remember the day perfectly well. I'd gone on one of those long, glorious rounds, embracing Skiddaw and Saddleback, a little off the beaten track of the average tourist, but one which I'd partly done before and wanted to explore still farther. I arrived back at my hotel about seven and settled down to a really satisfying dinner. It was one of those places that give you a good one if you want it. They realise patrons differ and that if you've merely been lolling in the back of a limousine all day, you require a very different kind of meal.

The waiter served my soup, and appeared to be full of something he was anxious to impart.

"Had a good day, sir?" he began.

"Splendid," I replied, "but unfortunately I ran out of cigarettes and had to walk the last three miles without a smoke. It's surprising how much more you want one, when you can't."

"Yes, sir, it is. By the way, sir, there's been a very sad accident today. Up on the Gable, sir. Gentleman from this hotel, too. Fell clean over and killed, sir."

"Good heavens!" I cried. "How awful! I was only up on the Gable yesterday."

"It was that tall, light-haired gentleman, sir, with the pretty wife, who used to sit over there in that corner."

Instinctively I turned my head, almost expecting to see him. I had got so used to his being there during the past week, that it was uncanny to find the table empty.

"Mr. Watson, his name was, sir. His wife, poor lady, is prostrate with grief. It wasn't actually their honeymoon, sir, but they'd only been married a short time. Easter, I think. Very devoted couple, sir."

"D'you know how it happened?" I asked.

"I'm not quite certain, sir. Mrs. Watson is hardly able to state clearly what occurred. As far as I can gather, a mist suddenly swept down on them, and while coming down the northern side towards the Green Gable, sir, Mr. Watson went clean over the edge. Fell about a hundred feet. Mrs. Watson fainted and two gentlemen came upon her about half an hour after. Carried her down somehow to Seathwaite and brought her home in a car. Meanwhile, some other gentlemen they met went after the body."

"Dear, dear!" I said. "A pity people won't keep still when there's a mist on. Unless they're on a definite path, they ought to wait until it clears."

"Of course, there are stones coming down that side of the Gable, sir. Mrs. Watson says they were following them quite carefully."

By stones, of course, the waiter meant a line or double line of whitened stones about a yard or so apart, placed on dangerous spots for just such emergencies as mist, or darkness, coming down quickly.

I finished dinner and retired to the smoking-room. I had a few letters I wanted to get off and for the moment the accident dropped out of my mind. It was just one of those sad occurrences that do from time to time obtrude into our lives and serve to warn us that we are after all merely mortal.

It was not until the next morning after breakfast that I was again forcibly reminded of the affair. I was on the point of starting out for the day, when the waiter approached me.

"Excuse me, sir, but would you see Mrs. Watson? She would deem it a great favour if you would speak to her. She has been talking to Mr. Hall, the proprietor, and he mentioned who you were. It seems that there is something not quite right."

I was rather annoyed, of course. When a man's on holiday, he wants it to be a holiday. However, Mr. Hall was an old acquaintance of mine, and I knew he would not have dragged me into anything without reason. I found Mrs. Watson in the office with Mr. Hall, and the latter introduced us. She was a short, dainty woman, pretty without being beautiful.

Mr. Hall began the conversation by going over the simple facts that I already knew.

"Mr. Travers," he continued, "Mrs. Watson would like your advice. She has already confided in me that she believes her husband's death to be not merely an accident. It is not a matter, at any rate yet, for the ordinary police. You must forgive me for taking the liberty of telling her that we had a Scotland Yard man here on holiday, but Mr. Watson was quite an old friend of mine; he'd been here many times before his marriage. Naturally, I feel bound to do all I can for Mrs. Watson, and introducing you is the first step."

"That's all right, Mr. Hall," I said. "I can't, of course, do anything officially, but I can ease Mrs. Watson's mind and tell her at once that the law will always stand by her. Now, Mrs. Watson," and I turned to her, "if you suspect foul play, there must be someone else involved. Now please begin right at the beginning. That is, as far back as the time when that other or suspected person, or persons, entered your life. You can trust both me and Mr. Hall."

I paused and waited and then Mrs. Watson began.

"Thank you very much, Mr. Travers. It is very good of you to listen to me. If I was not certain in my own mind, I would not trouble you, especially while on a holiday. Now I'll begin at the beginning. It chiefly rests on business, and I'll be as brief as possible.

"Some years ago, before we were married, of course, my husband was in business with a man named Howard Kent. I don't understand it absolutely, but there came a time when it ceased to prosper and began to lose. My husband wanted to close down or combine with a larger firm. Kent wouldn't. They began losing heavily. Naturally they quarrelled. My husband had to save himself somehow. He gave Kent every chance to come out, too, but he wouldn't.

"The upshot of it all was, my husband cut his losses, cleared out, and joined the other firm. Kent hung on and the concern eventually liquidated and Kent lost all he had in it. He swore all manner of things, including vengeance. My husband regarded it all as hot air; but Kent possessed a peculiarly vindictive character and, instead of forgetting it, allowed it to rankle.

"About this time I came along and, as luck would have it, both men fell in love with me. I disliked Kent from the start and did all I could to discourage his persistence. When I married Mr. Watson I thought that would end matters, but no, it only aggravated the situation. Kent used to make extraordinary threats against him, but my husband only laughed at them. I rather wanted him to see the police but he pooh-poohed the idea. If ever I saw hatred depicted in a man's eyes, it was in Kent's. I was afraid he might completely lose his reason some day.

"He went as far as to start a fire at my husband's new firm. Fortunately it was discovered in time and very little damage was done. Nothing was proved against Kent, but we had no doubt whatever that he was to blame. Then he left and went to live in London and I was very relieved and hoped that his hatred had worked itself out.

"Then, last week, we came up here for a holiday and ran across Kent. He ignored us entirely and didn't reply to my husband's 'Hullo, Kent, doing the Lakes?' After that we seemed to be meeting him almost every day and everywhere. I think, now, he must have been following us about; in fact, I'm sure of it. We met him at the top of Helvellyn once, another time on the Langdales, and, oh, many times in the course of our different excursions.

"Yesterday we didn't see him at all. We had a motor to Seathwaite and it was going to meet us in the evening at Buttermere. We were going to work our way round, over Great Gable, and across Scarf Gap and High Crag, you know the route, I expect. We had our lunch on the top of the Gable and then a thick mist came down on us. I wanted to wait till it was clear, but Jack said it was all right and he knew the track. Of course, there is a line of white stones marking it till you get right down to the gap which runs between it and the Green Gable opposite.

"Coming down there," said Mrs. Watson, becoming very agitated, "Jack just disappeared over the edge. Only a moment before he was singing, you know, just like a man does sometimes when he is happy. He was about four or five yards ahead of me. I could just faintly see his back, but everything beyond him was invisible. I heard him give an awful shout, and then I fainted. After that, two gentlemen found me and kindly brought me back. I can't remember anything more definite about it."

"Do you suggest," I asked her, "that anyone pushed him over?"

"I cannot say," replied Mrs. Watson. "I didn't actually see anyone. Jack was only just visible. I was continually looking down at my feet to watch my steps. I can't remember actually seeing him disappear."

Mrs. Watson broke down then, and it was a few minutes before I was able to question her further.

Presently she went on.

"All last night—of course, I couldn't sleep—I kept wondering how it had happened, and a growing conviction came over me that somehow, in some way or another, Jack had been murdered. There, that is all. You must forgive me if I seem overwrought. Possibly I'm imagining all sorts of absurd things, but I can't help it."

"You think, of course," I said, "that Mr. Kent had something to do with your husband's accident?"

"What else can I think?" she replied. "I'm sure of it, absolutely sure, but I don't know how. Could you—would you—Mr. Travers, go up and have a look round? Perhaps something might show you how it happened. I daren't go up again. Could you find one of the gentlemen who brought me down and take him with you? He could show you the exact spot."

Mrs. Watson showed unmistakable signs of being unable to control herself much longer.

"Very well," I said. "I will. I hope I may be able either to reassure you or—or confirm your suspicions. There's just one more thing, Mrs. Watson, I want to know. Can you tell me the exact time that it happened, or as near as you can guess?"

"Yes," she replied. "We'd just had lunch near the top, when the mist came down. We waited a bit for it to clear, but it didn't. Then Jack said: 'It's two o'clock. If we want to reach Buttermere by six we must be going'. It was only a few minutes afterwards, perhaps five or six, that—that it happened."

★

Poor Mrs. Watson then broke down completely and we left her to the tender care of Mrs. Hall.

Mr. Hall knew the men who had brought her down, and half an hour later I had made arrangements with one of them, a Mr. Gregory, to go up the Gable with him. What I expected to find, I didn't know. Nothing, really, but I was too sympathetic to ignore Mrs. Watson's plea. Besides, one can never tell, possible crime is always absorbing. On the other hand, when people suddenly suffer a shock, they are apt to think all sorts of preposterous things. They clutch, like a drowning man, at any chance straw of hope, or, failing hope, justice.

I explained, in confidence, to Mr. Gregory who I was and what was the reason of our errand.

"Just to satisfy a distressed widow," I told him. "She seems to think it was more than an accident. If it is a delusion, I hope to be able to give her some peace of mind."

We had a car to Seathwaite, as far as the road goes, and ate our lunch of sandwiches at the crest of the Sty Head Pass. An hour later we were on the top of the Gable. In contrast to the previous day, it was brilliantly clear. We picked out all the peaks of interest. Quite one of the most popular peaks in the district is the Gable, if you want a view. We paused a moment or two and then followed the track down towards the Green Gable.

"What time did you find Mrs. Watson?" I asked Gregory.

"I'm not quite sure," he replied. "Must have been nearly half-past two. I remember looking at my watch some time before and it was almost two. It must have been quite twenty-past, not earlier."

"Mrs. Watson says they left the top at two, so she must have been unconscious a matter of fifteen minutes before you found her."

"Here we are," said Gregory. "This is where we found her. Her husband must have fallen over just there, where the track bends slightly to the right. He must have veered to the left. How on earth he could have done it, I can't make out. Even in a mist, those stones are easily discernible. Must have been looking over his shoulder towards his wife and gone straight over. Eugh!" We peered over the edge. There was a sheer drop of nearly two hundred feet, then a sloping scree of stones, gradually falling to the valley below.

"Did you see anyone at all on your way up?" I asked him. "Let me see, you were coming up, not down, weren't you?"

"Yes, but we didn't see a soul. It was far too misty for one thing. We never heard a cry, we must have been half a mile or more away when it happened."

I examined the spot carefully, without finding a trace of anything unusual. It was almost preposterous even to suggest murder. No one could possibly have pushed the poor fellow over without Mrs. Watson seeing him, even in a dense mist. If she could see her husband, she could see anyone near him.

We sat down and lit our pipes. I reviewed in my own mind all the similar types of tragedies that figured in our records. In none could I find an exact resemblance. Plenty of cases where unfortunate persons had been pushed over precipices; but only when alone, none in full view of another person and yet without being seen. I was forced to the conclusion that it was a perfectly natural accident, but what to say to poor Mrs. Watson on my return I knew not.

Slowly we descended the path and followed it over the lower Green Gable and down beside one of the innumerable Sour Milk Gills which abound in the district. I resolved to put Mrs. Watson off with indefinite assurances and let time do its best to heal her fanciful illusions.

Next morning, I thought there would be no harm in having a talk with Mr. Kent if I could find him. After all, he had made a good many threats. It was enough to warrant my asking him his movements on that particular day. After inquiries I found what hotel he was staying at and ran him down about lunchtime.

"Mr. Kent," I said, "will you do me the favour of having a little chat with me?" I explained who I was.

Now, I'm not one who believes in prejudice, but I must say the nervous jump he gave impressed me. At the same time, anyone would feel uncomfortable in similar circumstances.

"Anything I can do—I'm sure—" he mumbled at last, safely.

"You see," I told him, "I must start somewhere and make inquiries of anyone who knew Mr. and Mrs. Watson. His death was obviously not suicide, yet I find it difficult to believe in accident. However, you may be able to reassure me at once. Where were you on that day? Anywhere on the Gable?"

"No—oh, no," replied Kent quickly. "I'd been on the Gable the day before. I was on Scafell that day."

"Scafell," I answered. "Oh, yes. Now I was rambling about on Scafell most of that day. Funny I didn't run across you."

("Half a minute," interrupted Johnson, "but Travers, old man, you told us you did Skiddaw and Saddleback, what—"

"Quiet," said Travers shortly, "and wait."

Johnson subsided into silence.)

Kent hesitated a moment (continued Travers), and then replied:

"Well, Scafell is a fairly big range, you know. As a matter of fact, I'm pretty certain I saw you, though. I came up to it from Bowfell and then worked back down to the Sty Head about tea-time!"

(Then we burst forth. "Aha," cried Johnson. "I apologise. You clever old bird, Travers. Got him nicely, eh? By Jove, I sometimes believe there are more brains in the Yard than I thought.")

Travers looked at Johnson witheringly, and then continued:

As Johnson has been bright enough to observe, I trapped Kent into making a false statement, merely for the sake of an impression.

Of course, he hadn't seen me, but he was anxious to pretend he had. It's an old trick and it pulled him. From now on I decided to take a real interest in Mr. Kent. My suspicions were nearly as fully aroused as poor Mrs. Watson's. All the same, I'd got to find proof. Motive is nothing by itself; neither is being on the same mountain any use. I'll admit I was somewhat stumped.

I had further long talks with Mrs. Watson and tried to draw out of her every item that might possibly be of use, but to little avail. She was always positive she saw no one anywhere near her husband at the time. I asked her how on earth she expected me to believe he was murdered, then. She couldn't say, she only knew—knew it absolutely. I know convictions of that kind. All sorts of people get them, sometimes rightly, but in most cases—only too wrong. However, I persevered with her. I persuaded her, at last, to come up the Gable again, with me, and that if we could choose a cloudy, dull day, we might succeed in meeting a mist on the top and be able to reconstruct the scene of the tragedy as nearly as possible. These attempts at reconstruction are often very successful. You try to get the exact atmosphere and then, if you do, something suddenly appears as daylight, where before there was darkness.

We climbed to the top and waited; waited for at least an hour. There were clouds about, but they would persist in avoiding the Gable. Scafell and The Pillar were constantly appearing and disappearing from view. At last our wish was fulfilled. We were suddenly swallowed up and might have been standing, for all we could see, in the middle of London, except for the colour.

We quickly reached the spot. I bade Mrs. Watson stop where she had fainted, and I strode on. Although the mist was dense, and the path a few feet ahead disappeared in it, all the same, one could hardly step over the edge. The whitened stones at short intervals warned one so easily where the track was. A man would almost have had to shut his eyes in order to go over.

"I cannot understand it," I told her. "Much as I would like to believe you're right, I cannot see how it could have been done. No one can be murdered without there being a second party."

"I can't help it," wailed Mrs. Watson. "I'm sure he was—Oh, I'm sure. If he wasn't pushed over, then he was tricked into going over. Tricked, Mr. Travers—somehow."

And then, like a flash, I saw it. Saw the whole thing. As simple as A B C. In front of my eyes, the whole time.

"You're right, Mrs. Watson, he was!" I cried out. "If we can only prove it. By God! What a fiend!"

I stooped down and picked up a white stone and then another. I moved them across just a few feet and then retreated. The guiding stones now led straight over the edge, and the mist hid everything beyond. It looked all right. It was a chance in a thousand that it would come off. Whoever had done it, risked that and nothing else. A hurried descent, and where were you? Watson must have cast a glance over his shoulder, gone a stride or two, and—

But my attention was immediately distracted by poor Mrs. Watson. The tragic associations of the spot and the discovery of the fiendish truth were affecting her beyond control. I speedily hurried her down the mountain, my mind full of my discovery, and wondering how I could bring it home to the devil who had executed it.

You see what the man had done. Watched them coming along through the mist, himself unseen behind some boulder. Gone ahead to this spot, transferred the stones and then hoped for the best, or rather the worst. He might have killed them both, probably hoped to. At any rate, one or other of them, it didn't matter which to him. At the first opportunity, in this case while Mrs. Watson was unconscious, he had replaced the stones and hurried away.

An almost perfect murder! Unless anyone had seen him, practically an impossible crime to bring home to a man. Suspicions, yes; theory, yes;

that nobody had seen him, he took jolly good care. If they had—well, by this time he would no longer have been enjoying liberty.

I can tell you, I thought it over and over, and the more I thought, the less hopeful the case seemed.

I climbed the Gable again the next day alone and sat down at the spot, and smoked pipe after pipe. One problem was solved, but the second defied me. How to prove what had been done, that was the job.

It's all very well for you chaps to think this and that. In all the stories you've ever read, the proof is arranged nicely beforehand. But in real life, it's another matter, you've got to find it. I did get a bit nearer, as near, I suppose, as anyone could get. I picked up the stones and examined them carefully for any signs of removal.

If you've ever lifted up a stone anywhere you'll know what is more often than not underneath—eh?—the humble wood-louse. I first examined a stone that had not been moved and about a dozen of the familiar but unpleasant objects started scurrying around. I waited, perhaps a minute, and replaced the stone. Lifted it up again, and, lo and behold— two wood-lice dead.

You see, when a stone is lying permanently, the little brutes run about between the earth and the inequalities of the under side of the stone. Directly the stone is lifted, all their landmarks disappear. Then when the stone is replaced, the odds are that one or two will have wandered on to virgin soil and be crushed. That is what happened when I tried it. I eagerly examined the vital stones; the ones that I suspected had been moved. I found exactly the same, one or two dead wood-lice under each.

But, alas, can you hang a man on the evidence of a humble wood-louse? Doubtful. Can't you picture the detective of fiction eagerly putting them in a pill-box and then producing them in court as evidence? Sensation, eh? Suspected man faints in the dock, and so on—one more feather in the detective's cap.

No, I didn't bother to save them, no use at all. Besides, if the possibility did ever occur, one can always turn up a stone in the back garden at home, eh?

All the same, it satisfied me at the time. I was certain Watson had been murdered in that horrible fashion and just as certain that Kent had done it.

I spent all my time, during the next few days, thinking about that situation. I went my usual long tramps, did a few climbs and so on, but that problem was never absent from my mind. I couldn't have dismissed it, if I'd wanted to.

Now, if it had been in America! I don't pretend to know a lot about American methods of detection, but I rather fancy they would have had their man on a system of third degree. Rightly or wrongly, we cannot do that in England. Sometimes I think wrongly—when I come across a case like this, for instance. But in other cases, no. It is open to possible abuse, there is such a thing as frightening a nervous person into an unjust and untrue confession. However, that is beside the point for the present.

What they would have done over there, I don't doubt, is something like this. They would have completely reconstructed the case, with actress and actors just as it happened. They would have selected a man of Kent's exact build, dressed him similarly and enacted the whole scene on the spot, faking, of course, the actual fatal fall. They would have had a film camera man there to shoot a picture of the whole thing.

Next they would have arrested Kent and calmly exhibited the film before him. If that didn't do the trick and extract a confession—well, they'd have done it over again; once a day, twice a day. It would take a very strong man to stand that, at any rate after a week or two. What d'you think?

But the method was not allowed me, so I was back again against hard facts.

I will admit, however, I was tempted, slightly tempted, to take a certain course, but somehow couldn't quite bring myself to it. If you think for a moment, there was one witness there—Mrs. Watson. Although she had fainted, she was there. I could coach her, and if she did not object to perjuring herself, we could get Kent hanged. All she had to swear was—that she fainted, came round, and saw a man, whom she recognised as Kent, moving the white stones back into their original positions; that she screamed and fainted again.

I was, I admit, slightly enamoured of the idea, but it was not honest. Again, it was somewhat late in the day to spring it. She should have told it at once, told it to the gentlemen who found her, told it to everyone, police included, on the day it happened. But four days later! Can you see the defending counsel tearing it to shreds? Perjury!

After a time I came to the conclusion that it was extremely doubtful whether I should collect sufficient evidence to have Kent arrested with any chance of making a winning case against him.

I decided to do the next best thing—frighten him. Possibly I might succeed in driving him to a confession. I moved over to the hotel where he was staying. I ascertained he had booked his accommodation there for another week. For him to leave hurriedly now would be the worst thing possible. I knew that, and he knew it. In that one week lay my chance.

I thought of asking him to climb the Gable with me and then at the fatal spot calmly show him what had been done. But I turned the idea down. It tended to show a certain weakness and he would realise my case was not strong enough.

No, I would pretend to collect evidence. First of all, I decided to have Kent followed. I could not ask for aid from the local police, of course, so I took Mr. Hall, my former hotel proprietor, into my confidence and he agreed to lend me William, the waiter. I dressed William for the part of shadower. I disguised him as the conventional detective and instructed him to follow Kent wherever he went. In fact, to overdo it to such an extent that Kent would be bound to know he was being kept under observation.

William acted his part well. If it were not for the tragedy of the whole thing, one might find considerable humour in following the daily round of these two men. During the first day, for instance, when Kent started off, William was at his heels constantly.

When Kent descended from a car at Wythburn, William got out of another a few seconds later. All the way up the long slope of Helvellyn, William was within a stone's throw of Kent. At the top he asked him for a match. Going down the Striding Edge, he inquired the time.

Later on, at Glen Ridding, he ate at the next table. On the steamer, on Ullswater, he borrowed a timetable. As they rounded Kailpot Crag, he asked for the loan of Kent's binoculars. I don't blame Kent for getting a bit huffy and refusing on the ground that one lens was broken.

At Pooley Bridge, they both tried to hire the same conveyance. William offered to share it, but Kent sulkily hunted up another. In the train back from Penrith—well, the story gets monotonous. William stuck to him like glue.

Next day it was the same, only round and about the Langdales. The day after Kent refused to go out and lounged about the hotel all day.

I rather fancied he was more frightened than fed up; he was beginning to fear that perhaps he had made a slip. However sure of himself a criminal may feel, there comes to him a time when fear takes a hold, something like a bulldog in its tenacity, and won't let him throw it off. But I didn't spare him, and staged a little effect for his benefit.

I chose a moment when he was alone in the vestibule lounge of the hotel. A little preparation in the garden and then a car drew up at the door. I got out, followed by William, who was staggering under the weight of a portmanteau. I had hardly reached the staircase when suddenly the bag flew open and half a dozen large white stones fell out.

I didn't half curse William for a clumsy fool, but I don't believe Kent heard me. He sat there, dazed, his eyes staring almost out of his head. He went as white as a sheet; his hands fiercely gripped the arms of his chair and beads of perspiration appeared on his forehead.

I ascertained afterwards he took a whole glass of brandy at the hotel bar.

From then onward he looked a hunted, even a hounded man. In a way, I felt sorry, but you cannot feel sympathy for a cold-blooded murderer. I had to try and get him in the only way I could. I assure you I would have much preferred to discover satisfactory evidence and have him arrested to stand his trial in the ordinary way.

Next morning I took the hotel pad of telegraph forms and pressing heavily with my pencil, wrote a telegram. It was addressed: "Headquarters, Scotland Yard", and read as follows:

"Gable case nearly through. Few minor details to collect. Expect return Wednesday."

I saw him deciphering the indentations left. Poor fellow, it was devilish work. Psychological, of course, but not so fiendish as the cause that made it necessary.

Every moment now I expected him to come to me and give himself up, unable to stand the strain. I began to rack my brains for a further demonstration of silent accusation. I had to keep him on the run. If only he held tight, of course, he would be safe. He knew he must be arrested in the course of a day or so. If he waited for it and it never came—became overdue—ran into next week—then he would know he was really safe and that no proof of his guilt was forthcoming. There lay my danger.

The following morning while Kent was trying to eat his breakfast and practically only drinking cup after cup of coffee, I slipped up to his bedroom and purloined a pocket-handkerchief of his. I selected one with his name in the corner and then proceeded to crumple it and dust the window-sill with it. Now, what I was going to do was not strict truth, and I don't want to bother you to give me your opinion of my morality. There are times when one can act a lie in the cause of justice and this I considered one. I descended and when Kent came out, I met him and said:

"By the way is this your handkerchief? I picked it up on the Gable a day or two ago; just where that poor Mr. Watson fell over. It's got your name in the corner, I believe."

His hand shaking horribly, he took it, looked it over and said, Yes, it was his. His face went a ghastly purplish white.

I took it back saying: "I think perhaps I'd like to keep it, if you don't mind, Mr. Kent—just as a souvenir."

I thought he was going to faint, but he pulled himself together and staggered away.

Although all the morning I hoped he would come to me and get his confession off his chest, he never did. William told me he sat at his bedroom window, which overlooked the main street, gazing apprehensively up and down. This gave me an idea. I slipped along to the police-station, got hold of the chief inspector, and after confiding certain of my suspicions to him, arranged another effect. Twenty minutes later two constables came marching up the far pavement, halted opposite, turned sharply and strode across into the hotel.

I had planned to chat with them a few minutes and send them out by the back way. Would Kent realise the game was up and come to me? I only wanted the slightest gesture from him, to help him out with his story. I wanted him to come and say, "I suppose I might as well get it over", then I could carry on.

But at that moment, the game ended, conclusively, somewhat unexpectedly, and in a way I did not altogether anticipate.

William dashed downstairs and hurried up to me.

"He's done it, sir!" he cried. "He's shot himself."

"Good," I said. "Sensible fellow. Saved all of us a lot of trouble."

I was surprised, of course, more surprised than you are, who do not perhaps realise that a murderer seldom has the pluck to commit suicide *after* an interval. If they do it at all it is usually at once. Premeditated, you know—murder *and* suicide. If they once let a gap grow between the two, it becomes harder every moment. That is why we hang so many murderers. At first they think they won't be found out. Later on, they find out how hard it is take their own lives. There are exceptions, it is true, and Kent was one of them. The only one I ever had, anyway.

I turned to the two constables.

"There's a fellow shot himself upstairs," I said. "William here will show you up. He only managed it since you entered the hotel. That's what is called an uncanny sense of anticipation, don't you think?"

They stared, a trifle bewildered, and then followed William. It's as well to impress local constabularies sometimes, gives the Yard prestige, you know.

I wrote Mrs. Watson that evening, and if my letter comforted her in any way, I was glad to be able to do it.

That was the end of the Gable case. I didn't get a man hanged who deserved it, it is true. It was one of my lucky yet unknown cases, and not one I care to think of over much. When you fellows talk about the romance and excitement of being a detective you ought to have a go at it for a time. Anyone like to enrol?

There was a deep silence and no one had the apparent desire to follow in Travers' footsteps.

"No, thanks," said Johnson at last. "All the same, I'd rather be Travers than one person in particular."

"Who?" we cried.

"The man he's after," remarked Johnson thoughtfully.

UNLUCKY DIP

Andrew Garve

Andrew Garve was a pen-name of Paul Winterton (1908–2001) who also wrote as Roger Bax and Paul Somers. His father Ernest was a Labour MP from 19290–31 and Garve twice stood for Parliament as a Labour candidate, but without success. He became a journalist and from 1942–45 he was Moscow correspondent for the *News Chronicle*. His experiences in Russia transformed his views about Communism, to which he'd been sympathetic in his younger days. Several of his books were filmed, perhaps the best adaptation being *A Touch of Larceny*, based on *The Megstone Plot* (1956).

Garve's love of boats and sailing surfaces in many of his stories, so it's unsurprising that several of them are holiday mysteries. The suspenseful "inverted mystery", *Murderer's Fen* (1966), is an enjoyable example. We are introduced to Alan Hunter, handsome and persuasive, while he's on holiday, eyeing up the girls. Before long we realise that he's actually a nasty piece of work, a sexual predator with little or no empathy for the girls he seduces. Soon, he contemplates murder…

"Unlucky Dip" is a short piece, part of the "Murder on Holiday" series published in the *Evening Standard* in July 1956.

M Y INQUIRY INTO THE DEATH OF JOHN ANGEL BEGAN AS A PURELY routine affair. Three weeks after taking out a £5000 accident policy with the Century Insurance Company, Angel had been drowned on holiday. It was the sort of coincidence that insurance companies liked to look into, and I was asked to investigate.

I called first on the widow, Edith Angel, at her semi-detached house in Beckenham. She was, I discovered, an attractive brunette of about 30. The strain of the tragedy still showed in her face, but she answered my questions with composure. The facts as she gave them to me were as follows.

Her husband—whose photograph on a nearby table showed a bald and rather unprepossessing man of at least 50—had been an accountant at an office in the City. His salary had not been high but recently he had had a modest rise. He had always been morbidly anxious lest some accident to him should leave his wife inadequately provided for, and he had suggested using part of the money for an accident policy. There were no children and as Edith Angel said, she could always have got a job, but she had agreed simply to set his mind at rest.

That year they had decided to take their summer holiday early, and had rented a furnished bungalow near Renwich on the East Coast for the last two weeks of May. The idea had been that they should spend the first week there by themselves, and that in the second week an old friend and golfing companion of Angel's, a man named Frank Borden should join them. I met Borden later on in the inquiry—a good-looking well-set-up chap of 40 or so.

The tragedy had occurred on the Saturday when Borden was due to arrive. Angel, an active man who believed in getting the most out of his annual leave, had gone off for his pre-breakfast swim, which he took with clock-like regularity at seven-thirty every morning, whatever the weather. That Saturday had, in fact, been fine, but with a rather cold east wind. Edith had stayed behind to prepare breakfast for three, since Borden had written to say he proposed to drive down early and would be there about nine.

At eight o'clock, John Angel had still not returned from his swim. Edith had grown worried and had gone out to look for him. The tide had been out, and she had had to walk several hundred yards to the water's edge. There washed up on the sand she had found his body. She had fetched help at once, and neighbours had carried him to the house. Borden had arrived in his car just as his old friend's body was being taken off to the mortuary for examination.

The medical report had been quite straightforward—he had died from drowning possibly as a result of muscular cramp. Some bruises around his shoulders had been attributed to his having been hurled on to stones by the breakers before his death. There had been no question of foul play, for at least four people had been out on the upper beach at the time and they had been unanimous that no one else had gone down to swim early that morning. Angel had had the sea to himself.

However, I was sufficiently intrigued by the set-up to visit Renwich after my talk with Edith Angel and made an on-the-spot check. I sought out all the witnesses and got them to go through their evidence again but they were quite unshakable. My last informant was a Mrs. Peterson, who occupied the bungalow next to the one the Angels had had. She had spent that Saturday morning in bed with a chill, and her bed looked out over the beach, and she said she was positive that no one but Angel had gone down to the sea before breakfast. In fact, she added, only one other person had bathed all morning—and that had been Mr. Borden who had gone in about 11.

I could scarcely believe my ears. It seemed such an extraordinary thing for Borden to have done. There he was alone, with the bereaved wife, and distressed, one had to assume, by the loss of his friend—and he'd gone off on that cold morning to take a dip! It took me quite some time to work out why he would have done a thing like that. But there was only one explanation I could think of, and presently I went off to the police.

Two days later they arrested Borden for the murder of John Angel. At my suggestion they had searched the sand dunes which ran parallel with the road along which Borden had come on that Saturday morning, and in a hollow quarter of a mile from the bungalow they had found tyre marks corresponding to the tyres of Borden's car. At first, he'd tried to pretend that he'd stopped there for a rest, but they'd also found the marks of his bare feet going towards the sea and in the end he'd broken down and admitted everything. Edith Angel was, of course, his mistress and they had plotted her husband's death together. It had been she who had suggested the accident policy. Borden had changed into swimming trunks in his parked car, swum for a quarter mile along the shore, found Angel in the water as he'd expected seized and drowned him and swum back the way he'd come. No one had noticed his bobbing head so far down the beach.

When I told my wife about it that night she looked puzzled, "But why *did* Borden go in for a dip that day?" she asked.

"Well," I said. "he knew the body was being examined and he knew there might be bruises and there was always the chance the police might come and ask questions. And he was in possession of a piece of damning evidence which he disposed of in the simplest possible way."

"What evidence?"

"His wet bathing trunks," I said.

QUARREL AT SEA

Victor Canning

Victor Canning (1911–86) was a popular thriller writer whose novel *The Rainbird Pattern* (1972) was filmed by Alfred Hitchcock as *Family Plot*; this was the Master of Suspense's final movie, and although the screenplay was very different from the novel, both remain enjoyable to this day. Among his successes was a series of four books featuring the private eye, Rex Carver. He made good use of foreign settings in many of his books, including *Venetian Bird*, which was filmed and also televised, in much-altered form, as a two-episode show in the long-running American private eye series *Mannix*.

Canning's first three novels, published in the 1930s, were comic stories rather than mysteries; they featured a character called Mr. Edgar Finchley going on various trips. In the first book, Finchley is told by his boss to go on holiday for the first time in his life; the story of his escapades became a bestseller, enabling Canning to give up his own job and write full-time.

T HE ROAD DOWN TO THE CREEK DIPPED THROUGH THICK OAK
woods and then ended in a small open space fronted by a narrow
jetty. A hundred yards away the oak slopes of the creek were bathed in
early morning sunshine. A small yacht lay alongside the pier, just afloat
on the rising tide.

Doctor Stephens got out of the police car. He was a small man with
a round, mild face and a mild manner to go with it.

"Lovely morning," he said, polishing his glasses. "Going to be hot
later."

Detective-Inspector Gregson came round the car and joined him.
"This way, doctor." He never wasted words. Hard, tall and spare, he
began to walk towards a small cottage set back in the oak trees a few
yards from the water's edge. A police constable waited for them by
the garden gate. Not that there was any garden. It was just a mass of
overgrown grass and weeds.

"Well, Brown?" Gregson nodded to the constable.

"Good morning, sir. Morning, doctor." The Devon accent was thick
in the man's voice. He walked up the path with them, talking, knowing
what was expected of him. "Nothing been touched, sir. Just as I found it
after Mr. Milton called. Walked to the top of the hill, he did, and phoned
from the old farm."

"Mr. Milton?"

"Rufus Milton, doctor. He's the elder brother. The other one—
Harold—is there. Mr. Rufus is on the boat. I told him to stay there until
you came."

"Cut-up?" asked Gregson sharply.

"Quiet like. Must have been terrible shock. Here we are." The constable waved a hand at the cottage porch. Two untouched and folded daily papers lay on the stone slab bench. "Terrible lonely spot this. Paper boy comes about mid-day. Just throws the paper to the porch and goes. Poor fellow must have been lying there for three days… until Mr. Rufus came back and found him—."

"All right, Brown," said Gregson. "You stay here." He pushed open the door and waited for the doctor to enter. He followed him and shut the door.

The cottage consisted of a large living room with a kitchen and scullery beyond it. A rough stairway led to two bedrooms over the living room. It looked what it was, a holiday cottage, rough, but adequate enough for two people who spent less time in it than on their yacht.

The place was a shambles. Chairs were broken and overturned, and a couple of bottles of beer had fallen from a table and been smashed. The drawers of a large chest were open and in disorder. Upstairs there was more evidence that someone had been through the place.

"Some opportunist broke in and then was discovered by Harold Milton…" The doctor let his words trail away, glancing at Gregson.

Gregson shrugged. "These holiday cottages are fair game for some gentry. What about him?"

They stood at the bottom of the stairs and he jerked his head towards the far window. Under it, lying on his back, was a man. He was about 28, fair-haired, well built, wearing flannel trousers, canvas shoes and a loose blazer over a white shirt.

There was a great bruise on the side of his face, and the fair hair above the left ear was matted with blood. Near by on the floor lay a stout piece of chair back. Both men went on their knees alongside him.

Their eyes on the body there was a long silence between them. Harold Milton lay there, quiet in death, his arms outflung. The bright sunlight through the window glinted on his fair hair, picking up reflections from the silver buttons of his blazer and from the glass of the wristlet watch on his left hand.

The doctor said, "What do you know about these brothers?"

Gregson, his hands professionally busy on the body, said, "Not much. Not local people. Come here every summer for the sailing. Often go out for four, five days at a time in the Channel. Run a business together somewhere in London. Quiet... Don't use the pub over the hill much. Keep to themselves. That's how we like holiday folk down here."

The doctor nodded. "Finished? Can I move him?"

"Yes. Nothing in his pockets of interest."

The doctor reached out and unbuttoned the shirt front of the dead man. Between them they stripped off the blazer and shirt. The chest was marked with dull purplish-red patches. The doctor grunted. "Dead a good three days, all right. Don't like it, though, do you?"

Gregson stood up. "I don't know what you don't like, doctor. But I know what I don't like." He shook his head. "Some tramp breaking in for a quick haul, a fight, murder... Could be. But why is his watch still going after three days?"

The doctor put out a finger and gently touched the blotched torso. "Post-mortem hypostasis... discoloration of the skin due to the gravitation of fluid blood into capillaries and small blood vessels of the *rete mucosum* of the most dependent parts of the body. Thirty years ago I learnt those big words... Forensic medicine and Toxicology—"

"And which word is it," asked Gregson, who knew his doctor very well, "that you have in mind?"

"Dependent."

"I think we'll go and see Mr. Rufus Milton."

Rufus Milton was, maybe, a couple of years older than his brother. Dark, good-looking, shorter, but more muscular than his brother. He came up out of the cabin of the yacht *Siskin* as the doctor and the inspector dropped aboard.

The formalities over, Gregson said, "When did you get back, Mr. Milton?"

"Last night, about three on the top of the tide. I made fast and went up to the cottage and found Harold and then—."

"Yes, you went up to the farm and telephoned. How long had you been out?"

"Three days. The weather's been good. I went down as far as Falmouth. I was ashore there for a few hours. Spent the night anchored off St. Mawes and then I went out and had a night in the Channel. Came back late the next day."

"Why didn't your brother go with you? He was all right when you left?"

"Yes. He was OK. He didn't come—frankly, because we had a quarrel. We run a largish florist's business in London. It isn't doing too well. I think because of his handling. I wanted to pull out, sell my interest. He wanted me to put more money in... You could find this out for yourself, but I'm telling you. I wish now I'd been more reasonable and he had come with me. Then, whoever broke in would have just gone off with a few odds and ends and he would still be alive..."

Gregson was silent for a moment. A pair of swans went flying cumbersomely up the creek and from the woods on the far side came the sound of a dog barking. Then Gregson shook his head.

"I'm sorry, Mr. Milton, but I don't think it was like that at all."

"What do you mean?" Milton frowned.

"Just this. I think your brother went out with you. He brought up this business affair when you were at sea. You fight. I don't know whether you meant to... but you killed him. A blow on the side of the face and head with a tiller bar or something—"

"But this is nonsense!"

"No, Mr. Milton. You killed him and you were scared. You didn't know what to do. The weather was too good to dump him overboard and pretend he'd been lost in bad weather. Good swimmer, I'd say, and a good sailor. So you dumped him in the cabin for three days while you milled it over—"

"Face downwards on the cabin floor," said the doctor. "Hypostasis set in, Mr. Milton. It always does. It's a kind of discoloration caused by the gravitation of the blood to the lowest parts of the body. Your brother is lying on his back in the cottage. You'd expect to find it on his back, wouldn't you? But no, it's on his chest. Yes, face downwards on the cabin floor."

Gregson said. "You came back last night at three o'clock. No one to see you. You carried him up to the cottage and arranged the robbery-with-violence set-up. Quite well done, too—but not good enough. Even without the doctor's hypo-whatever-it-is, you were in the soup. Your brother wears a self-winding watch, Mr. Milton. If he'd been lying there for three days it would have run down. They only go for about thirty hours if left alone… say forty-eight at a pinch.

"But your brother's watch is still going, Mr. Milton. Why? Because for three days the body's been swaying up and down with the motion of the boat. That kept it wound up…"

But Mr. Rufus Milton wasn't listening. His head had dropped into his hands and he was breathing heavily, the stocky frame trembling from time to time.

THE HOLIDAY

Ethel Lina White

Ethel Lina White (1876–1944) was born in Abergavenny, a market town in Monmouthshire. One of nine children, she spent the first half of her life in Wales before moving to London. She served her literary apprenticeship as a writer of short stories and did not publish a full-length novel until after her fiftieth birthday. *The Wish-Bone* (1927) was described by one reviewer as "a charming little romance" and was followed two years later by another novel with a strong love interest, *Twill Soon be Dark*. *The Eternal Journey* (1930) blends an unconventional murder story with elements of fantasy and the supernatural. The following year, she turned to more orthodox crime fiction with *Put Out the Light*. At this stage of her career, she was still experimenting with her writing, trying to find which genre best suited her talents as a novelist while continuing to write short stories.

Fear Stalks the Village (1932) was an accomplished village mystery, which has been published as a British Library Crime Classic; so has her most famous novel, *The Wheel Spins* (1936), which was successfully filmed as *The Lady Vanishes*. "The Holiday", one of her most enjoyable short stories, appeared in 1938 in *Britannia & Eve*, a popular monthly magazine with a predominantly female readership.

N EARLY EVERYONE IN THE SMALL BLOCK OF OLD-FASHIONED mansion-flats seemed to be going on holiday, with the exception of Charles Bevan.

Checked in his ambition to become one of Trenchard's young men, for the past eight months he had been lying in a back ground-floor flat, which looked out into the well of the courtyard. He disliked reading, so had nothing to do but listen to the rush of bath-water down the pipes from six o'clock in the morning, and to watch the lights appear in the opposite building until the final eclipse.

The walls were thick, so that he could not hear the voices or footsteps of the other tenants. He had but few visitors, and depended mainly on the society of the porter—Tory—and his wife, who looked after him. That was his life.

In the circumstances, it was hardly surprising that his energy had corroded to mental irritation, his ambition had turned to poison, and all hope had soured and died. On this particular hot August morning he had sunk to a stage when he doubted not only the doctor's assurance of his ultimate recovery—but his own power to endure…

At the top of the building, Janet Lewis—the girl in a fifth-floor flat—was going on a holiday. She did not want to go, but as there was a lull in her typing-commissions it seemed prudent to take advantage of the chance, for reasons of health.

Her suitcase was packed and lay on the floor; inside the tradesman's lift was placed a note to Mrs. Tory who shopped for her, asking her to send up no more provisions until further notice. Before she left, she was finishing an article intended for a woman's journal, which contained hints on holiday preparations.

As she typed it, she checked its points for her own benefit.

"Turn off gas, water, and electricity at the mains." She would do this just before she left.

"Make provision for pets." She had none, for lack of room.

"Dispose of all perishable food." While she thought of it, she would crumble up the remains of the loaf for the birds.

Plate in hand, she unlocked her front door and ran up the last flight of stairs to the roof. It was hot weather, and as she gazed down at the forest of chimneys pricking through the smoky haze, she suddenly realised that she was stale and overworked.

In spite of her youth, she had known the horrors of poverty, as a result of which she had begun a twenty years' plan. This involved continuous work to secure an annuity at the age of forty, when she would live in a cottage in the country and grow her own spinach.

Although she was sacrificing everything to her purpose—leisure, exercise and amusement—she remained surprisingly healthy and attractive, with fresh colouring which accompanied the dash of red in her brown hair. She was too busy to worry or question, while her flat which consisted of two rooms—a living-room and kitchen, with a hall which held the usual offices—seemed a luxury apartment to her.

But as she looked down at the city, for the first time, she welcomed the prospect of a holiday, when she would be free to wander, according to her whim and without a single plan.

Next door to the mansion-flats, the cashier of a small branch-bank was thinking also of his holiday. He had booked rooms at Eastbourne, and was due to meet his wife and young family at Victoria Station, in half an hour. Anticipating his emancipation, he was wearing grey flannel bags, and he sported in his buttonhole an orange carnation, from his garden.

There only remained two minutes to closing time, so he looked up with a slight frown, at the entrance of a latecomer.

The man walked to the counter, but instead of a cheque, he presented a revolver at him.

Even as he realised that he was being held-up, the cashier rushed at the bandit. The next second, he lay, crumpled upon the floor, with a bullet in his brain—while his wife was watching the clock at Victoria Station and his children sucked toffee-apples.

The bandit worked swiftly, but even as he packed his bag, the alarm was raised. He reached the door just in time to see his partner scorch away in the car, either to save his own skin or to draw the pursuit. Panic-stricken, he darted into the entrance hall of the flats and tore up flight after flight of stairs until he reached the haven of an open door.

A minute later, Janet ran down from the roof and entered her flat. The first thing she saw was a leather bag on the floor of the hall. She was wondering where it came from, when someone behind her sprang on her and gripped her throat.

"One squeal and you're dead," he whispered. "I've just killed a man."

Too stunned with shock to feel fear, she realised the strength of his position. He could shoot her and be invulnerable to reprisal, since the law could not hang him twice.

In any case, she could not have cried for help, because of the pressure on her wind pipe. She was beginning to choke, when she heard the sound of heavy footsteps ringing out on the stone stairs.

They stopped on the fifth-floor landing and then someone hammered on her door. With a throb of deep gratitude, she realised that the hunt had picked up the man's trail and was hot on the scent.

She was waiting for the end of a brief yet concentrated thrill when the man pushed her forward.

"Open the door," he whispered fiercely.

As he spoke, she felt a ring of metal against her back. Flinching from the contact, she drew back the catch of the lock with trembling fingers.

The porter and a policeman stood outside; both were out of breath and appeared hot. She looked at Tory with beseeching eyes as he mopped his face. Although she could touch him, she was divided from him by a gulf she could not bridge.

"Did you hear anyone pass this way?" asked the policeman.

Her unwelcome guest stood behind her where he was screened from view; but she felt the increased pressure of the metallic ring. It was a hint whose nature she could neither mistake nor ignore.

"No," she replied quickly.

"Has your door been open?"

"No."

As she spoke, a hope flared up that they would insist on searching her flat; but Tory crushed it immediately by a suggestion.

"We'd better try the roof, to satisfy you."

Once again Janet was left alone with the man. He took no notice of her, but looked around him with intent eyes which missed no detail.

"Yours?" he asked, kicking her suitcase aside. "Are you going away?"

"Yes," she replied.

"How long?"

"A fortnight."

"Do your friends know?"

"Yes."

She answered mechanically, for she was listening for the sound of footsteps coming down from the roof. It was a cheering reflection that the man was only waiting for the chance of a safe getaway. She was wondering how long he would linger in the building, and whether he would force her to act as his scout, when he snatched her note to Mrs. Tory, off the lift.

She swallowed her indignation as he tore it open and read it.

"Does this woman send up all your food?" he asked.

"Yes," she replied.

"Don't you ever go out?"

"Yes, sometimes, when—"

"Shut up."

The threat of his revolver made her realise that Tory and the policeman were returning from the roof. They tramped across her landing, passed her door, and went down the stairs.

When they reached the hall, Tory had the satisfaction of reminding the policeman that he was right.

"I told you he couldn't be here. All the flats are kept locked and there's nowhere he could hide."

He was still very pleased with himself when he entered the ground-floor back flat, to give his gentleman a second-hand thrill. His idea was to cheer up the invalid, so he was taken aback by the glum misery of Bevan's face, as he interrupted the tale.

"He came in all right. I heard him on the stairs, but I didn't give it a thought. Even if I had. Amusing, isn't it? On the spot and able to do nothing, while some decent chap is sent west, and his murderer gets away with it. I'm a valuable member of society."

"Now, sir," protested Tory, "you'll soon be all right again. The doctor says—"

"Don't quote that comedian. It's his daily joke. Of course, it's obvious what happened. The man went up to the roof and came down by the fire escape to the back entrance, while you were on the tiles. He's well away by now. Will you tell Mrs. Tory not to trouble to send me in lunch. Thank her very much."

When Tory repeated the message to his wife, her jolly face grew grave.

"I don't like it," she objected. "He's too polite. If only he'd buck up and swear. I'm getting afraid of going in to his room, for fear of smelling gas."

*

In contradiction of Bevan's statement, the bandit was in a state of nervous tension when he experienced the aggressive terror of a cornered rat. Since he had been followed to the flat, he felt sure that the building would be kept under observation, and he dared not leave, for fear of walking out into an ambush.

But Fate had provided him with a solution of his problem. He reasoned that the police would count on his being starved into submission, in the event of his having found some hiding place on the premises. Therefore, if he remained in this girl's room for a definite period, their suspicions would be destroyed and they would call off any guard.

Whistling under his breath, he considered the possibilities of his scheme. The girl would not be missed at her place of business for the duration of her holiday, while supplies of food would arrive daily. The fact that she did not go out would not be noticed unless a deliberate watch was set on her movements. In this case, there would be nothing to attract attention, since apparently she would be carrying on her usual routine.

The flaw seemed to lie in her holiday arrangements. He knew it was useless to question her about these, since she would lie; but he counted on the fact that anyone who was puzzled at her non-arrival, would ring up the flat—when he could compel her to reassure them.

Fortunately for his conspiracy, the telephone, speaking-tube and tradesman's lift were all in the kitchen, where he could control them. Success depended on whether he had the nerve to lie low and sit tight. Spinning a coin for luck, he tore up Janet's note to Mrs. Tory, countermanding supplies.

"Listen, *you*," he said. "You're not going away. I'm staying here—and you've got to stay too. You've only one chance. *Keep quiet.*"

Too terrified to protest, Janet stared at him with dull wonder that he should look so average and normal. He did not resemble the gangsters of the screen, neither did he use their slang. Hard-eyed and tight-lipped, with smooth hair, there was nothing to distinguish him from any keen young business man, who determines to rise.

Yet, in spite of her fear, she found it impossible to believe in such an amazing situation.

"It can't last," she told herself. "Someone is bound to come to the flat—Tory, or the postman. I must make them suspect something is wrong."

Her hope rising at a sudden inspiration, she ventured to speak to the bandit.

"I think I had better send a message for extra supplies. I don't eat much and you won't like my food. I don't have meat."

His sneer at her flimsy ruse shrivelled any expectation of success. He did not even trouble to reply, but asked a sudden question.

"Has the porter a master-key of the flats?"

"Yes, in case of fire," she told him.

"Well, if he uses it, *for any reason*, he's a dead man. That goes for anyone who tries to come in. And the next bullet will be yours."

He went to the door, locked it, and put the key in his pocket, thus formally making her his prisoner.

She was too stunned to protest. His last speech had reminded her of the hideous truth that he had just killed a harmless citizen in cold blood, and that any unsuspecting person who entered her flat would meet with the same fate.

It would be an invitation to be murdered, if she incited Tory to come to her rescue, unless she could smuggle through a note to him, telling him the facts. If he communicated with the police, she knew that they would devise a means to draw the man's fire and take him by surprise.

But, pending such information, she must do her utmost to keep the porter—or anyone else—away.

"Directly I've a chance, I'll write to Tory," she decided. "I don't suppose *he'll* let me get near the lift—but I can throw it out of my window."

As though he were playing into her hands, the man went into the living-room and wheeled out the divan, which served as her bed, by night, and a couch, by day.

"I'm sleeping in the kitchen," he told her. "There'll be no monkey business with the lift. You stay in the other room."

Even as her heart lightened at the prospect of privacy, he went into the living-room and jerked the pictures from the walls. Wrenching out the long nails, he drove them through the frame of the window, so that it was impossible to open it. Then he came close to her and stared into her eyes.

"It's a noisy business to try and break glass," he said. "I don't advise you to try. *I shall hear you.* And now listen I don't like you. I don't want you here. Keep out of my sight. Don't speak to me. If you call out, or try to attract attention, I'll shoot you like a rabbit. And this is to show you I *mean* it."

His fist shot out and she fell down limply to the floor.

Her holiday had begun.

When the man had gone back to the kitchen, Janet sat in the living-room and tried to think. Although she felt mentally bruised, and her cheek was beginning to swell, in one way, she was vaguely relieved by the man's attack. It expunged the human element from the situation, and made him seem almost disembodied, like a destructive force of indiscriminate and universal hatred.

As she lit a cigarette to soothe her nerves, he reappeared at the door.

"So you smoke?" he muttered. "Fags, too."

He snatched up the packet of cigarettes as he nodded at the typewriter.

"Carry on as usual with that," he then commanded.

The incident made her realise the cunning of his imagination, which foresaw every possible pitfall. In his determination to avoid any discrepancy, he had refrained from smoking, until he had learned her own habits.

He meant to shield himself with her identity. It was fortunate for her sanity that she was allowed occupation. In accordance with her principle of never refusing work, she had accepted some heavy monotonous matter, which was poorly paid, but which she was privileged to deliver them in instalments.

She now set herself the task of clearing it off in bulk. As she tapped away, her thoughts circled around her imprisonment. She could see no shred of hope anywhere. The other tenants of the fifth floor were away on holiday, and no one could possibly miss her, or know of her predicament.

When she set out to compass her twenty years' plan she had isolated herself rather too well. All wires were cut, while signals were worse than useless.

"I could keep flashing the light, when it is dark," she told herself. "But whoever noticed it would only tell Tory and send him up. Sherlock Holmes is the only person who could help me now."

Presently, when Tory whistled up the tube—as a preliminary to winding up the lift with her supplies—the bandit ordered her into the kitchen.

"Thank you, Tory," she said faintly.

"Have you got a cold, miss?" he called up. "Your voice sounds rather queer."

As the bandit flourished his revolver, she forced herself to speak brightly.

"No, thanks, Tory, I feel splendid."

Then the lift was wound down, empty, and her brief interlude of intercourse with the world was ended.

"Is this all?" snarled the man, as he looked at the small supply of wholemeal bread, butter, an egg, and salad.

"I warned you," she told him.

"Then take this."

As he handed her the lettuce and fruit as her portion, she managed to pluck up her spirit.

"I'd better smash the window and let you shoot me," she told him. "It's quicker than starvation."

She could not know that the man's calculations were seriously upset by the food shortage. While her own rations were sparrow's food to him, and he did not scruple about reducing her to a state of semi-starvation, he did not want to lose his official voice, whose function was to quell any outside suspicion. Therefore he was relieved by her suggestion to order a tin of biscuits.

"I always have one in stock," she told him. "The last one is practically finished."

When he had tested the truth of her words by finding the empty container in the cupboard, he allowed her to whistle down the tube to Tory, who was not too pleased with the request.

"Won't tomorrow do, miss?" he asked.

"No, today, please," she told him. "I'm terribly hungry."

"Very good, miss."

As he expected, his wife was annoyed at the prospect of having to go out again, when she had finished her day's shopping.

"Give me a man to do for every time," she declared. "If she can't remember, she shouldn't order in penny numbers. She can wait till tomorrow."

Tory, as usual, saved the situation with a suggestion.

"There's Mr. Bevan's new tin, not opened. He never eats now with his tea. You can get in another tin for him by the time he asks for them again. If he ever does."

In spite of the calendar, that day was the longest in the year for Janet, but at last, it came to an end. As she dozed—fully dressed—in an armchair, she kept reminding herself of her identity, and also that there was a time-limit to her ordeal.

"I'm Janet Lewis," she told herself. "Something has happened to me—but it will pass. In three weeks' time, he will be gone and I shall be here. I'll still be Janet Lewis."

During the hideous days that followed, the fifth-floor flat was not a dwelling, but a temporary shelter where two alien personalities shared an intolerable situation. Except for unavoidable contacts, they kept apart. Sometimes the man gave her an order in a penetrating whisper, but otherwise they remained silent.

Janet grew pale and thin from semi-starvation, but she suffered most from the enclosed atmosphere. In spite of the relief of an almost continuous wind which whistled down her chimney, the air grew daily thicker and fouler, so that she had to deny herself the consolation of smoking. She made cups of tea over the gas-ring in her room, when she forced herself to nibble biscuits, but all appetite for food had deserted her.

As she tapped away at her machine, she lost all sense of place and felt suspended in a curious dimension outside space, even while she was enclosed within the walls of her flat. She could hear people pass by her door and see them cross the courtyard, yet she was cut off from all intercourse with humanity.

Sometimes she wondered whether Tory would remark her closed window, but he never appeared to look up. In any case, it was almost screened from observation by the high coping of the small balcony in front.

Besides—she did not want him to notice any unusual feature—lest it should prove his death-warrant.

Although she welcomed the end of every day, as one stage nearer release, the nights were even worse, when she sat, in her clothes and dozed, starting awake at every creak of the divan in the kitchen. The man, too, scarcely slept, for he was strung up to a state of nervous expectancy which exceeded her own, and which kept him continually on guard.

Through the day, he lay on the divan, smoking and counting his piles of new notes; but while he was obsessed by his fortune, his main object was to get away in safety. He always turned on the wireless to get the news, in case of a police SOS; and he strained his ears for the movements of the porter and other tenants, in order to get a clue to their time table.

Although he ate Janet's daily rations, after his first outburst, he seemed indifferent to food. At night, he removed only his boots and slept with one eye open—his revolver beside him—ready for instant flight.

As he grew daily more red eyed and unkempt, Janet shrank from him. She guessed that he was maddened to a pitch when, at her first false move, he might shoot her from panic. Being shut up with him was about as safe as sharing a confined space with an infernal machine, but she endured because of her confidence of the end.

One hot muggy night, however, when she was panting for fresh air, this certainty of release was replaced by a new and ghastly dread. Suddenly she remembered a picture she had seen at a cinema, when a gangster shot the doctor and nurse who had rendered him a service, in order to secure their silence.

For the first time, she asked herself the question—"What will my own fate be?"

Meanwhile the occupants of the fifth-floor flat were not the only sufferers. Bevan, too, was feeling the heat acutely and was more than usually depressed. In his morbid condition, he seemed to assume responsibility for the fact that the criminal who had shot the bank cashier, was still at liberty. He feverishly searched numerous newspapers for news of his capture, and practically ceased to eat.

One afternoon, however, he staggered Tory by a request for biscuits with his tea.

"I'm afraid you've finished your tin," he said. "The missus will slip out and get you some in two minutes."

"It doesn't matter, thanks." Bevan's voice was listless. "It's very quiet," he added. "I suppose everyone this side of the building is away?"

"All but the young lady up there."

Glad to change the subject, Tory pointed to a window set high in the side of the wall.

"She sits typing all day," he told Bevan. "She's so set in her ways, you could put a clock by her, for all she's young and pretty. My missus shops for her too, as she doesn't get out much."

"Sounds unhealthy," yawned Bevan, who had lost all interest in young and pretty girls.

"But she looks blooming," Tory told him. "She eats well, too. I'll confess now we let her have your tin of biscuits because she told me she was extra hungry."

"Oh, confound the blasted biscuits," said Bevan with unfamiliar vigour.

While the two men chatted, life went on somehow in the fifth-floor flat. Every morning, Janet told herself, "This can't last another day," but the hours crawled on until she was faced with the torment of another night, with its question of haunting suspense.

"What will my fate be?"

A week passed, every day of which left its mark upon her. She lost all personal pride and stopped looking in the mirror. Because of her shrinking dread of passing through the kitchen, in order to reach the hall, she did the minimum of washing—although she powdered her face with some vague notion of covering up deficiencies.

Nothing seemed to matter in this nightmare, except the fact that the end must come. Whenever she typed, her thoughts winged on strange journeys. Gradually she became a kind of split personality, when she carried on conversations with herself. Semi-delirious from strain and hunger, she listened to a girl of twenty—her own age—who reproached a woman of forty.

"You're a selfish introvert. You've never considered *me*. I've never been to dances. I've had no time to make friends. I've had to slave for *you*... Why couldn't you wait till you were fifty-five to get your cottage in the country?"

The voice droned on in unison with an imprisoned fly which buzzed maddeningly over the window-pane. But in the lucid interlude which followed, Janet admitted the truth of her ravings. She had wasted her youth and was losing the present for the future.

In this connection, she remembered with a pang, that Tory had told her of a bed-ridden young man on the ground floor, to whom she could have lent books, in token of sympathy. Now, as though in punishment, it was her turn to feel completely cut off from the world.

On the eighth morning, the bandit returned from the hall, completely altered in appearance. He was cleanly shaved, his hair shone, and his coat was well brushed. He looked like any smart young business man, except for the revolver with which he drove her into the kitchen.

"Whistle down to the porter," he commanded. "Tell him to stop sending up food, as you are going away on your holiday."

Too excited to think clearly, Janet rushed to the tube and delivered the message to Tory.

"Will you want a taxi?" he called up.

"No, thank you," she replied, obedient to the shake of the bandit's head.

"Then, a pleasant time, miss," said Tory. "If you should want me for anything. I'll be over in the back block, after eleven, as I'm showing some people a flat."

Janet noticed the sudden glint of the bandit's eye, and realised that, unconsciously, Tory had revealed the exact time when the entrance hall would be unwatched.

The next half-hour was an agony of suspense, when hope struggled with fear of her fate. Suddenly the man glanced at his watch, and, laying his revolver on the table, came towards her.

"If this was a picture, I should seize it and hold him up," she thought wildly.

Even while she was trying to nerve herself for the attempt, the man threw a double of laundry cord around her and the back of the chair on which she was sitting, pinioning her to her seat. Too terrified to cry out, she struggled silently and vainly, while he bound her wrists together and fastened her legs to the rungs.

"What will happen to me?" she whispered.

"Shut up," he growled. "You'll be all right."

These words were all she had to guide her to make a terrible choice, as the man took a kitchen cloth from the table drawer. She told herself that if he meant to leave her gagged and bound in a locked flat, her end would be so terrible that she had better scream, and so ensure the swift mercy of a bullet. But, on the other hand, there was a glimmer of hope that he might send information to the porter, which would lead to her release, once he was safely away.

It was taking a desperate chance, for she had noticed no scruple or sign of ordinary humanity in the bandit; yet the passion for life was so overpowering, that she resolved to remain silent.

As the man folded a strip of linen into a pad, there was an unexpected interruption. A loud scrape and rattle against the outside wall of the building was followed by the appearance of the top of a ladder against the kitchen window.

"The cleaner," gasped Janet.

With an oath, the man pushed her chair towards the window.

"Tell him to go away," he ordered.

His back was turned to the door, so that he was unable to gauge the significance of that psychological moment of distraction. But even as Janet remembered that the window cleaner was not yet due, she realised that the noise of the ladder had covered the silent entrance of Tory with two policemen.

With the fury of a tidal-bore, they rushed at the bandit. Unarmed and taken completely by surprise, he fought like a maniac; but after a period of noise and confusion, he was overcome and handcuffed.

After the police had tramped away in triumph with their prisoner, Tory stayed behind to release Janet. Now that her ordeal was ended, she had become hysterical, and she overwhelmed him with blessings and thanks.

"How did you know about me?" she asked, when she had grown calmer.

"I didn't," he told her. "It was Mr. Bevan, the gentleman in the ground-floor flat. He fixed everything up. If you are all right now, I must go down and tell him everything went off according to plan."

"I'm coming, too," said Janet. "I must thank him."

She drew out her pocket mirror and then gave a scream.

"Is that *me*?" she gasped. "You'd better go down without me. I won't be long."

When Tory opened the door of the ground-floor flat to her, ten minutes later, it was evident that Bevan also had prepared for a reception. He looked as gorgeous as a Sultan in a new dark purple dressing-gown, while his thin face wore an unaccustomed grin.

"Don't tell me who you are," he called out, before Janet could speak. "You're the six o'clock bath. I've known you for eight months. You're punctual to the dot. And you're *cold*."

"How could you tell that?" gasped Janet.

"Because no steam ever issued from the overflow. I knew the exact point in this antiquated plumbing where to expect to see you. And since a cold morning bath is a Spartan habit which, once acquired, is not lightly or wantonly abandoned, I noticed the fact when you stopped running down the pipe."

"I *had* to give it up," explained Janet. "You see, the bath is in—"

"In the kitchen," finished Bevan. "I knew that, from the arrangement of my own flat. At first, of course, I paid no attention to your lapse, as it was obvious that you were either ill, or away. But when Tory told me that you were still in residence, and eating rather above form, I grew reflective."

Suddenly Janet began to feel hungry.

"He ate all my food," she said piteously.

"That's why you are going to have lunch with me at once. Mrs. Tory has kindly promised to arrange it."

Tory caught his wink and beamed at the new development. While he hurried away to tell his wife, Bevan went on with his explanation.

"As, providentially, I had nothing to do but lie still and puzzle it out. I came to the conclusion that you might be entertaining an uninvited visitor of a certain type, in your kitchen. I remembered the scare over the bank bandit, as he was still at large. I thought I might connect the two. After that, the significant feature of your continued silence pointed to the threat of a bullet."

Janet forgot to shudder as she gazed at Bevan with shining eyes.

"I can never thank you," she told him. "It was marvellous of you."

"Oh, that part of it was elementary," he told her lightly. "The difficult bits were, first, to prevent the gallant Tory from using his master-key on his lonesome, and then to sell the idea of a surprise visit to the police. By the way, you appear to have the remains of an old-fashioned black eye."

"Yes. He knocked me down."

"Good luck for you. He might have been amorous. When I'm up again—and that will be very soon—we must go to the pictures together and see a gangster film, to criticise its technique."

"No," shuddered Janet. "It will bring it all back."

"Now, don't be sorry for yourself. I know it's Satan rebuking sin, but we're both alive—and that should be enough for us. You've been jolted out of your rut, and I—"

He lowered his voice as he added, "You'll never know what this has meant to me. I had lost my faith. Everything seemed a futile mess and waste. But now I know *why* I had to lie like a log for eight months, and listen to water rushing down the pipes. It was because I had to miss the six o'clock bath. You."

EVEN MURDERERS TAKE HOLIDAYS

Michael Gilbert

Michael Gilbert (1912–2006) led a double life, combining a successful career as a solicitor (whose clients included his friend Raymond Chandler) with a remarkable output of crime fiction—novels, short stories, plays for stage and radio, and television scripts. He created numerous series characters, but his admirable determination not to repeat himself meant that he was equally at home whether writing thrillers, spy fiction, police stories, or traditional whodunits. He received the CWA Diamond Dagger to mark his outstanding achievement in the genre, and in his obituary in *The New York Times*, his American publisher said: "He was always so utterly urbane and civilised. He wrote about a sordid world from the perspective of a gentleman. There was something comforting as well as exciting about that."

Gilbert had the knack of making it look easy to write entertaining mysteries; in fact, his smoothly readable fiction was the product of an accomplished craftsman. During his lifetime, remarkably, no fewer than ten books of his short stories were published. Even then, a good many uncollected stories remained, and thanks to the efforts of John Cooper, four posthumous collections of his work have appeared. The following was the title story to one of them, having first appeared in the *Evening Standard* on 9 October 1950.

CROFT WAS A PROFESSIONAL MURDERER.

Where a murder became expedient for business reasons, it was usually Croft who did it. Business was the operative word. His talents were not at the beck and call of private passions. So far as Croft was concerned the amateur murderer could continue to use the blade and the blunt instrument, the noose and the poison bottle and when discovered (as amateur murderers usually were) he could hang for it himself.

But not Croft. Croft was a specialist.

His trade was one which is perhaps more associated in the public mind with the great United States of America, where, if one is to believe all one reads, it is possible to purchase murder for cash down over the drugstore counter. Yet, in any country, demand will create supply.

Even in England there were company directors whose obstinate honesty constituted a threat to their fellow directors. Perverse shareholders who would persist in voting against carefully planned amalgamations. Irritating and officious employees who read letters not intended for their eyes.

In most of such cases Croft would be consulted.

At the beginning of his career when he had been, as it were, fumbling after his technique, his methods had been various.

At one time he had favoured pushing people from railway carriages. This was a safe method so far as the operator was concerned, but had the drawback that it did not always result in the death of the victim.

In his middle period, after some very disappointing experiments with a silenced automatic, specially imported for him from the Continent he had explored the possibilities of drowning. It was necessary, of course, to bring the victim to the water, but time and patience usually worked for him in the end, and he had had several successes in this medium, when an unfortunate incident rendered it distasteful to him.

He was following, one evening, an elderly grey-haired woman, a majority shareholder whose ideas of commercial honesty were proving exceptionally tiresome to her fellow-members. Choosing his moment carefully, he had pushed her from the towing-path into the grey, flood-swollen waters of the Thames above Bell Weir Lock, but to his indignation she had struck out vigorously, crossed the river at a controlled, but powerful, trudgeon and climbed out nimbly on to the opposite bank.

It hardly softened the blow to his pride when he discovered that she was an ex-Channel swimmer.

Now, however, those days of groping and experiment were past. His execution had achieved a certainty of touch, a maturity, which one can only compare to the later period of a Rembrandt or a Mozart.

He simply stole a car and ran his victim down from behind. If the road was lonely and the operation had not attracted attention, he might even reverse once or twice over the body: but, in most cases, a single well-judged blow from the radiator in the small of the victim's back was more than sufficient. The car was then abandoned.

It was late in the summer when Croft decided that he must have a holiday.

His business was not without its stresses and strains, though not as dangerous as the thoughtless might imagine.

The penalties for instigating murder are almost as unpleasant as the penalties for murder itself. And Croft never acted until he had taken the precaution of getting his instructions *in writing*.

No—in such a transaction neither side had very much fear of being given away by the other. Nor had he much to fear through his victims. He had never met them before they happened to become the objects of his professional attention. How then should he, personally, come to be suspected?

Anonymity was one of the advantages of professionalism.

Nevertheless, there's no denying, he sometimes felt the strain. And when you feel strain you need a holiday. A quiet holiday, with all business barred. A holiday beside the sea.

At random Croft had selected Blymouth, on the South coast.

The season was nearly over and the first gales of autumn were emptying the promenades and bringing down, with the yellow leaves, the prices at the many boarding houses.

Croft had no difficulty in getting a room in Haven House (proprietress Mrs. Byles) at a price well suited to his pocket. Having established this *pied à terre* he set about looking for amusement.

"There's the cinemas," said Mrs. Byles, "though why anyone should come to the seaside to go to the cinema which they can just as well do at home, don't ask me. There's the Pierettes—but they're nearly done with, now, poor souls, their noses were so blue with cold last time Mr. Byles and I went to see them they hardly needed to paint them. There's the racecourse, if you're that way inclined—or the Red Ribbon dance hall—"

Croft thought he would try the dance hall and it was here, on the very first evening, that he met Miss Green.

It was an acquaintanceship which began over an invitation waltz and ripened over a rumba. Miss Green revealed that her name was Rita and, that she lived with her family who were residents of Blymouth.

Croft could see that she, too, was lonely. They arranged to meet on the following evening.

In such circumstances, matters are apt to progress rapidly. Croft thought that Miss Green was a very nice girl. A nice, simple, girl. Not so simple, however, that she was prepared to agree to his propositions— phrased so as to sound vaguely matrimonial—without taking certain precautions. She displayed, indeed, quite a remarkable business sense.

"I'm very fond of you," she said one evening, towards the end of the first week. "But how am I to be certain that you are not one of those horrid adventurers that come to seaside towns and pick up girls—"

"How indeed?" thought Croft.

In higher-class circles, Miss Green continued, it was not unknown for both parties to put down substantial sums of money as pledges of the purity and disinterestedness of their intentions. It was called, she believed, a marriage settlement.

By the time they met again Croft had devoted a good deal of thought to this aspect of the matter. The drawback, as he very reasonably stated to their settling large sums of money on each other was that neither of them, so far as he knew, possessed a large sum of money.

Might not the same effect, however, be achieved if they both insured their own lives—for, say, £5000 a-piece, and then made over their policies to each other. Both would then acquire a solid interest in the other at the cost of no more than the premium for keeping up the policies.

Rita, eating the cherry off the top of the nut sundae which Croft had just brought her, said it sounded all right to her, but how did they do it?

No difficulty at all, said Croft. He was himself an agent for several reputable insurance companies and he knew a little man in Blymouth who would settle the whole matter in a twinkling.

Nor was he boasting. In the course of his profession he had found it expedient to know, under a number of different names a great number of little men who could settle matters for him.

Rita finished off the sundae and said she would talk to her father about it all.

Several times, in the course of the ensuing days, Croft warned himself not to be a fool. He reminded himself of the old saying that you should never mix business with pleasure. A holiday was a holiday.

Worse, he was stepping outside his own strict line of business. But however hard he argued he could not argue away the tangible figure of five thousand solid, indisputable, Bank of England pounds.

For years he had been acting as an agent. Now was his chance to become a principal.

For years he had been removing unwanted persons in return for—what? A pittance, a salary. Here was the big money, waiting to fall into his hands.

His mind turned more and more to a cliff path which he and Rita had recently climbed together. A narrow, winding path with an absurdly inadequate barrier separating it from a drop of a hundred feet on to the rocks below.

A dark evening, with enough rain to keep people indoors and enough wind to drown noise.

The insurance had been neatly and safely concluded. He might be suspected when he claimed the money, but it could hardly go further than suspicion. There would be no shadow of proof. He was prepared to put up with a good deal of suspicion for £5000.

His mind was made up, and on the Thursday night he sat contentedly in Mrs. Byles's parlour listening to the weather forecast for Friday. "Stormy," said the wireless, "with occasional showers. Deteriorating towards the evening."

He might have been less content, if he could have been present at a conversation which was taking place at that very moment between Rita and her family, in a private room behind a public-house near the racecourse.

She was talking to her father, and her two brothers were also present.

Croft might not have recognised her father, since he was not a racing man, but it is a safe bet that every bookmaker in Blymouth would have done so. Most of them had, at one time or other, either paid for, or attempted to avoid paying for his protection and the protection of the gang which he led. Either way it had proved a painful operation.

"What's his lay?" said Mr. Green, senior.

"Search me, dad," said Rita. "I can't make it out at all?"

"Doesn't sound like any racket I've ever heard of," said the elder brother.

"Perhaps he's really fallen for Rita," suggested the younger brother. He was the sentimentalist of the family.

"Perhaps he has," said Mr. Green. "But I don't like it."

"Whatever he's up to," said the elder brother thoughtfully, "it seems to me there's one obvious way of handling it—"

He talked and the others listened.

Croft stood at the junction of Seaview Avenue and the old Coast Road. It was a grey evening. One shower had just passed and another was coming up.

He was feeling pleased with himself. He had arranged the rendezvous with some skill. It was normally a lonely spot, at times like this absolutely deserted.

He had impressed on Rita that she must tell nobody about their meeting. He had hinted at an important secret which he had to divulge. She had agreed readily.

"A very nice kid," thought Croft, with a last-minute touch of sentiment, sternly repressed.

And here she was punctual to the minute.

"A lovely evening for a walk, I must say," she said. Croft thought she seemed a little nervous.

"That's all right," he said. "We'll go up the cliff path. We'll be nice and dry in the shelter at the top, and we can have a good talk without being disturbed."

"All right," said Rita. She was standing with her head on one side and might have been listening. If there had been anything to listen for but the crying of the gulls and the blustering of the wind.

"There's just something I ought to show you before we start."

She stepped out into the middle of the road and started fumbling with the catch of her bag.

"What is it?" said Croft curiously, as he stepped after her.

"Nothing much," said Rita, and leaped back to the safety of the pavement.

At that moment, through the noise of the wind, Croft heard the purring of tyres on the asphalt and started to jump after her.

As he jumped, the radiator caught him neatly in the small of the back.

"MR. BEARSTOWE SAYS..."

Anthony Berkeley

Anthony Berkeley was the pen-name under which Anthony Berkeley Cox (1893–1971) wrote innovative detective stories, often featuring Roger Sheringham; several of his novels have been published as British Library Crime Classics, including the ingenious mystery for which he is best remembered, *The Poisoned Chocolates Case* (1929). Cox also wrote as Francis Iles, and the remarkable Iles novel *Before the Fact* has also been republished as a Crime Classic. Berkeley was educated at Sherborne School before going on to Oxford, and he endowed the School's Francis Iles Prize, an essay prize awarded for "clear, accurate English"; prize winners have included Robert McCrum and the actor Hugh Bonneville.

This story, originally published in *The Saturday Book 3*, edited by Leonard Russell, illustrates Berkeley's penchant for the restless re-working of ideas and material. It was, in effect, a new version of "Razor Edge", a Roger Sheringham story apparently unpublished in Berkeley's lifetime, which I included in *Resorting to Murder*, my previous collection of holiday mysteries for the British Library Crime Classics series. George Locke, a rare book dealer and expert in Berkeley's work, privately published a collection of Sheringham stories in 1994 under the name Ayresome Johns, in which he discussed Berkeley's synopsis for a novel simply titled *Seaside Story*, but clearly intended to be an expansion of the original storyline of "Razor Edge". He speculated that Berkeley, a strange and troubled man who liked to cultivate an air of mystery, might have written up the novel and published it under yet another pseudonym, but this seems unlikely, and certainly no such novel has ever come to light.

F OR THE FIRST FEW MONTHS OF THE WAR BLOOMSBURY WAS ABLE to carry on much as usual. Besides, to give a beer-and-sausage party, or even to attend a beer-and-sausage party, seemed a subtle defiance of Hitler and all his wars. That, at any rate, was the impression that Roger Sheringham was receiving at a party which he found himself unaccountably attending in the month of November 1939.

Roger did not care much for parties, even beer-parties; nor did he care much for Bloomsbury. For that matter Bloomsbury cared even less for Roger Sheringham. Either it knew him not or, if it did know, despised his best-selling capacities—and was inclined to go a few steps out of his way to let him know it. In due course, therefore, Roger, tired of being snubbed, betook himself and his tankard into a corner and surveyed the smoke-wreathed hubbub with a surly frown.

Like gravitates to like. Into Roger's corner there imperceptibly edged a woman, obviously as lonely as himself but wearing in place of a surly frown a fixed and determined smile. Roger surveyed her. She was a somewhat faded lady, of middle middle-age, who had once been prettier than she was now. Her clothes were worn as wrong as even female Bloomsbury can wear clothes, but unlike theirs, were expensive. She was clearly out of place, and Roger decided that behind the fixed smile she was unhappy.

"Do you want to get away?" he asked suddenly. "I do. Let's go."

The lady started. She seemed unused to being addressed by strangers, even at a Bloomsbury party. "Go away?" she repeated vaguely. "Oh, no! I think it's wonderful!"

"Do you?" Roger said glumly. "What in particular?"

"Oh, well—everything. I mean, all these authors and—and poets and people. Oh, I do so wish I could write. Perhaps you write. Do you?"

"No," Roger said firmly.

"It must be wonderful to be able to, don't you think? Well, Mr. Bearstowe says he believes I could, if I could find a theme. Er—you know Mr. Bearstowe's work, of course?"

There seemed so much appeal in the question that Roger, rather to his own surprise, succumbed. "Of course."

She's in love with him, he thought without enthusiasm, as he noted the pleasure, singularly tinged with relief, or even gratitude, which at once illumined his companion's face. He wondered who this Bearstowe was, and why he was not looking after his own, as he prepared for the worst.

He received it. A flood of Mr. Bearstowe promptly poured over him. "Mr. Bearstowe says..." Roger wondered how Mr. Bearstowe found time to say so much.

But all is salvage that falls into a novelist's dustbin. Fascinated, Roger began planning a short story. It would be called "Mr. Bearstowe says...", and it would be about—well, it would be partly about Mr. Bearstowe, of course.

"By the way, is Mr. Bearstowe here?" Roger asked. It is as well to have a working idea of one's characters' appearance.

"Oh, yes," the lady said eagerly. "He's over there." Her glance appeared to indicate a group of three bearded young men, one tall, one short, and one middling. There was nothing to show the height of Mr. Bearstowe. Roger could not decide whether he should be the tall, cadaverous young man, the short, bouncing young man, or the middling, might-be-anything young man.

There must be a triangle, of course. The faded lady's husband—"Of course my husband isn't much interested in that sort of thing," the lady supplied, rather wistfully.

"Of course not," Roger said with gratitude. No, of course the husband mustn't be interested. The husband must be a self-made man, who married a little above him and now thinks he married below him: a self-opinionated, self-satisfied man, who—

"You see, my husband doesn't care for me to go to concerts without him, and as he doesn't care to go himself—"

"Exactly!"—who rules his wife out of school as well as in, and won't let her go to concerts. Excellent. Probably one of those short, pompous little men.

"How tall is your husband?" Roger asked abruptly.

The lady looked taken aback. "How tall? Well, I don't really know."

"Oh, come you must know whether your husband's tall or short," Roger said impatiently. Ridiculous woman! It was important that the husband should be short, because then Mr. Bearstowe could be the tall, cadaverous young man.

"No, I think he's just about—average."

"In a country of dwarfs the average man is a giant," said Roger, inaccurately as well as inanely; but he judged that this was the sort of thing that the lady attended Bloomsbury parties to hear, and it seemed a pity that she shouldn't have at least one gem to carry away with her.

He was going on to supply more, out of sheer kindness, when his companion uttered a sudden exclamation and made a rush for the door. Through the doorway Roger just had a glimpse of a blond head throwing an abrupt nod in her direction, and Mr. Bearstowe passed—the secret still unsolved. All three young men had been blonds. "Gentlemen prefer to be blonds," Roger muttered sourly.

"Was that an epigram, my sweet?" asked a familiar voice.

"Crystal!" Roger exclaimed with relief. "Fancy seeing you in this bear-pit. And talking of bears, who is Mr. Bearstowe? You know him, of course. You know everyone."

"Michael Bearstowe? Yes. Well, I don't know quite how to describe him. He would be a dilettante, if he had any money. But he hasn't. So he dilettantes on other people's."

"He's a sponger?" Roger asked delightedly. Oh, admirable, sponging, cadaverous Mr. Bearstowe, taking the wives of pompous average self-made men to concerts (wife paying)!

"I should say so. Why look so pleased about it?"

"Because it fits so nicely. Crystal, tell me more of this Bearstowe. My interest in him is insatiable."

"I don't know that there's anything more to tell you. He's the type who runs after the wives of rich men, and feeds them Culture and Literature in return for temporary loans. A literary gigolo, you might call him. I hear he's got hold of some groceress now and is toting her everywhere."

"Groceress, Crystal?"

"The female of a grocer. At least, I understand that the husband makes big noises in Mincing Lane. Isn't that where they groce?"

"No, I think it's where they drink tea and spit it out again. But this Bearstowe, Crystal—has he published much?"

"Nothing, that I'm aware of. Oh, yes, I believe he did have a short story printed in one of the cheap magazines once," said Crystal, whose job it was to know everything about everyone, and even a few things that they did not know themselves.

"It's perfect!" Roger said ecstatically. "I shall write the story this very evening."

Roger did not write the story that evening, or any evening; and within a week he had forgotten the very name of Bearstowe.

But Mr. Bearstowe's story was being written none the less, if by a different hand—and in a different medium.

"She seems terrible upset, sir," said the station sergeant doubtfully.

"Crying her eyes out already, and she doesn't even know the body's been found. I don't know whether she's fit to interrogate, sir."

"Well, try and get her to pull herself together," the superintendent said impatiently. The bathing is dangerous round Penhampton and one gets so inured to corpses after twenty years' police service that it is difficult to realise that the relatives are not equally hardened off. In his home the superintendent was the kindest of men, and loathed killing mice.

"You won't want to wait for this, Mr. Sheringham," the superintendent added to his visitor. "A woman come to report her husband missing after bathing. As a matter of fact, we've got the body already, but she doesn't know that. I'm afraid she'll go a bit hysterical when she does. They often do," added the superintendent with a sigh.

"No, I'll slide out," Roger agreed. "In any case, it looks as if the colonel isn't coming this afternoon; so—"

He broke off. The sergeant had returned already, with his charge. Roger, having no wish to intrude on the woman's grief, waited for them to pass before slipping quietly out. Then he caught sight of the woman's face and, after a moment of indecision, returned unobtrusively to his chair.

The woman was given a seat facing the superintendent's desk. She had pulled herself together bravely, but from the clenched hands on her lap it was clear that she was vibrating with nerves.

The superintendent made soothing noises. "Now, Mrs. Hutton, let me see—you're worried about your husband?"

The woman nodded, choked, and said: "Yes. He went out bathing this morning. I was to join him later. His clothes were on the beach, but—oh, I'm sure—I'm sure—"

"Now, now," said the superintendent mechanically, and asked for further particulars.

These took some minutes to obtain, but amounted to very little. Mr. Edward Hutton, described as a wholesale provision merchant with an office in the City and a home in Streatham, had been staying with his wife in the little village of Penmouth, some five miles west of Penhampton. He had left the house at about half-past ten that morning, telling his wife that he was going to bathe. Mrs. Hutton had arranged to join him about noon, but when she arrived there was no sign of her husband, though his clothes were behind the same rock that he always used for undressing purposes. Mrs. Hutton had called and searched, and then returned to her lodging. In the afternoon, being now thoroughly worried, she had decided to take the only bus of the day into Penhampton and report to the police.

The superintendent nodded. "Very proper, madam. Now as to your husband's description, can you give us some idea of his appearance?"

Mrs. Hutton leaned back in her chair and closed her eyes. "My husband is five foot seven—no, eight inches tall, not very broad, thinnish arms and legs, 34 inches chest measurement, rather long hands and feet, medium brown hair, clean-shaven, grey-green eyes, and rather a pale complexion; he has an old appendicitis scar, and—oh, yes, there is a big mole under his left shoulder-blade."

The superintendent could not restrain his admiration. "Upon my word, Mrs. Hutton, you reeled that off a treat. Very different from some of them, I assure you."

"I—I was thinking it out in the bus," the woman said faintly. "And—his passport, you know. I knew you'd want a description."

"Yes. Well." Surreptitiously the superintendent studied the description of the body now in the mortuary. It tallied in every particular.

With much sympathetic throat-clearing he proceeded to the distasteful task of warning Mrs. Hutton to prepare for a shock. He was very much afraid that in the mortuary now, if Mrs. Hutton would come along for just a moment—

He sighed again as the woman gave every sign of imminent hysterics.

"He's here already? Must I see him? Must I? Won't—won't the description do?"

It took five minutes to get her into the mortuary to identify the body.

But once there she regained her calm. A curious dead-alive look came into her face as the superintendent gently withdrew the sheet that covered the dead man's face.

"Yes," she whispered, tonelessly. "That's my husband. That's—Eddie."

And then Roger noticed a very curious thing. Like the others' his gaze had been fixed on the sheeted figure on the slab; but happening, by the merest chance, to glance round at Mrs. Hutton, he saw that her eyes were slightly closed. For all she knew, she might have been identifying a piece of cheese as her husband. He nudged the superintendent.

The superintendent understood and nodded back. "I'm afraid, madam," he said, as gently as he could, "you must *look* at him you know."

Mrs. Hutton started violently, opened her eyes, looked at the dead man in front of her, and uttered a horrible, hoarse scream.

For a moment Roger thought she was going into hysterics again. He jumped forward, as did both the superintendent and the sergeant, and between them they hurried Mrs. Hutton back to the office. The sergeant produced a glass of water, and within a few minutes the lady was able to stop sobbing and assure them that she was quite all right now, it was just the shock of seeing her own husband, actually lying there—

"Shock, yes," said the superintendent hastily. "Nasty thing, shock. I remember—"

When at last Mrs. Hutton got out her powder-compact, all three men heaved sighs of relief.

Roger, who had at last solved a problem which had been worrying him ever since he first saw Mrs. Hutton in the doorway, deemed it a good moment to introduce himself.

"Do you know that we've met before, Mrs. Hutton?" he said, with his best social smile.

She looked at him vaguely. "No. Have we? Where?"

"At a party. I didn't know your name, nor you mine, and I've been wondering why your face seemed known to me. Now I remember. It was at a deadly beer-party about two years ago, soon after the beginning of the war. Do you remember? In Bloomsbury. By the way, have you seen Michael Bearstowe lately?"

Mrs. Hutton jumped to her feet, her face dead-white. For a moment she gazed wildly at Roger, then she collapsed on the floor in a dead faint.

"That wasn't kind of you, Mr. Sheringham," said the superintendent reproachfully, when Mrs. Hutton had been finally tidied away into the care of the police matron. "I thought we'd got her round—why, she'd got her powder-puff out and all!—and then you go and do a thing like that."

"I didn't do anything," Roger said indignantly. "I only reminded her of a party we'd both been to and asked after an old friend of hers. Do you faint when people ask after your old friends?"

"You upset her."

"Apparently. But that's no reason for you to upset me. I might even try to upset you, in return. I might tell you, for instance, that the last time I saw that lady she was so vague that she couldn't tell me whether her husband was a tall man or a short one. Yet now she not only knows his height to an inch but his chest measurement too."

"Well, why not? She remembered it from his passport. She said so."

"They don't put your chest measurement on your passport."

The superintendent frowned. "What exactly are you suggesting, Mr. Sheringham?"

Roger laughed. "Now don't get official, Super. I'm not suggesting anything. I merely hand you a queer little discrepancy, and you can do what you like with it. But," Roger added thoughtfully, "do you know, I would like to have another look at the body, if you've no objection."

"Oh, I've no objection. But you won't find anything. The doctor's been over him already, and death's due to drowning all right. Still, have a look at him if you want I'm afraid I can't stay myself; I'm late already; but—"

Roger assured the superintendent that for nothing in the world would he detain him longer.

Roger did not have the mortuary to himself. There were two other men already there. The sergeant who had been appointed Roger's conductor, indicated that they were the police surgeon and the detective inspector in charge of the C.I.D. of the Penhampton police force; and he left him to them.

The sheet had been withdrawn from the body and both men were standing by the slab, gazing down. Roger joined them.

"Pasty-faced beggar, eh?" remarked the doctor cheerfully.

"Certainly no advertisement for Penhampton's Bonnie Sunshine," Roger assented absently. He was remembering more and more.

Yes, and the husband was to have been a pompous, paunchy little bully, who wouldn't take his wife to concerts and wouldn't let her go by herself. Well, here he was face to face with the husband at last; and he certainly wasn't paunchy, and could hardly have been pompous. But that wasn't to say that he might not have been a bully, Roger thought, looking at the rather weak face and the indeterminate chin: the kind that bullies out of weakness instead of out of strength. Perhaps he was even that pathetic type, the artist *manqué* (his hands seemed to indicate the possibility), *manqué* and condemned to an office desk in Mincing Lane, and in consequence soured. Yes, and he had inherited the office-desk too, not achieved it; for this man had never made money, or anything else, if Roger knew faces. Well, it was a story, whichever way it went.

"Notice anything, Mr. Sheringham?" the detective inspector asked eagerly.

"No. Why?"

"I thought you were looking at him a bit hard."

Roger laughed. "Afraid not, this time. Except that Mr. Hutton wasn't as spruce as he might have been."

"How do you make that out, sir?"

"He hadn't shaved this morning."

"Sorry, but he had," the doctor corrected with a smile. "That cut's fresh, at the side of his mouth."

"Well, he wanted a new blade," Roger said feebly.

"Like most of us," the doctor agreed. "But if you're really looking for queer details, what do you make of his back?" He signed to the inspector, and the two of them turned the corpse over.

Roger saw that the skin on the back was badly lacerated from the shoulders to the small of the back, and the elbows were almost raw. "Barnacles?" he suggested.

The doctor nodded. "Rocks covered with them. And it was among the rocks that the body was found. Still—"

"I see what you mean. If the body was washing about, why was it lacerated only in that particular area?"

"Yes, it's queer, isn't it? No doubt there's some simple explanation. Probably the man who found him pulled him in by the legs. That's all."

"No, doctor," put in the inspector. "The body was wedged under a big rock at the side of a pool. Trewin, the farm-hand who happened to find him when he went down for a pail of sea-water, says he picked him up straight from the pool."

"There's an abrasion on the front of the right thigh, where he was wedged," supplemented the doctor.

"Yes, but that's natural," Roger said. "Those scratches aren't."

"And here's another thing. I've an idea those lacerations were made during life. There were signs of free bleeding—freer than I should have expected."

"Very interesting," Roger commented. "Very queer."

"Don't think there's anything wrong, do you, sir?" asked the inspector, hopefully.

Roger's reply was lost in the sudden entrance of the superintendent. "Well, it seems we've caught a tartar," he announced, not without triumph. "Just had Scotland Yard on the phone. Caught me in the nick of time; another minute, and I'd have been gone. Seems this fellow was wanted by the Yard for black market stuff. They've got a warrant out against him, and they'd just heard he'd been seen in this vicinity."

"Well, fancy that," observed the inspector.

Roger stared down at the dead man. "You never know, do you? Still, that weak chin—"

"Yes, yes; criminal type, obviously," pronounced the superintendent. "Well, doctor, this is bound to raise the question of suicide. Any chance, do you think?"

"None that I can say. Of course, he may have swum deliberately too far out, but there's nothing to show it."

"Are you going to check up on Mrs. Hutton's statement, Super?" Roger asked suddenly.

The superintendent stared. "We'll make the usual routine enquiry at her lodging. Why, Mr. Sheringham?"

"I only wondered," Roger said mildly. "It would be interesting, for instance, if she took a bathing-dress out this morning, wouldn't it? Or if she left the house soon after her husband, and not at noon?"

"Why, Mr. Sheringham," said the detective inspector, whose job it would be to make these enquiries, "you don't think—?"

"I only think it might be quite an interesting case," Roger said.

As he trudged along the coarse sand the next afternoon Roger wondered if he were wasting his time and energy. That Hutton had been murdered, he felt convinced; and the method was fairly obvious. But could the woman have done it? Physically, yes. But psychologically? Hardly. She was too vague, too woolly, too—too silly, poor woman.

Or did silliness not debar one from murder? Murder itself was usually very silly. Mrs. Hutton might not be the stuff of which strong, silent murderers were made; but mightn't she be a silly murderess? She was a hero-worshipper. How far would hero-worship carry her?

Roger's plodding feet seemed to be picking out a shambling refrain. "Mr. Bearstowe says... Mr. Bearstowe says..."

And suppose Mr. Bearstowe said, "Pick up your husband's feet when he's bathing and hold them up in the air for a few minutes, out of sheer girlish *elan*, and then I shall be able to marry your Mincing Millions."

Oh, Mr. Bearstowe was in it all right. Why else faint at the mere mention of his name?

Yes, and of course there was the evidence of guilt all the time. First she wouldn't look at her murdered husband at all; then, when she was made to, took one peep, turned pea-green, and screamed. If that wasn't presumptive evidence of guilt what was?

And reeling off the description in that silly way! Roger could almost hear the voice of tuition: "If they wonder how you've got it so pat just say you were thinking it out in the bus, or remembered it from his passport or something. They won't bother." And pat she certainly had got it like a child repeating a lesson. Mr. Bearstowe should have devoted more time to his artistic effects.

But the superintendent had smelt no rat. Roger thought the superintendent rather a foolish man. Now that inspector—Yes, there the inspector was, already. Then this must be the place.

The inspector was feeling a little guilty himself. "You know, I oughtn't rightly to be doing this, Mr. Sheringham. The super would be wild. He says it's a straightforward case of accident if ever he saw one, and you've got a bee in your bonnet about murder."

"I never so much as mentioned the word," Roger protested.

"No, but it was obvious what you thought. And I couldn't but agree that there seems something fishy about Mrs. Hutton. More I think of it more it seems to me that she acted queer—very queer indeed."

"Have you checked up at the lodgings?"

"Yes, but more of a country house than lodgings. Must have been costing them a tidy packet to stay there. They've got money to burn all right those Huttons, in spite of the taxes and all. Still, her story's all right so far as it goes. She did leave at the time she said, and she didn't take a bathing-dress."

"Any signs of—worry?"

"No!" said the inspector emphatically. "I asked that specifically, and she was just as usual before she went out. Didn't answer her husband back when he laid down the law at breakfast as usual, or anything. But when she came back! Tears? Floods of 'em! And before he'd been missing long enough to make any ordinary wife do anything but curse about him making her wait for lunch, mark you."

"Umph! Remorse? I wonder." Roger felt a little puzzled. Bearstowe would hardly be the type to spring an unexpected murder on a foolish, possibly unreliable woman. He pushed the point aside. "Anyhow, where's the rock?"

The inspector pointed it out. The tide had gone down far enough for Roger, balanced precariously on slippery seaweed, to be able to inspect the crevice in which the body had been wedged. It told him nothing.

He gazed thoughtfully round on the broken, rocky shore, with little waves slapping whitely here and there and the seaweed waving in the pools.

"Well, sir, if you don't want me anymore, I think I'd like another word or two with Trewin. You never know. He might have noticed something."

"Do," Roger agreed. "I shall be poking round here for an hour or so if you like to pick me up on your way back."

But it did not take Roger an hour to find the thing which he had hardly expected to find. In only the third pool which he explored after the inspector's disappearance, shining merrily on a bunch of seaweed only a few inches below the surface, was a gold ring, simply asking to be found. Scarcely able to believe in his luck, Roger examined it. It was a man's wedding-ring, and the inside was inscribed, "E.H.—B.G. 18 November 1932."

Roger turned it slowly over in his hand. It was a chance in a million. And yet what did it prove? That Edward Hutton had been murdered in that particular pool, and none other. Not very much. No hint as to who had murdered him, for instance.

Roger dried himself on his handkerchief, and sat down to await the return of the inspector.

He came an hour later, bursting with news. "The woman's in it all right, Mr. Sheringham. By a stroke of luck I found a man who was working in this field yesterday afternoon. He says he saw a woman on the beach about half-past three, and the description of the clothes tallies near enough."

"Mrs. Hutton didn't mention being on the beach then?"

"No, sir, she did not. But that's not all. There was a man with her."

"Ah!"

"You expected that, Mr. Sheringham?" asked the inspector, a trifle disappointed.

"In a way. Well, what did they do?"

"By the looks of it they came out of a little cave under the cliff here. I must have a look there later. The farm-hand thought they might be a larky couple, so he watched; but after a minute or two the man went back into the cave and the woman went off along the beach."

"Did you get any description of the man?"

"Nothing particular. Orange pullover, grey flannel trousers. Clean-shaven."

"Clean-shaven, eh? Yes, well, he would be, of course."

"Sir?"

"He had a beard last time I saw him, but beards are much too distinctive. Look here, Inspector, it's time I told you a few things. Sit down."

They found a rock and made themselves comfortable in its lee. Roger lit his pipe, and then told his tale.

"Mind you," he concluded, "there's no evidence that the man's Bearstowe. After all, it was over two years ago and she may have got a new hero by now. But it's worth making a few enquiries."

"I certainly will, sir. This alters everything. The super's bound to OK me spending a bit of time on the case now. And what are you going to do, sir?"

"Me? Do you know," said Roger, "I should awfully like to ask Mrs. Hutton why she fainted at Bearstowe's name. I do so wonder what she'd say."

Roger did not put this interesting question, however. (For one thing was not sure that he had the moral courage.) Instead, he left Mrs. Hutton in peace and went up to London.

His objective was Crystal Vane, and he was lucky enough to catch her the first time he rang up her flat. Crystal was writing what she called one of her "sob-articles" when he arrived, but she put it aside readily enough to answer Roger's questions.

Yes, so far as she knew the affair of Michael Bearstowe and his groceress had survived the war to date; Michael was on a good thing there, and it wasn't likely he'd let it go; no, he hadn't been called up—total exemption on some grounds or other, oh, yes, conscientious objector, naturally.

"Would you say that Bearstowe was utterly unscrupulous in attaining his own ends?" Roger asked carefully.

"If you mean, would he boggle at a little thing like seducing his groceress if it was going to pay better dividends?" Crystal began.

"No, no. Worse than that. Stick at absolutely nothing, I mean."

But Crystal's journalistic nose scented news, and Roger had to promise her the first chance when the story broke. Then they discussed the possibilities. In the end Crystal gave it as her opinion that Mr. Bearstowe was probably quite unscrupulous enough for murder if driven to it but it wouldn't be *like* him.

"I see," Roger said thoughtfully. "Then I wonder what did drive him. Something big, presumably. Money-troubles, do you think? They can be big enough, in all conscience. But what drove *her*? She doesn't look to me unscrupulous at all. It must have something even bigger. Love, I suppose. You know, there's something queer about this case, Crystal. It doesn't seem quite to fit?"

"Why do you suppose Mrs. Hutton was driven at all?" Crystal asked. "You say she was perfectly normal that morning. A woman of her type couldn't appear normal with her husband's murder in the offing."

"No. In fact she may not know it was murder at all, even now. Why shouldn't Mr. Bearstowe have said it was an accident, and she must just keep his name out of it for convenience? Yes! That explains her part much better. And yet—that excessive grief, for a husband she couldn't have loved? I don't know. No, it doesn't fit, somehow. I think I'll take a walk to Streatham."

But Streatham, it seemed, had nothing to tell Roger. Nor had Mincing Lane, where the offices of Hutton and Edwards were ominously closed. Enquiries as to Edwards showed only that there was no Edwards.

But at Cartwright Mansions, W1, where Mr. Bearstowe had a flat of surprising opulence for one with no means, the porter told Roger that Mr. Bearstowe was away on holiday; nor was it known when he would be back. Nor was it even known where he was; the porter thought, camping.

So that was one point established, at any rate, Roger considered, or perhaps two—or even three. At any rate, he might as well take them back with him to Penhampton the next day, little though they amounted to. What I want, Roger thought, is a couple of nice, juicy coincidences.

He got one at Paddington the following morning, when he ran into Mrs. Hutton by the bookstall.

Mrs. Hutton appeared confused, and dissembled her joy at the meeting; but Roger was officiously helpful, and gladly paid the excess fare over his third-class ticket for the privilege of travelling first with Mrs. Hutton. Mrs. Hutton could not escape without rudeness and she lacked the capabilities for that useful gift, which in this country is the prerogative of the Very Upper or the Pretty Well Lower classes.

But Roger learned little. The carriage was too full of people (with third-class tickets) to allow of intimate conversation, and Mrs. Hutton was obviously far too scared of her companion to respond to intimacy even had they been alone in the middle of the Sahara. In fact all Roger could learn was that Mrs. Hutton was very, very much on her guard. And why should she be that, if innocent?

As the train got into its rhythm, Roger listened to the refrain of the wheels.

"Mis-ter BEAR-stowe-says, Mis-ter BEAR-stowe-says…"

"You don't need to look at him when you identify him. Just keep your eyes closed and say it's your husband. They won't notice."

Had Mr. Bearstowe said that?

But why not look at a dear husband, so sadly and accidentally drowned? Is one frightened of a dead husband, that one cannot look at him? No, it didn't fit. Mrs. Hutton must have some guilty knowledge, even if she wasn't privy before the fact.

Roger looked at the faded, once-pretty face. Mrs. Hutton caught him at it, started violently, blushed unnecessarily, and looked away.

Dash it, Roger thought; the woman's as nervous as a kitten—Why? By the time the train reached Penhampton he still had not found the answer.

But if Roger felt that he had little to show for two days' work, that was certainly not the case with Detective-Inspector Brice. Almost before Roger had had time to ask for a cup of police-station tea, the Detective-Inspector had burst into his story.

"You were right, Mr. Sheringham. We've found Bearstowe. Got on his track, that is. He was camping on the cliffs, not a mile from the scene of the crime."

"Ah!" said Roger, and noted that it was now officially a crime.

"And about half-past one—that's a couple of good hours after the murder, by our reckoning—at half-past one he was seen by the farmer on whose land he was camping, he was seen taking his tent down. And he bolted for it, Mr. Sheringham. Packed his tent and things, all lightweight stuff, into the holder on his bicycle, and rode straight off. Didn't even wait to pay the farmer what he owed him for milk and such."

"I don't think I should pay too much attention to that," Roger murmured. "I should say that was fairly typical."

"Anyhow, he did. Now here's another point. When the farmer saw him, about half-past one, he hadn't shaved off his beard (yes, he still wore a beard; I found that out). When he was seen round about three o'clock, on the shore, he had."

"Ah!" Roger said again. "Yes, that's interesting. Sure of it?"

"Absolutely. The farmer was doing a bit of hedging, not fifty yards away. He says he could see Bearstowe quite plainly."

"How was he dressed?"

"The same. Pullover and grey trousers."

"Any trace of the tent or bicycle?"

"None. He must have hidden 'em before he doubled back to meet

Mrs. Hutton, and afterward he picked 'em up and he's made off with them. We've put out an all-stations request for any solitary camper to be interrogated, anywhere."

"Quick work. Now here's another point I take it that your times are correct? What time does the doctor say that death occurred?"

"Round about eleven o'clock, he thinks. Anyhow, not before ten or after one. He was dead when Bearstowe took down his tent, if that's what you mean, sir."

"Yes, partly. And when he was taking down his tent, at one-thirty, Bearstowe had his beard. Less than two hours after he hadn't. Well, here's my point. How did Bearstowe get hold of a razor? Men with beards don't carry them."

The inspector beamed. "That question occurred to me, sir."

"I'm sure it did. I just meant if he had a razor with him, wouldn't that show that the murder was premeditated? If he hadn't it was probably done on the spur of the moment."

"Well, he hadn't," the inspector said with pride. "He got hold of one, and I can tell you where he got it from. Look at this schedule, please, Mr. Sheringham."

Roger looked. The paper contained a minute inventory of the belongings of the late Mr. Hutton, as left in his rooms; it was complete down to spare collar-studs. Roger ran his eye quickly down the column. A shaving-brush and soap were listed; there was no razor.

"I say, good work," Roger said warmly. "You mean Mrs. Hutton took it to him at three o'clock?"

"That's what she met him for, the second time," said the inspector, flushed with pleasure.

"The second time? Oh, I see. You mean, she met him first at twelve, and took instructions. Yes, of course." Roger drank his tea. "Well, that certainly seems to put the case in the bag, Inspector. So all you've got to do now is to find Bearstowe."

"Yes, and Mrs. Hutton," said the inspector, not without resentment. "Gave us the slip yesterday she did, and got away to London. Went up to meet Bearstowe, for a tenner. We'll pick her up again, all right, but she may have tipped him off that—oh, there you are, sir."

"Ah! Mr. Sheringham!" said the superintendent genially. "Well, you were right, sir. I don't mind admitting it. And now we've got you and Mrs. Hutton together again. Yes, our chap picked her up at the station and brought her along. Didn't want to come, not a bit. What do you say, Brice? It's your case, but I think it's time we asked Mrs. Hutton a few questions. Eh?"

"I quite agree. Well, we'll see her in here. No, don't go, Mr. Sheringham. You were in at the beginning, so you may as well see the end." He leaned over the inspector's desk and pressed a bell.

In less than two minutes Mrs. Hutton was once again sitting on a police-chair confronting the superintendent; but this time it was a frankly terrified woman, and a police official who no longer spoke kindly. Roger looked at her, waiting like a cornered mouse for the spring of the cat, and felt rather sick. She was such a silly woman. Who but a woman of almost sublime silliness would bring her lover a razor with which to shave off his beard, but omit to bring shaving-brush and soap?

Suddenly something in his brain went "click!" and he saw the whole thing.

He glanced quickly from the superintendent to the inspector, calculating his chances. No, there was not a second to lose. In another moment the superintendent might ruin the whole thing. He must charge in, and brave the wrath that would certainly come.

"Superintendent, may I ask Mrs. Hutton one question first?"

The superintendent looked surprised but gave permission, not very graciously.

Roger moved his chair so that he could look at the woman more directly. "Mrs. Hutton, do you mind telling me this: are you sure you really know what happened on Penmouth beach that morning?"

Mrs. Hutton's jaw dropped. Obviously she had not expected the question; equally obviously, she did not know how to answer it.

Roger followed it quickly with another. "Do you know, for instance, that *murder* had been committed?"

Mrs. Hutton started to her feet, prepared to scream, thought better of it, and fainted.

"Mr. Sheringham!" exclaimed the superintendent, in real anger.

Once again Mrs. Hutton was borne unconscious into the back regions.

"Listen, Super!" Roger pleaded. "The whole point was that Mrs. Hutton never knew that murder had been committed. If you'd broken it gently, you'd have given her time to adjust herself to the idea; and she might have decided to help cover it up. Now she's had a bad shock—and she'll talk!"

"Humph!" The superintendent chewed his moustache, by no means mollified.

"We've been making a mistake from the beginning," Roger continued urgently. "A fundamental mistake. I've only just realised it. You see, this murder *was* planned. A long time ago, I fancy. A pit was carefully dug for us, and we fell into it. At first sight, I must say, it looks a terrific gamble, and yet—police procedure is so rigid. Yes, that's the clue. Police procedure is so rigid. Your own procedure protected the murderer, Super. He'd banked on it."

The superintendent raised heavy eyebrows. He did not look convinced.

"It was clever," Roger continued musingly. "He killed two birds with one stone, you see. That warrant for Hutton's arrest—he must have got wind of it somehow. By the way, was Hutton insured? I think you'll find he was. Yes, of course he must have been. Heavily. That's another thing Mrs. Hutton was intended to do: collect the insurance money. That was to be a tidy windfall for him to cash in on, you see, even if everything else went up the spout. Of course the bathing appointment was carefully arranged. Right time, right place, deserted beach and all the rest. And then—up with his heels in some convenient pool, and what does it matter if his back gets scratched on the barnacles so long as his head stays under water? Nothing simpler! Then wedge the body where with any luck it won't drift loose for a few tides; and even if it does, what's the odds?

"Mrs. Hutton of course knew nothing in advance. That puzzled me from the first. How could such a foolish woman, however amiable, be trusted with murder-plans? Obviously not. And naturally, when she met him on the beach, he told her it was an accident. But what a convenient accident! It could be made to fit right in with their own plans. So he told her the tale and about the warrant and everything, and how the authorities would probably confiscate everything by way of a post-mortem fine except the insurance money, and why he must be kept out of it all, and what she must do. I expect he had some difficulty in rehearsing her, owing to floods of tears; that's why he didn't emphasise the importance of details as he should have done. And so, of course, she managed to give things away. She would. That was the one flaw in his plan, having to rely on poor Mrs. Hutton. But of course he had no choice. Lucky for us that he hadn't.

"So that was that. And if things went right there was his future all nicely secured, and—his hated rival out of the way! Yes, I think he was really jealous. He must have been fond of Mrs. Hutton in his own way.

"After all, she suited him very well. Anyhow, he couldn't stand having a rival in her regard, so—exit rival! Hence those tears. She was fond of the rival, you see. Much too fond, in his conceited opinion.

"Now shall I tell you what suddenly gave it away to me? It was that shaving-brush and soap. How like Mrs. Hutton, I thought, to take her lover a razor to shave off his beard with and not take the shaving-brush and soap; and I wondered if even Mrs. Hutton could have been so silly.

Well, of course she wasn't. The shaving-soap wasn't taken because soap doesn't lather in sea-water, so it would be no use. Ridiculous little point for such a case to hang on, isn't it? But the case does hang on it. Because Mrs. Hutton wouldn't know a thing like that. Therefore it wasn't she who left the shaving-soap behind, therefore it wasn't she who took the razor, therefore—"

"Then who did take the razor?" interrupted the superintendent.

"Of course, the murderer! Just as he brought that false beard to Penmouth with him, bought probably months ago. By the way, how delighted he must have been with that orange pullover. You see, any bearded face surrounding an orange pullover is just the same at fifty yards as any other bearded face surmounting—"

"Here, what's all this?" The superintendent looked his bewilderment. "False beards? Orange pullovers? What do you mean, Mr. Sheringham?"

"I mean," said Roger gently, "that you shouldn't have relied on Mrs. Hutton's sole identification of her husband's body. You see, the body you've got in that mortuary isn't Hutton's. It's Bearstowe's."

IN THE PICTURE

Nicholas Bentley

Nicholas Clerihew Bentley (1907–78), best known as Nicolas Bentley (his preferred spelling), was the son of Edmund Clerihew Bentley, who himself can fairly be described as a founding father of Golden Age detective fiction on the strength of his ground-breaking whodunit *Trent's Last Case*—and who also invented the clerihew verse form. Nicolas was probably better-known as an artist than as a novelist, but he did make a number of interesting contributions to the crime genre, and two of his crime novels were filmed. One was *The Floating Dutchman* (1950), the movie version of which made little impression, though it was scored by Eric Spear, now remembered as composer of the melancholy theme tune for *Coronation Street*.

The other was *Third Party Risk* (1953), in which a man holidaying in Marseilles is rescued from drowning only to become enmeshed in a criminal plot. The film version, made in 1954, starred Lloyd Bridges, Finlay Currie, and Maureen Swanson, and—despite various changes to the plot—is also a holiday mystery, albeit set in Spain rather than France.

YOU WOULDN'T HAVE THOUGHT TO MEET HIM THAT PAUL WAS anything but what he seemed, an ordinary young man—ordinary meaning the slim-witted product of a not quite first-class public school; young, that he was approaching thirty. He was good-looking in an undistinguished way, and to women who demanded nothing more he seemed attractive.

He didn't ask much from life, and consequently no doubt, didn't get much out of it. But he was not worried by this, having too little imagination to see that it has certain gifts to offer even to someone like himself.

His ambition was to lead an unobtrusive life (preferably with a pension towards the end of it), and as he was shy and found little handicap in being lazy, he was well endowed for the purpose.

Only Katherine knew that the impression he made when you first met him—and, in fact, maintained until you got to know him as well as his reserve would allow—only she knew how different this impression was from the reality.

She knew it because she was his wife. She had experienced his long taciturn spells of introspection, his sharp outbursts of anger about trifles, and the scenes of remorse laced with self-pity that often followed these outbursts.

True, he had not been like this to begin with, though as time went on Katherine had got so used to it that she hardly noticed that such occasions were gradually growing more frequent. Or, if she sometimes suspected that they were, she did not suspect the reason.

The reason was simple; it was jealousy. He was jealous not only of other men when they admired Katherine—and she was lavishly admired, being extremely pretty, though she had no thought for anyone except Paul—not only was he jealous of them, he was jealous of Katherine herself.

He would like to have shared better still to have monopolised the admiration that was hers. But beside her he was a flop, and he knew it.

He was a flop, too, in his own right. He coupled shyness with mediocre ability, and lately he had begun to realise that the kind of success that would have meant most to him, success in terms of power and adulation and money, were never likely to come his way.

Yet, all things considered, they were not too badly off, and managed to keep up appearances without elaborate subterfuge. Their holidays were spent abroad as a rule, and in the year when all this happened they had made plans with William and Moira to drive across France.

In the ordinary way the prospect would have pleased Paul as well as Katherine. William and Moira were old friends: there would be no obligations or need for formalities on either side.

It was William who had suggested their joining forces, and in his suggestion lay the seed of Paul's preoccupation. He grew obsessed with the idea that William was in love with Katherine, and he fed his suspicions by covertly watching their behaviour towards each other and by raking over incidents from the past which were, in fact, quite innocuous and explicable in the most innocent terms.

Having no one with whom he could or would have cared to discuss this illusion, and who could have shown him its silliness and injustice, it grew in his mind, feeding on itself until it became like a wen, thrusting aside the normal tissues of reason and probability and good faith in its unnatural growth.

To no one, least of all to Katherine, did he give any sign of his suspicions.

Towards the end of August the four of them set off by car, driving south-eastwards from Cherbourg towards the Bouches du Rhone. From the moment it was decided that they should go together, Paul's mind was made up.

In the few months that elapsed before they started, he perfected his plan, whittling away at it, reducing it to its simplest terms so as to eliminate any possibility of miscalculation. Just when to put it into action remained to be seen: as long as they stuck to their route, the opportunity was bound to arise sooner or later.

Paul knew the road and knew the countryside through which they were to drive pretty well. A partisan brigade had sheltered him in the Puy de Dome after he had escaped from a prisoner-of-war camp, and the lie of the land was almost as familiar to him as it had been around Hindhead when he was a boy.

Between Le Puy and Aubenas, the high hills—hangers he would have called them in those days—were so steep that it seemed hardly possible for the trees massed on their slopes to get a hold on the shelving earth.

The road was slow and almost deserted, with sharp bends every few hundred yards. Each bend was buttressed by a low stone wall and on the other side of it was a long drop on to the steep plantations of ash and oak and chestnut that grew far below.

Each day they had stopped for a picnic beside the road, and Paul had been as he could be when he decided to make the effort, as cheerful and as expansive as anyone in the party.

The third morning had begun with a stillness and a radiance in the air that made it seem certain the day would be very hot. By half past twelve the sun's heat was relentless, and on an empty stretch of the pass they decided to stop for lunch.

An hour later with paté and a foot of French bread, some cheese, some fruit, and half a bottle of wine under his belt the vaporous sensations, the prickling of his scalp, and the chilly sweat on his palms, that Paul had felt all the morning were beginning to wear off.

He got up from the grass under the red-berried ash and stretched himself. As he stepped out from the shade into the sun the heat struck him as though an oven door had been opened. "You folks smell delicious cooking?" he said. "That's me."

He walked over to the sun-baked wall and sat down on it gingerly. The stones were almost uncomfortably hot against his bare legs.

William gave an appreciative gurk and got up. He came over to where Paul was sitting and straddled the wall beside him, looking down into the leafy abyss.

"Hold it. I'm going to take a film," Moira said. "You boys stay as you are."

She went to the car and got out her camera and stood juggling with it for a moment, frowning as she peered, at the range-finder, the edge of her tongue showing itself between her lips. "Now then hold it—"

"I *say*—look at these!" Katherine was standing up on the bank across the road. "Wild strawberries! Just enough for me."

"Is that *so!*"

Moira put the camera down and shot across the road. "Kate—you're a *pig*—!"

For the space of a cry that was never uttered Paul and William were hidden from sight behind the car. William, still straddling the warm stones of the little parapet, was taken unawares as Paul flung himself against him with all his weight. There was no time to struggle, none to cry out: he simply pitched over sideways and disappeared.

It was several seconds before the girls up on the bank heard the sound that came from Paul's throat, a sound that was something between a sob and a cackle of laughter. He came running round from behind the car, white-faced, and stood there for an instant, blabbing and gesticulating. But in a moment he was himself again.

★

During the sickening confusion that followed and on the grim journey across France and back to England, Paul's solicitude for Moira, was something that she thought she would never forget. And she was right, though her remembrance of it was not quite what she imagined it would be.

It was six weeks later, on a cool October afternoon, when detectives came to the flat and asked her to go with them. Something, it seemed, had cropped up about William's death.

Not knowing in the least what to expect, she was surprised all the same to find when she got to the station that there was someone there she knew, someone she was used to seeing in a white coat behind the counter at the chemist's.

It was the young man in the photographic department.

Gently, and with formal solicitude, a beetle-browed officer began to ask her questions about the accident. There was not much that she could say, but she told him all she could remember.

What she had forgotten—because at the time she had hardly realised it—was that when she had put her ciné-camera down, she had left it running.

AND THE POLICE WERE NOT CALLED

Bernard J. Farmer

Bernard James Farmer (1902–64) was born in Kent, and trained as an engineer, before emigrating to Canada. While convalescing after a work-related accident, he wrote a short story for the *Saturday Evening Post* which won an award and set him on a new path. In 1936, having returned to England, he published a novel based on his experiences in Canada, *Go West, Young Man*. After the Second World War he joined the "J" branch of the Metropolitan Police Force and subsequently worked as a journalist. A bibliophile, he published *The Gentle Art of Book Collecting* in 1950.

In 1953, he decided to make use of his experience in the police by turning to detective fiction and published *Death at the Cascades*, which introduced a police constable called Wigan. Wigan returned three years later in *Death of a Bookseller*, which was crammed with book lore; the novel became the hundredth British Library Crime Classic when it was republished in 2022. Farmer's career in the genre was relatively short-lived, but with Jamie Sturgeon's help I have uncovered this story, which was syndicated in various newspapers, including the *Leicester Evening Mail* on 21 July 1951.

I T WAS A BOILING HOT DAY. POLICE-CONSTABLE WARDOW, SPENDING his annual holiday at Extown-on-Sea, was enjoying a swim. He went along with a leisurely yet powerful crawl-stroke. His son and daughter swam behind him.

"Steady on, dad!" called Jack, his son.

Wardow grinned. He could still show the youngsters something. He eased up, turned on his back, and with the sea as a most luxurious cushion, gazed restfully at the sky.

"I say, dad," said Jack, "you know the old dear sitting at the corner table in the dining-room? As Joan and I came through the hall after fetching our swimsuits, she wasn't half in a state!"

Wardow grunted. For fourteen days he had left the public and its troubles far behind.

"She was telling Mrs. Mings that she had lost five pounds from her handbag," said Joan.

Wardow turned over and faced his off-spring. "Did you two tell her I'm a copper?"

It is a recognised thing that a policeman on holiday never discloses his profession, for if he does he may be drawn into arguments over the pros and cons of the law; all of which he wants to forget for a time.

"Not likely," said Jack, "after what you told us. But I thought it might interest you, that's all. She said it was stolen from her room while she was at breakfast."

Wardow had quite a name in his force for detective work, but he grunted again. "Let the locals get on with it."

And pleasantly conscious of what his uniform would feel like this hot weather, and how he was now free, he went for another swim.

He returned to the boarding house after his bathe to find it in a state of emotional upheaval. Gathered in a group in the lounge were Miss Prosset, who had lost the money (not so old despite Jack's disrespectful description), Mrs. Mings, the proprietress, Dulcie the maid, Miss Haughtibar—dubbed the Blonde Venus by Jack and Joan—and a middle-aged bachelor named Mr. Vanting.

"I demand the police," Mr. Vanting was saying. "This casts a slur on all of us."

"Most unpleasant," said Miss Haughtibar.

Mrs. Mings intercepted Wardow. "Could you advise me?" She gave the facts as already known to him.

Jack nudged Joan. He had already heard his father referred to as "such a sensible man."

Wardow turned to Miss Prosset. "You're certain you've lost the money in the house?"

"Positive. I left my bag with five one-pound Bank of England notes in it on the dressing-table before locking the door and coming down to breakfast. When I went up after, they were gone."

"Phone the police station," said Wardow.

Mrs. Mings was reluctant. "It will make a dreadful scandal. The other boarding-houses will say I'm not respectable. Do you want the police, Miss Prosset?"

"I want my money back. If the person who took it owns up now, I shan't prosecute. We were all at breakfast together—except Miss Haughtibar who came down late."

"Oh! How dare you? What a vile insinuation." She looked to Mr. Vanting for support. He said: "No-one who knows you, Tilly, would dream of such a thing."

"Unfortunately, one must face facts, dear Mr. Vanting," said Miss

Prosset. "To my knowledge Miss Haughtibar was short of money. She was talking about it to Mrs. Mings when I went in the office yesterday."

Dulcie cut in: "As soon as Miss Prosset went down to breakfast I unlocked her door with my key and went in to do the room. I was still there when Miss Haughtibar went downstairs, so I don't think she could have taken it."

"There! You will please apologise, Miss Prosset."

Miss Prosset sniffed. "That was probably when you saw my bag. You may have slipped back when Dulcie was out of my room. Your room faces mine across the landing. It could be easy for you to enter. One door-key will fit another lock. Can you swear you were near my room till I came up, Dulcie?"

"No, I can't. But if Miss Haughtibar came upstairs again I think I should have seen her."

"You might not. You were in the office this morning, Miss Haughtibar. Did she pay her bill, Mrs. Mings?"

"Yes," admitted Mrs. Mings.

"I…" Miss Haughtibar looked as if she were going to faint.

Wardow said no more about 'phoning the local police. "Can you identify your money, Miss Prosset?" he asked.

"I can identify one note. As it happens, having no scrap of paper handy a day or two back and recollecting the date of a friend's birthday, I wrote it down in tiny figures on a pound note—one of the stolen ones."

"Let's see your cash-box, Mrs. Mings."

Mrs. Mings brought the box. She opened it and handed Wardow five one-pound notes paid to her by Miss Haughtibar. He examined them carefully. Then he said: "What was the date you wrote down, Miss Prosset?"

She told him.

"Yes. That is on this note."

Miss Haughtibar burst into tears. "Oh dear, I didn't think I was doing wrong. I found the money on my table last night when I went to bed.

I thought Mr. Vanting had put it there. He knew I was in difficulties because Mum is ill and I had to send her money I put by for my holiday. He has asked me to marry him. I took it as a loan and meant to repay it."

Vanting tugged at his moustache. "I was going to lend you the money, Tilly."

"A likely story," said Miss Prosset. "You're a thief, Miss Haughtibar. However, I shan't bother to prosecute. I shall ask Mrs. Mings to send you from the house at once."

"Did you put the notes in Miss Haughtibar's room, Miss Prosset?" said Wardow.

Miss Prosset turned scarlet. She tried to out-face them, but could not.

It is always tragic to see anyone cry, and Wardow turned his gaze away as Miss Prosset's eyes filled with tears.

"All right, I did. Before she came here, Mr. Vanting and I were friends."

Miss Prosset turned to go upstairs to pack. But Wardow could not let her go quite so easily. "What you did was a wicked thing," he said sternly. "And had you succeeded and driven Miss Haughtibar from the house, your own happiness would not have prospered. One cannot found happiness upon a lie."

Later Wardow said to Mrs. Mings: "Dulcie seemed a reliable witness, and she practically let Miss Haughtibar out. I suspected Miss Prosset when she mentioned that one door-key would fit both rooms, for it meant that she had tried Miss Haughtibar's room herself. A motive became apparent when she made a dead set at Miss Haughtibar, though Dulcie, honest girl as she undoubtedly is, would come under some suspicion."

"You ought to be in the police yourself, Mr. Wardow," said Mrs. Mings.

Wardow never batted an eyelash. "Thank you, Mrs. Mings. Now, I think, I'll collect my family and we'll go on the promenade before lunch."

CONSIDER YOUR VERDICT

Anthony Gilbert

Anthony Gilbert was the principal pen-name used by Lucy Beatrice Malleson (1899–1973). She published a couple of novels as J. Kilmeny Keith before the first Gilbert book, *The Tragedy at Freyne*, appeared in 1927. *Murder by Experts* (1936) introduced her main series character, the solicitor Arthur Crook. *Death in Fancy Dress* (1933) has been published as a British Library Crime Classic, as has the dark Christmas mystery *Portrait of a Murderer* (also from 1933), which was published under the name Anne Meredith.

In *He Came by Night* (1944), Crook goes on holiday in the countryside, visiting the little Mereshire village of Bridget St. Mary, where he stumbles upon a body. Before long, he is defending a woman charged with the crime. A later novel, *Passenger to Nowhere* (1965) sees Sarah Hollis heading off on holiday to a villa in the French Pyrenees, only to find herself in need of Crook's services.

I MET GIL ARNOTT THE SUMMER I INHERITED A HUNDRED POUNDS from my Aunt Emily and went to the Langley Towers Hotel in Lakeland instead of my usual Bournemouth pension. He was about my own age, the not-quite-young thirties, and very handsome in an Italian sort of way. We were each of us on our own and we seemed to gravitate to one another from the first.

He had a car and was a magnificent driver, and I had spent some of my legacy on clothes, so it seemed worth while when he began to pay me attention. He took me driving and made me try the wheel. You'd learn in no time, he said and I could put you on to a chap who'd see you weren't fleeced if you wanted a second-hand car. Which should have warned me, but didn't.

He told me about himself, how he was a partner in a flourishing motor company, and travelled all over the place. He encouraged me to talk about myself, so I told him I had a house in London, which was true and impressed him rather—but I didn't add I ran it as a rooming-house for my living. Holidays, I thought, are the time to get away from reality.

Besides driving we used to go bathing together. I thought it must be rather poor fun for him, since I'm not much of a swimmer, and he had all sorts of silver cups and trophies at home, but he said he could swim at any time, and he'd rather have my company. I was in the seventh heaven, of course. This sort of thing had never happened to me before.

He was clever about money, too. Twice during that first fortnight he told me he'd had bonus shares from companies in which his capital was invested. He said he could put me on to a good thing if I had any spare cash, and I tried to look mysterious and said I must think about it.

I suppose you're thinking this is the oldest story in the world—but mine doesn't end in quite the conventional way.

Other people noticed us, of course, but we didn't care about them. Everything went smoothly until Rose Laxton came to the Towers. I was in the bar with Gil one evening when she appeared; I could see at once she recognised him and seemed rather surprised to find him there. He just bowed and turned back to me, as cool as a cucumber.

"Who was that?" I asked, when she'd gone.

"Oh, Just a client," he told me. "But I'm on holiday now."

I couldn't help noticing she seemed very much interested, but she didn't speak to me till the third day. Then I was hurrying through the lounge to meet Gil on a spit of land overhanging the lake that was known as the bluff—we didn't always set out together, because of the gossips—when I heard someone say my name.

"Miss Lambert. Just a minute."

I hadn't seen her in her deep chair. "Well only a minute," I said, "I have an engagement."

"If it's with Arnott," she told me, "the longer you keep him waiting the better."

I froze. "Mr. Arnott," I began, but she interrupted me: "Not much Mister about him. I suppose he's been at his old tricks, spinning yarns. Who is he this time?"

"I can't imagine what you mean, Mrs. Laxton," I told her, but my heart began to shake. I suppose all along I'd had the feeling it was too good to be true. "I know he's a partner in a motoring concern…"

"That's one way of putting it. Did he suggest selling you a car?"

"It wouldn't be any use," I told her. "I haven't any capital." I wasn't going to let her have it all her own way. "This holiday is the result of a windfall."

She actually chuckled. "So he's hoist on his own petard for once. Wait till he learns that. You won't see him for dust."

"You're quite sure it's only money that attracts him," I exclaimed, nettled.

It was her turn to look astounded. "My dear girl, you weren't born yesterday or the day before. You can't believe your virtue was ever in danger." I could have killed her for that. "I suppose he didn't mention that his partner in the motor business—actually a rather small garage off the Fulham Road—is Mrs. Arnott, to whom I believe he's devoted?"

I know what people mean when they say they've had a mortal blow. I couldn't speak. She didn't seem to notice, but went on. "Since you haven't any money there's not much harm done. Are you still going to keep your appointment, or would you like me to go instead? I'd like to see his face when he learns that for once he's been led up the garden."

I got away somehow up to my room and began flinging things into my case. I decided to go down to the town and send myself a telegram; then I could catch the late train to London. I couldn't spend another night at the Towers. But, as it happened, I had to.

I sent the telegram, as I'd planned, and then I went into the woods for rest and shade; but what with the flies and losing my way, I got precious little of either. When at last I got back to the hotel I found the lounge packed with people who all turned to stare, like feeding cattle. A woman said, "Here she is," and I could see at once that Mrs. Laxton hadn't kept her big mouth shut. I was a fool to imagine she would.

"I've been lost like the famous Babes," I said, trying to carry it off. I looked round for Gil, but he wasn't there, and a minute later I knew why.

Because it appeared that some visitors to the lake had found him there drowned, near the bluff, about an hour before. I didn't believe it, naturally. How could he drown, a man who held all those cups for diving and swimming? It had been a sort of joke between us. Take care you don't slip he'd say, because it would be quite easy there. The water's fathoms deep. And I'd laugh and reply, It wouldn't matter, because you could dive in and rescue me.

Then I had my next ghastly shock. Because it appeared that the tro-phies were of a piece with the flourishing motor concern: the truth was he couldn't swim any better than I could, which was why he'd always stopped with me at the shallow end.

I felt quite faint and someone brought me a chair. A man I hadn't noticed before said: "Weren't you going to meet Mr. Arnott this after-noon, Miss Lambert?" and I said: "After what Mrs. Laxton had to tell me—she knew him before I did, it seems—I changed my mind. She can explain. I suppose you didn't go to meet him at the bluff?" I added. I told you I felt I owed her something for that cruel taunt about my virtue.

"I didn't even know he'd be there," she said.

"I told you…"

"That you were going to meet him, but not where."

The awkward part about it from her point of view was that she'd actually been near the bluff that afternoon, but she swore there was no one in sight. It had been one of those grilling days when all sensible people stay indoors. I told them I hadn't seen a soul either, coming or going, except, of course, in the town itself.

We were both called to the inquest and thoroughly grilled. I was in a spot all right, means, motive and opportunity. I had them all. I could have gone down to the bluff first and pushed him in and then gone to the town and sent the telegram. And Rose could have done it, too, though she swore again in the witness-box I'd never mentioned the bluff. But she couldn't shake me, really she shouldn't have expected to get off so easily.

No one remembered the actual time I left the hotel, so the time of the telegram didn't help. In fact, there wasn't enough evidence against anyone to swing a cat; nobody came forward to say they'd seen two figures on the bluff, and there'd been a fatal accident there a few months before. The jury brought in an open verdict, which shows you what they thought.

A truer verdict would have been Death through Vanity. If he hadn't boasted of his swimming prowess Gil might be alive today. You see, I hadn't been able to resist the temptation to go down to the bluff to say "Hullo, I'm not stopping, I just dropped by to tell you the laugh's on you. Because I haven't got a penny to my name. I keep a boarding-house, that's all. This is one of your investments that won't yield any bonus shares." And I laughed like a drain, as they say.

It was his reply, that I can't repeat, that made me see red and give him the unexpected shove that caught him off balance and sent him toppling into the lake. I was still laughing as I heard the splash. All the way to the town I pictured him crawling back to the Towers like a drowned rat. He was what's called a snappy dresser and thought a lot about his clothes.

Let him laugh that one off, I thought.

How could I know I was signing his death-warrant? How *could* I know? The bank was only a few yards away, child's play to the swimmer he'd made himself out to be.

There's one thing that puzzles me still. Seeing I never meant to do him a mortal injury, no malice a forethought, you might say, am I a murderer?

I still don't know the answer.

CROOKED HARVEST

Shelley Smith

Shelley Smith was the pen-name under which Nancy Hermione Bodington (1912–98) wrote crime fiction. Like her contemporary Margot Bennett, she began with a couple of relatively orthodox whodunits featuring a series detective, but gained sufficient literary confidence to move on to produce rather more sophisticated novels of psychological suspense. Like Bennett, too, she was far from prolific. *An Afternoon to Kill* (1953) is an exceptionally clever novel, while *The Party at No. 5* (1954) and *The Lord Have Mercy* (1956) show her ability to create intriguing characters as well as scenarios of quietly developing tension. Her 1961 novel *The Ballad of the Running Man* was filmed as *The Running Man* (not to be confused with the Arnold Schwarzenegger movie with the same title, or indeed its 2025 remake), and starred Laurence Harvey.

After that success, however, she only wrote two more novels. Her sister Barbara, to whom she dedicated two books, was also an author, and her novel *Dramatic Murder* (published under the name Elizabeth Anthony) has been published as a British Library Crime Classic. In their later years, both sisters lived in Steyning in Sussex. This is one of the few Shelley Smith short stories; it first appeared in the *Gerald Swan 1947 Crime Album* and I'm grateful to Jamie Sturgeon for drawing it to my attention.

NIGEL ARMSTRONG WONDERED DISCONSOLATELY WHY HE HAD ever imagined that a quiet holiday in the country would be fun. It was dull, unbearably dull. No one to talk to, nothing to do but walk. He kicked an inoffensive stone along the lane. It wasn't true that country folk were friendly, they were hatefully reserved and stuck up. That adorably pretty Miss Brown, for instance. Her house was a stone's throw from his, they saw each other daily, and yet he could not get into conversation with her.

He leant against a convenient stile and lit his pipe, his strong brown hands cupping the little flame protectively. Why wouldn't the girl speak to him? Was he a leper or something? They could have had such fun together, there were so many things *two* people could do—why, even walking was enjoyable if you had a companion. And she looked such a darling. He mused idiotically about her cute trick of blushing when he said good morning to her; and then passed easily into a daydream wherein he rescued her from a burning house, or a bull, or—oh, there were hundreds of variations—and thereby earned her undying gratitude.

He walked on, immersed in his dream. The faint humming in the distance became a sudden roar in his ears. Instinctively he flung himself into the hedge. The huge, cream-coloured car flashed past him and disappeared round the bend.

"Brute!" muttered Nigel, and wiped his forehead. "Coming at that speed down a country lane."

When Nigel arrived back at his little cottage, he saw the cream-coloured roadster standing outside Miss Brown's gate. There was something vaguely familiar about it. Could it be—? No, it was ridiculous to think of it. There must be hundreds of cream Sandham Super Twelves on the road. His eyes puckered at the corners as they strained to read the number-plate.

He exhaled in a long-drawn whistle. So it *was* Oscar Thark's car! He bit savagely on his pipe-stem as he recalled how Thark had swindled him a few short weeks ago. Thark had walked into Nigel's little antique shop as cool as an iceberg—and just about as dangerous—chosen something, paid for it on the spot, and walked away. It was only later, when the shop was shut and Nigel was making up his books, that he discovered that the notes he had been paid with were counterfeit. He had wasted much time and money in trying to trace Oscar Thark—and now to run into him in this absurdly unpopulated spot! The gods were indeed sportive! Were they playing into his hands at last, he wondered.

But what was his car doing outside Judy Brown's cottage? Was he a friend of hers? Did she know he was a crook? Obviously, she didn't, or he wouldn't be there. Well, why was he there? Supposing he was up to his tricks again? Something, Nigel decided, must be done about this. He must let the girl know what she was up against. But how? You couldn't just walk into a girl's house and say, "Hullo! I just dropped in to tell you that your friend is a crook." No, it wasn't done.

Funny to think that barely an hour ago he was inventing dozens of ways of rescuing her from peril, and now that a most unpleasant peril was sitting in her best armchair he couldn't think of a thing to do about it. Life was like that, he decided bitterly.

Hastily he bolted some lunch, his mind still groping for a solution. No good! He straightened his tie, smoothed back his rumpled hair, and rose to his feet. He would have to trust to the inspiration of the moment, that's all.

His long legs covered the short distance between the two houses in a few minutes. The gate squealed hideously as he pushed it open and strode up the little path.

She must have heard the gate, for the door opened before he had time to knock. She gazed at him, her brown eyes wide with surprise, one small hand clenched at her side.

Gosh! She looked sweet in that little flowered dress. He swallowed convulsively. "Miss Brown, I hardly—well, I don't—but we are neighbours, aren't we? You see—er—oh, Lord, you must believe me—" it was harder than he had imagined. He hadn't felt such a fool since he'd gone up to collect the Scripture Prize on Speech Day; then, too, his hands had swelled up like Balloons and his tongue had felt like a lump of boiled flannel.

The girl smiled. "What is it, Mr.—?"

"Armstrong, Nigel Armstrong," he supplied hastily. "Look here, you're going to think this the most awful bit of cheek, I know. But—" he was stuck again. He ran a finger desperately round the inside of his collar.

"Do you think you could be a little more explicit, Mr. Armstrong? You see, I have somebody waiting inside," she blushed delightfully, as if she had been overbold in speaking to this strange, male creature.

"But it's just about that that I'm here," he said eagerly. "Do you know who that man is? Miss Brown, I don't know if he's a friend of yours or a complete stranger, but I do beg you to be careful, very careful."

"Careful!" she echoed. "Careful of Mr. Thark?" and a frown patterned her smooth, white forehead. "Why?"

"He's a crook," he burst out.

Her face blanched and she braced herself against the door-frame. "Are you sure?" she said, her voice so low that it was almost inaudible.

"I give you my word," Nigel said solemnly.

"We can't talk on the doorstep like this, it's absurd," she said with a gallant smile. "Won't you come in? No, I don't mean to meet Mr. Thark, I mean in my little study."

He followed her into the small, pleasantly furnished room. She motioned him to a chintz-covered armchair and sat down opposite him with a little sigh. "I can't believe that he's a crook," she said. "It seems impossible. Of course, I don't really *know* him, but he seems so nice. He's a sort of dealer, isn't he? He came down here to buy some things of mine, you see, and he really has been awfully kind about it. He has offered me full value for the things he wants to buy."

"Thank God I came," said Nigel devoutly. "That sounds just like his little game. And do you know what he would do then? He would pay you in counterfeit notes, just as he did me."

Judy Brown gasped with horror. "But whatever shall I do?" she wailed. "I need the money so badly, and he did promise to pay what I asked. Oh, surely he wouldn't cheat me, I can't believe he'd do a thing like that," she implored. "Here is the ring he wanted to buy, for which he offered me three hundred pounds." She opened her clenched fist and disclosed it on her palm.

Nigel uttered a wordless exclamation. It was a lovely thing! A large cabochon emerald in an ancient silver setting, cunningly chased. For a long moment he stared at it in silence. Then he made up his mind.

"I'll buy it from you," he said firmly, "at the same price suggested by Thark." That killed two birds with one stone, didn't it? He felt pleased with himself, excited.

"No, no," she protested, "I couldn't possibly allow it. You have done quite enough for me already."

"But I insist. You must look on it as a purely business proposition. I have taken a fancy to the ring, and I want to buy it. You, I happen to know, want to sell it—you said just now that you were in need of the money—and you might just as well sell it to me as to Thark." Nigel was eager.

Judy hesitated and a warm blush spread over her face. "You're sure you're not just doing this for—my sake?" she murmured.

"Of course not," he assured her heartily. "Will you sell to me? I'll write you out a cheque immediately," he pulled out his wallet as he spoke.

The girl nodded dubiously. She seemed stunned by the unexpected turn of events.

With a firm hand Nigel signed the cheque and exchanged it for the ring. "There," he said, "now we're both satisfied."

"I don't know how to thank you," said Judy softly. "You've been so kind." And then, with a sudden change of tone: "Good heavens, what am I going to say to Mr. Thark? Whatever excuse can I make?"

"Just tell him you've changed your mind and that you don't want to sell after all. He can't eat you, don't be scared."

"Oh, dear, I suppose he can't hurt me, but it is rather awkward, isn't it? I'd better get it over at once. I'll just have to remember that he's a crook, and that'll give me courage," she smiled. At the door she turned back. "Oh, Mr. Armstrong, I am being a nuisance to you, but have you by any chance got a car here? You see, I would like to get this cheque banked right away—for safety—and my bank is at Bichester."

"I'm sorry," said Nigel regretfully, "I'm afraid I haven't a car. I wish I had."

"And I've missed the afternoon bus," she bit her lower lip pensively, and a mischievous glint came into her eyes. "Do you—do you think I could ask Mr. Thark to drive me in on his way to the station?" she dimpled.

"You might try," Nigel grinned. "It would be a wholesome change for someone to get something out of *him*. Well, I wish you luck. I suppose I had better be toddling along now."

She grasped him firmly by the hand. "Thank you again for coming to my rescue. You've been very sweet about it all. I hope you won't regret it."

With a swift gesture, Nigel bent and kissed her full on the lips—and was gone before she could protest.

From his cottage window Nigel watched them set off in the cream-coloured car. He was glad he had kissed Judy, for he had an idea that he wasn't going to see her again. He tossed the ring meditatively in his hand. Funny to think of the demure little Miss Brown being in league with Oscar Thark. He had recognised the ring instantly as the one Thark had swindled from his shop. Thark must have just given it to her as a present. She must have had the dickens of a shock when he appeared out of the blue to tell her that Thark was a crook. And she was a quick thinker to have found a way out of the difficulty with such rapidity. Well, he was glad that she had thought of selling it to him as if it were her own; it was a bit of luck for him getting it back, he had certainly never thought to see it again.

No, the country wasn't so dull after all, he'd enjoyed himself this afternoon. He chuckled suddenly. He would give a lot to see their faces when the bank clerk handed them back the cheque. He had prudently signed it "N. AMESWRONG."

CYANIDE IN THE SUN

Christianna Brand

By the time Christianna Brand (1907–88) published her first novel in 1942, the Golden Age of detective fiction was drawing to a close. However, Brand—who in the post-war years became a stalwart member of the Detection Club—was emphatically a writer in the Golden Age tradition, an author who prized highly ingenious plotting. The cleverness of her stories, coupled with her lively characterisation, has led to her becoming one of the most popular authors whose novels have been brought to the attention of a new readership by publication as British Library Crime Classics. Her gifts are evident in novels such as *London Particular, Tour de Force, Death of Jezebel*, and *Cat and Mouse*, but perhaps her masterpiece is *Green for Danger*, which was made into a hugely enjoyable film starring Alastair Sim.

Brand was as skilled at writing short stories as she was at concocting full-length mysteries. In her lifetime, three collections of her short fiction were published, while more recently Tony Medawar has done sterling work in rescuing several uncollected stories from oblivion. This story first appeared in the *Daily Sketch* in August 1958, and a revised version was published in *The Realm of the Impossible*, a splendid anthology edited by John Pugmire and Brian Skupin.

THE ATTRACTIONS AT SCAMPTON-ON-SEA ARE MANY AND MRS. Camp, plump proprietress of the Sunnyside Guest House, exploited them all but one.

(A+)BPR+O wrote Mrs. Camp crisply across the top of her letters, promising every comfort and happiness to prospective holiday-makers.

With much turning back and forth of the pages of accompanying leaflets, they might discover what these cryptic letters stood for.

But nowhere would they find any mention of Scampton's major claim to fame—the Cyanide Murders.

Once she had them netted, however (terms payable in advance), Mrs. Camp regaled her guests freely with gossip upon this delightful theme.

She was particularly well-equipped to do so.

Widowed under distressing circumstances (her husband had choked on a crumb and suffocated himself) she had worked for many years as a district nurse before settling down to run Sunnyside.

And in this capacity had no less than three times been called to the scene of one of the now famous murders. And once had been accidentally present.

Not that this was the full tally. Several others had taken place quite without benefit of Mrs. Camp's attentions.

On these, of course, she was less informative. "The first was just an old tramp," she explained rather disparagingly, doling out soup on the Saturday evening of their arrival to the new batch of guests sitting round the communal dining-table.

"Quite well known in the town, he was. Sat down on a bench on the front to eat a sandwich—and suddenly...

"Frightful it was, they said. And they do arch up dreadfully, of course, dear.

"Let nobody tell you it's all over in a second... Mind, I didn't see that one," admitted Mrs. Camp regretfully. "I'd gone up to London that day. But I can show you the very bench."

She paused to wipe a small splash of soup from her apron bosom. "And in his hand a scrap of paper: Just saying in block letters, PREPARE TO MEET THY DOOM."

"There's always a warning isn't there?" said Miss Pratt. "I've read about it in the papers." She gave a shudder and put her soup-spoon down suddenly in her half-finished plate of soup.

Miss Pratt had come down from London on the afternoon train.

She worked in one of the big stores in their "medical and surgical" department.

She had been, like Mrs. Camp, a nurse at one time, but had abruptly given it up and now dealt with medicines but not with invalids direct.

She was perhaps 35; not pretty but very fresh and spruce. If one is 35 and not pretty, the next best way to make oneself attractive is to be fresh and spruce.

"'Prepare to meet thy doom'—such a shocking message," said Miss Pratt. "They might at least have put it a little less horribly. Even 'Prepare to meet your end' would be better than 'doom.'"

"Only that might sound a bit like a whiting," said Mr. Culham. "Cooked with its tail in its mouth."

He smiled at Miss Pratt. And Miss Pratt's poor heart did a little somersault and was severely ordered back into place again. Mr. Culham was a married man.

Mrs. Camp continued to dole out with a pretty equal generosity horror and haricot mutton.

"Now the second murder, I did see. Helping out, I was, at the fête in the garden at the Old Ladies' Home. And an old lady went that time."

Miss Jones gave a little shudder.

Miss Jones was a model, it seemed, free-lancing in London, and naturally must keep her figure and couldn't touch a potato. The bare idea had made her go pale.

She was an entrancingly pretty girl and considering her evident success at her glamorous job—for she seemed to have money to spend—very modest and simple.

Mrs. Camp, oblivious of the shudders, continued to regale them with the details of the passing of the poor old lady and her Devonshire Split.

Mr. Culham looked at his wife in some alarm. Her white, peevish face—powdered whiter than ever to attract the more sympathy for her purely imaginary ailments—was more peevish than ever.

He knew that when they got to their room she would rail at him for bringing her to a place where such dreadful things could happen.

He plunged his head in his hands, his pale, soft hair sticking out spikily through his fingers in a little-boy way that made poor Miss Pratt's heart stand on end again.

"John," said Mrs. Culham sharply, "Don't sit there with your elbows on the table!"

Mrs. Gerald did not wait to get to her room before declaring her opinion about the suitability of Scampton for a holiday. "We should have been informed. I call it false pretences, Mrs. Camp, not warning us first."

"It's been in all the papers," protested Mrs. Camp. "And anyway there hasn't been a murder for months now. I daresay it's all over."

Mrs. Gerald was a monstrous old woman with a high colour and a high, hard, hooting voice. "Everywhere else will be booked," said Mrs. Culham, joining forces with her. "Or we should demand our money back and leave at once."

"A maniac at large!" cried Mrs. Gerald on a top note. "None of us is safe. We may all be murdered in our beds."

"We must be careful not to eat Devonshire Splits in our beds," said Mr. Raie.

Hugo Raie was the sixth and last of Mrs. Camp's guests: A tall, thin young man with a permanently sorrowful expression which had quite gone to Sharon Jones's heart already. And a faintly foreign accent which by no means detracted from his interesting melancholy.

"But where iss this cyanide supposed to come from, Mrs. Camp? It iss not part of the natural attractions of Scampton. We do not breathe it in and out with the ozone?"

"The murders are not all in Scampton," said Mrs. Camp.

"One was in the train. A girl, that was. All by herself in the carriage and not a corridor train. And it didn't stop anywhere.

"But when they got to London..."

She described with loving detail the scene when the train arrived at the terminus. "And nothing to show for it but a roll and butter she'd bought at the last minute at the station buffet."

She stood up once more, serving-spoon in hand. "A bit more pud, Mrs. Gerald, no *do*?"

If it was Mrs. Camp's plan to counter the lavishness of her table by putting off the appetites of her guests, she had found the perfect solution. Nobody by this time fancied a second helping of pud.

It was a slightly uneasy little group that wandered out to the promenade on that first evening (averting their eyes from the bench, kindly pointed out by Mrs. Camp, where the tramp had expired).

All about them happy holiday-makers were strolling and laughing, evidently oblivious of the prevailing perils of their chosen resort.

"I think it's dreadful," insisted Mrs. Culham, her dark-rimmed eyes blazing in her sick, white, peevish face. "We must leave tomorrow, John. You should never have brought me here."

"I don't think anyone will want to kill *us*," said John, mildly.

"Who would want to kill those others? A tramp, an old woman, a young girl, all the rest of them. It's a maniac, there's no motive in it, it's someone who gets a pleasure out of doing it…"

"So it might just as well be one of us, you mean?" said Miss Pratt in her pleasant, grave voice.

"What are the police doing about it?" said Mrs. Gerald. "That's what I'd like to know."

"Baffled," said Sharon Jones, and tried a little exchange of amused glances with Hugo Raie.

But young Mr. Raie was not laughing. "Do you think this iss funny?" he said. "For my part I do not. I think it iss frightening.

"Here in England, you don't believe in 'feelings' in premonitions— you call it 'witchcraft' and you dismiss it. But in my country we believe in premonitions—and in witchcraft, too.

"And I tell you frankly that I have 'feelings' about this horrible thing. I tell you frankly that standing here in the sunshine with the sands so yellow and the sea so blue and the sky so fresh and clear, I am cold inside and dark, and very much afraid."

And he swung about and cried out suddenly, on a sharp note of fear. "What did I tell you? It *is* witchcraft! Look there—look there!"

Very slowly, slowly and surely moving down the long, golden promenade, a black blot in the colour and movement and gaiety of the holiday crowds in their bright summer dress—an old, old man.

An old man, black as a carrion-crow in his black suit and black hat and black-gloved hands. Carrying aloft a banner as black as himself.

And on the banner, in letters of gold, the words: PREPARE TO MEET THY DOOM.

They swung about and stood staring with thundering hearts and faltering breath, caught for a moment in that age-old web of darkness that the word "witchcraft" thrice repeated had spun about them.

And then—a shrug, a rather forced smile, a careless word.

For what was it after all?

An old man carrying a banner with a warning sent out by some killjoy religious sect.

But: "You see!" said Hugo Raie, with a touch of triumph. "You cannot say there iss not something of witchcraft, even here."

And he stooped, carelessly, and picked up a scrap of paper from the ground. "Hass one of you dropped this?"

A scrap of paper—which had not been there a minute, half a minute, ago. Dropped by one of them: by one of the Culhams, by Miss Pratt, by old Mrs. Gerald, by Sharon Jones—by Hugo Raie himself.

A small scrap of paper: printed upon it in large, black, pencilled letters, PREPARE TO MEET YOUR END.

Within 24 hours one of the six people staring down at that scrap of paper was to die.

What Hugo Raie had said was true. It was a dreadful thing to be among gay holiday-makers in the blue and gold of the summer evening's sunshine by the sea—and to be dark and cold inside and very much afraid.

"A joke," said Mrs. Camp, dismissing it, when the huddled, uneasy little group, clinging together with some sort of forlorn trust in security in numbers got back to Sunnyside.

"A trick. One of you trying to be funny."

"Or some stranger perhaps, in the crowd," suggested Hugo Raie, doubtfully. "We were surrounded by people, up there on the promenade."

"No," said Sharon Jones.

"No?"

"Don't you see—it *must* have been one of us. One of you two," she said to the Culhams (though anyone less likely than Mrs. Culham to play practical jokes it would be hard to imagine).

"Or Miss Pratt or yourself, Mr. Raie. Or me. Because of the way it was put."

"'Prepare to meet thy doom'?"

"But it wasn't," said Sharon. "It usually was 'Prepare to meet thy doom.' But it wasn't this time: It was 'Prepare to meet your end.'

"And only six of us not counting Mrs. Camp who wasn't there—could have known that Miss Pratt had said only an hour before at supper that that would have been a less shocking way to phrase it."

"A joke," insisted Mrs. Camp again.

But next morning, round the Sunnyside breakfast table, five people sat ashen-faced. Mrs. Culham, the sixth of the party, being, as was her habit, still upstairs in bed.

For a letter arrived by the post, addressed in thick pencilled capital letters that made Mrs. Camp gasp and clutch at her bosom when she saw them.

"It's the same! It's the letters on the message the old lady had. I saw it in her hand. And the others—they were reproduced in the newspapers, the other warning messages.

"After the murders, I mean—to see if anyone might recognise the writing and inform the police.

"I've seen all the messages: Actual or reproduced. And these letters are the same."

The envelope was addressed to Mrs. Culham.

"To Lena! To my wife!" cried John Culham, hardly able to believe his eyes. "Who on earth would want to—to do Lena any harm?"

"This murderer doesn't want to murder anyone in particular, you see," said Mrs. Camp. "He just wants to—well, murder."

"But Lena! Why Lena?"

"Why the tramp? Why the poor girl on the train? Why that poor old Colonel Thomas?" said Mrs. Camp, unhappily shrugging. Colonel Thomas had been the Scampton Murderer's No. 5.

"Do you think I'd better open it?" said John Culham, at last. He looked round at them with agonised, anxious eyes. "My wife, she's so—nervous already. Don't you think I'd better?"

And, after all, it might not be the murder message. It might be an ordinary letter. Why frighten her needlessly? They all agreed: "Yes, yes, open it yourself, before she comes down."

Inside the envelope—a scrap of paper. Bearing in the same block capitals five words, PREPARE TO MEET THY DOOM.

"I dare not tell her," said Mr. Culham. "She—well, she suffers from her nerves already. You've all seen her."

"If it's not a joke," said Sharon, her lovely blue eyes as wide and blue, in her terror, as a Siamese kitten's, "you do realise that it's one of us? One of US."

It was agreed at last to say nothing for the moment to the police: Not to risk unnecessarily distressing Mrs. Culham. Joke or no joke the sender of the notes was one of themselves.

Surely, then, it would be safest to keep together, so that the innocent might watch the guilty and so best guard Mrs. Culham from harm.

"He can hardly strike while the rest of us are on the look-out all the time. But if we disperse…"

Well, there was the girl in the train, the man at the theatre. To be out of Scampton, once one had received the warning, was by no means to be out of harm's way.

Better by far to stick together, to watch one another, to vet every mouthful of food Mrs. Culham ate.

For the poison was always conveyed by means of food.

The second Sunday in August is Landladies' Day in Scampton. By long tradition, the small private hotels and guest-houses entertain their guests to an evening picnic on the beach.

Each lady takes a hamper of food and drinks for her own little group.

The moonlight bathing, games, dancing, music and jollity are common to all.

To this junketing, Mrs. Culham, the only member of the Sunnyside ignorant of the threat to her safety, in her whining way consented to go.

And true to their joint plan for her protection, the rest went, too. It is, after all, no easier to poison a person's food at a picnic than it is indoors.

"I'll keep everything very, very simple," said Mrs. Camp, talking it over with the little Safety Committee. "No prepared stuff that might be doctored in advance. I can't be watching my kitchen every moment of the day.

"Everything fresh, still wrapped—just as I buy it. And some of you shall come with me to each of the shops. And nothing particularly marked for Mrs. Culham—everyone will take just what comes as it comes."

And no one person, she suggested, should wait on Mrs. Culham. "Each of us will do our bit—passing things, pouring the drinks and so on."

It was clear that not much idle holiday-making was coming the way of any of the Sunnyside guests for the next little while. Always excepting Mrs. Culham.

But none of them felt much inclined for jollifications, anyway.

And the meal when it came was certainly simple enough. They sat in a ring on the hard, dry sand, all scuffed with the feet of the merrymakers, the checked tablecloth spread in the centre.

And all about them other little groups sat laughing and talking and carefree each with its own presiding Mrs. Camp.

"Now," said Mrs. Camp, "here's the loaf and some butter. And that's the lettuce in front of you, Miss Pratt, and a packet of ready-carved ham in front of Mr. Raie.

"So now you take the knife, Mr. Culham, and cut the loaf, and pass each slice to me and I'll butter it.

"Miss Pratt can pop a piece of lettuce on it, Miss Jones can shake a little dressing on the lettuce from that bottle, and Mr. Raie shall lay a slice of ham on top of the lot.

"And Mrs. Gerald," said Mrs. Camp, determinedly gay, "shall be Queen of the Mustard Pot!

"Now—one, two, three: Off we go!"

They had eaten little lunch and not much tea, all watching Mrs. Culham's every mouthful as they ate.

Surely now they might relax a little under so foolproof a plan?

"Bags I the crust!" cried Mrs. Camp, still dreadfully gay, as the first slice went its round.

If there's been any tampering with the ends of the loaf, her glance said to her fellow-conspirators, that's my responsibility, and I shall take the outside to show good faith.

The crust passed round, was duly buttered, piled with salad, dressing, ham and a dab of mustard.

Mrs. Culham watched with offended astonishment while their landlady reached out her hand for it and took a large bite.

Mrs. Culham sat waiting with irritable impatience for her own slice.

Mr. Culham cut the slice, Mrs. Camp, using the same knife as before, digging the butter from the same part of the half-pound block as the first had come from, slapped on butter.

Miss Pratt forked a leaf of lettuce from the heap before her.

Sharon Jones shook a little dressing over it from the bottle.

Hugo Raie speared a slice of ham and laid it reverently on top of the lettuce.

Mrs. Gerald added a touch of mustard and passed the heaped open sandwich to her next-door neighbour.

All so safe, so simple, so utterly foolproof.

A moment of agonising uncertainty, a moment of petrified astonishment, an eternity of horror—all compressed within 60 seconds of watching that terrible, jerking, gasping marionette, threshing about in its death-throes on the dry, scuffed golden sand.

Exactly one minute after taking her first mouthful, Mrs. Culham was dead.

Saturday, Sunday, Monday, Tuesday—it had settled down to be a wonderful August.

And the ninth of the Cyanide Murders was the only blot on the blue and gold of those shining summer days at Scampton-on-Sea.

Monday had begun a week of carnival—little damped, it seemed, by headlines screaming the news that the Scampton slayer had struck again.

But down at the end of the pier it was almost deserted. Sharon Jones leaned there on the wooden rail with Hugo Raie.

"It's so dreadful, so dreadful…"

But one had said it so many times that the words and even the emotion itself had almost lost meaning.

"And so frightful for poor Mr. Culham."

"Also for poor Mrs. Culham," suggested Hugo dryly.

"But they had him down at the police station for hours and hours."

"If a gentleman iss not getting on so well with hiss wife," said Hugo, in his soft foreign voice, "and thiss wife suddenly dies…"

"How can you suggest such a thing?" cried Sharon, horrified. "Mr. Culham has never even been in Scampton before. How could he possibly be the Cyanide Murderer?"

"Mr. Culham *says* he has never been in Scampton before.

"And I do not say that he is the Cyanide Murderer. Perhaps *A* cyanide murderer—but that's a different thing."

"But…"

"My dear Miss Jones—a maniac in Scampton kills off half a dozen people at random, first sending the message PREPARE TO MEET THY DOOM.

"This need not prevent anyone else killing off one person or more, not at all at random—warning message and all.

"Especially," added Hugo, "if the message can be conveniently prevented from ever reaching its destination. And the message to Mrs. Culham was prevented from reaching its destination."

"Why should poor John Culham do such a thing?" said Sharon.

"Have you not noticed," suggested Hugo in his young-old way, "that Mr. Culham looks upon Miss Pratt with a very friendly eye?"

"They never even saw one another before Monday."

"How do you know?" said Hugo, complacently.

"Well, I think you're perfectly horrid," said Sharon again.

"And anyway, as it happens he can't have done it. I know he can't. I watched him. He cut off the crust and passed it on the tip of the bread-knife to Mrs. Camp.

"And then he just sat and waited with the knife sort of poised in the air, and then he cut the next slice and passed that on in exactly the same way.

"And the other hand didn't touch anything, not anything.

"So," said Sharon, triumphantly, "as you're such a great detective— where does that lead us?"

It led them, said the great detective quite unperturbed, to the only remaining corner of the triangle—it led them to Miss Pratt.

And so absorbed was Sharon in considering the case against Miss Pratt that she failed to observe that in his absorption, Mr. Hugo Raie had quite ceased to talk with a foreign accent.

The Rock Gardens, too, were deserted in favour of the carnival procession.

And here on a bench overlooking the formal (and really quite hideous) patterns of marigolds sat Mrs. Gerald and Mrs. Camp.

Mrs. Gerald was still in a high stage of indignation at Mrs. Camp's having allowed her to come to Scampton at all.

"But I can't turn away business," pleaded Mrs. Camp, almost tear-fully. "And you must have read the papers. Anyway, you can't be the Maniac, can you?"

"I?" Mrs. Gerald's high nose flamed more crimson than ever.

She got up and stood towering over stout little Mrs. Camp with uplifted parasol as if for two pins she would strike her.

"I? The Maniac! Why it's you," squawked Mrs. Gerald, "who's the Maniac if anyone is.

"You're the only one that's been in Scampton all this time while these murders were going on."

"Any or all of you may have been in Scampton," said Mrs. Camp, calmly. "How do we know? None of us knows anything about the others."

"We know something about you," insisted Mrs. Gerald. "We know *you* were in Scampton. And very fishy, I call it, you being at the scene of the death so many times."

"I've been at the scene of more deaths than that, my dear," said Mrs. Camp. "I'm a trained nurse."

"Deaths, yes. These happened to be murders."

"I don't inquire first," said Mrs. Camp, still equably, "what my patients are proposing to die of. I just help them."

"Help them to die," agreed Mrs. Gerald.

"If you like to put it that way—yes," said Mrs. Camp. "Help them to die." But not, she added, by offering them doses of cyanide. With or without mustard.

"What do you mean?" cried Mrs. Gerald.

"I mean that I buttered that slice of bread—same pound of butter, same knife, and all of you watching me. And you put mustard on the ham—same pot, same spoon and all of us watching *you*.

"So don't suggest silly things to me," said Mrs. Camp, "and I won't suggest them to you.

"And as for her having been in Scampton at the time of the murders—two could also play at that game also.

"And I have a good memory for faces," concluded Mrs. Camp.

"So you recognised her, too?" said Mrs. Gerald.

It wasn't quite what Mrs. Camp had meant. But she listened with growing enthusiasm to Mrs. Gerald's indictment of Miss Pratt.

And in the empty lounge at Sunnyside Miss Pratt sat with poor, sad, anxious, remorse-stricken Mr. Culham.

"Dear Mr. Culham—you shouldn't reproach yourself. You and Mrs. Culham weren't happy."

"She changed," acknowledged Mr. Culham wretchedly. "We were happy enough at first, you know, but—she changed."

But his mind wandered away to the ever-recurring question. Who could have wanted to kill her?

"Me, Mrs. Camp, and yourself, Miss Pratt—we've been through it all so many times. Then that little Miss Jones.

"All she did was shake dressing from a bottle on to the lettuce."

"A proprietary brand. The bottle had never been opened."

"And young Raie. A slice of ham. Any slice of ham. Out of a foil-wrapped package he had never set eyes on. He just speared a piece and put it on to the bread."

"On to the lettuce," corrected Miss Pratt. "*I* put the lettuce on the bread."

"From a bundle of salad rolled in a damp table-napkin to keep it fresh."

"Which I, also, had never seen before," observed Miss Pratt.

"Of course, of course. I noticed," remarked John Culham, idly, "that on both occasions you held the fork in your left hand."

"Yes, I'm left-handed," agreed Miss Pratt. But her mind was elsewhere.

She said delicately: "Have you ever just wondered, Mr. Culham...? I mean, your poor wife—always fancying herself ill and unhappy...?"

"You mean suicide?" said John Culham bluntly. "But it's impossible. She wasn't truly distressed; She had nothing on earth to commit suicide *for*.

"And then in such a way! As if she—or anyone would!

"Everyone knows that a death from cyanide is dreadful. And after all those descriptions Mrs. Camp gave us... My wife was quite upset... She couldn't get them out of her mind—that wretched tramp on the bench, the old lady in her garden chair..."

"It was a bath-chair," corrected Miss Pratt. "One of those old fashioned ones, wicker-work..."

She had gone very pale, she spoke in a dreamy, far-away voice. "She was—half in, half out of it.

"All—all crooked, arched-up as you say and—and froth you know, and..."

Suddenly the light came back to her eyes, she flung up her hand to her mouth. "What have I been saying? I didn't mean to—to say anything. I just—just mean I pictured it all..."

"You were there!" said John Culham. "You were at the Home when the old lady was murdered. You pretended you were never in Scampton before, but you were here when at least one of the murders happened."

And he caught at her wrist and pulled her hand away from her face and said, "Weren't you? Weren't you?"

It was the following morning that the second warning came. PREPARE TO MEET YOUR END.

It was addressed to Miss Pratt.

Now it was Miss Pratt's turn to spend hours and hours with the police.

John Culham waited for her, leaning wretchedly over a low wall, watching with unseeing eyes while elderly gentlemen in white linen caps padded about the velvety bowling green.

She appeared at last, exhausted and much distressed. "They wanted me to go away. But I won't.

"We have the murderer in our midst, one of six people—you or Mrs. Camp or Mrs. Gerald, or one of those two young people, Hugo Raie or Sharon Jones.

"Or me, of course," said Miss Pratt, trying to smile. "And, incredible, impossible though it seems to say it here, in all this sunshine and colour and light-heartedness all around us—incredible though it seems, one of us is a murderer, a homicidal maniac.

"And he's out for blood—he or she, whichever it is. The mood is on him. He's killed and he wants to kill again.

"If it's not me, he'll go for someone else. I can be protected: but if I run away and hide, he'll go for someone else in my place and that person won't be known in advance and can't be protected.

"So I must stay. We must all stay. Once we disperse, the whole horrible business will begin all over again." She took a deep breath. "And what is more, we're repeating that picnic tonight."

"No," said John Culham, violently, "NO!"

"It's the only chance."

"I refuse. I won't allow it. Do you think I want to see *you* die—as my wife died...?"

"No more people must die as she died," said Miss Pratt. "That's why we must trap the killer."

He consoled himself. "The killer will know it's a trap. You'll be safe. He daren't strike."

"You forget that the killer's mad. Perhaps he's too mad to understand his own danger."

"You aren't very consoling," said John Culham. And Miss Pratt's heavy heart contrived a tiny leap, dejected though it was, at the anxiety in his voice.

★

It was a dreadful day. At the instance of the police, anxious to prevent panic, no mention of the warning note was permitted to reach the public outside Sunnyside.

Isolated among all the gay holiday-makers, the little group must carry their terrors in their own shrinking hearts.

Nor did they trust themselves now in one another's company. Solitary, they crept off to their long interviews with the police, solitary they crept back to Sunnyside.

To lunch at the communal table was unthinkable. Each alone, they slunk into unfrequented shops and bought biscuits and buns to stave off hunger till the evening meal should come... looking fearfully over their shoulders choosing only wrapped foods.

The lunch hour came and passed. Mrs. Camp, all by herself, presided at her dining table. She ate a good meal. But then the food had been prepared for herself, by herself.

Even she felt the need to be alone. She went up to her room and let out the strings of her corsets a bit and kicked off her shoes and lay down on her bed.

The photograph of the late Mr. Camp gazed back at her as she lay. She got up and put him away in a drawer.

"You're better out of the way for a bit, Tom," she said to it. "You get on my nerves, dear."

She lay down on the bed again. And her nerves can't have been too much tormented, for in a very short while she was soundly sleeping.

And John Culham in his room also lay wearily on his bed, and also stared at a photograph—and also addressed it.

"Don't look at me so reproachfully, Lena," he said. "It wasn't my fault. I just can't—can't help myself. I'm not to blame, truly!"

Through the flimsy wall he could hear the sound of many matches scraping against the side of a box, and he wrenched away his wounded thoughts and wondered incuriously what old Mrs. Gerald might be up to.

A smoking pile of old letters, invitation cards, bridge scores in process of feverish destruction would have answered him had he been able to see through the wall as well as hear.

And above in two little top rooms, two young people stared into two mirrors; and each thought: "I must not look so pale; they'll begin to suspect."

So Sharon Jones applied pink rouge, paused and went to a drawer.

She prised up the lining paper and took a peep at a legal-looking document—or copy of a document—hidden there, hastily pushed it out of sight again and went back to her dressing-table.

Hugo Raie sloshed half the contents of a bottle of brown-tinted lotion into his forehead, cheeks and chin.

Leaving off only to make an occasional dash to the window and peer out and up to where the lead guttering ran along the edge of the sloping roof.

But there was nothing to see there: not a sign, not a hint of a sign of that fat black pencil pushed away out of sight in a crack between guttering and roof—a thick black pencil with a very soft black lead in it...

So the long day passed. And suddenly the day was over and, all too soon, it was evening.

Wearily, anxiously, they trudged down to the picnic spot, spread the checked tablecloth, arranged themselves in a circle around it: Not one of them without dread in his heart—murderer and all.

And in the shadows behind them, dodged behind rocks, crouched between the flower-beds in the terraced cliff armed with heaven-knows-what paraphernalia of telescopic lenses, tape-recorders, first-aid sets and all the rest of it were the police.

Mrs. Camp slowly opened her hamper. The last stage in the case of the Scampton Cyanide Murders had begun.

The bread, fresh from the bakers, the bread knife, the unwrapped butter, the butter knife, the lettuce, the unopened bottle of dressing, the ham, the mustard pot.

Mrs. Camp, her round cheeks not so healthily pink as usual, shoved the load over to John Culham.

"We'd better begin."

But suddenly John Culham couldn't. He couldn't. "You all seem to forget, it was my wife who died. How can I sit here, how can I go through that same routine?"

"I'll change places with you," said Miss Pratt. "I'll take over the bread."

The crust was sliced off, buttered, garnished: came round full circle. "The order has changed a bit of course," Hugo Raie pointed out.

"With Mrs. Culham not—not here, the numbers are different. Who's eating the crust this time? Who's eating the first slice?"

"I'm eating the first slice," said Miss Pratt, quietly. "I'm the one threatened. That must be as it was before.

"It was the first slice that Mrs. Culham ate and it'll be the first slice that I eat. It's all arranged."

As to the crust, she said, the crust was harmless, that had been proved. It didn't matter much who ate the crust: or *if* anyone ate the crust.

"We should keep it the same," said Mrs. Gerald with her customary majesty. "Someone must eat the crust."

"Well, perhaps," agreed Miss Pratt.

"Anyone for the crust?"

No one seemed violently eager to take advantage of this offer. There was a short silence. Then into the silence a voice said casually: "All right—I'll eat the crust."

As they had sat on that Sunday night, stuck silent and motionless with tension while slowly and firmly Mrs. Camp had eaten her way through the garnished crust, so now they sat again, absolutely silent absolutely still…

And slowly Mrs. Camp's pink mouth opened, white teeth parted, thrust forward bit into bread and salad and mustard-crowned ham…

And suddenly all the night was filled with screaming: with one word screamed out between rapidly tensing jaws, through foam-spattered lips—one word jerked out in an eternity of agony that yet lasted for only one single threshing, writhing, arching, screaming minute of pain and horror and then was absolutely still.

One word: "LEFT-HANDED!"

And the night was filled with the sound of men's voices shouting, and the men's boots running over the hard, dry sand towards them.

The cries of the startled holiday crowds all about them on the beach.

But at the storm-centre, five people stood petrified to stone. Just staring. Staring at the writhing thing on the sands that writhed slower and slower even as, speechless with horror, they gazed upon it, and at last was still.

Would never move again, would never speak again…

AND WOULD NEVER KILL AGAIN. The Cyanide Murderer of Scampton-on-Sea was dead.

And one clue only to that death. "Left-handed!"

Mr. and Mrs. John Culham—that quiet, rather melancholy, very devoted couple, talked to no one about the Scampton murders except each other.

For to them it was not a matter for juicy gossip and scandal. Nine people were dead, among them the first Mrs. Culham. And now the murderer herself…

The infamous Mrs. Camp, maniac, was dead.

Her husband had died "under distressing circumstance"—had choked on a crumb of bread, been ignored as supposedly fooling. But had not been fooling… had suffocated and died.

Had died leaving her (already, no doubt, mentally unbalanced) with a grudge against the world which had failed to save him.

She had taken up her nursing again and gradually accumulated, as the years went by, tiny doses of stolen poison, adding up at last to enough to kill—and kill—and kill again.

At first she had gone cautiously, had not cared what victim she had selected, had not waited to see him die in agony, to avenge that other death.

A tramp well known in the district with a set routine of habits such as many tramps acquire.

Shuffling along the promenade, searching the litterbins for scraps of food.

And his murderer was innocently away for a day in London. And the old lady at the garden fête where kind Campy was helping Matron—in the refreshment tent…

And the girl in the train, buying her ham roll oblivious in the scrum round the buffet counter of the small, dumpy figure buying a similar roll just next to her.

And the Colonel, hastening away from her friend and fellow-landlady, Mrs. Boyle's—having broadcast his intention of taking his mother on the following Saturday to a matinée.

A tray of tea and bread and butter—passed so willingly along the row of stalls by the helpful hands of the unobtrusive little woman who had shortly afterwards departed…

"Always bread," said Mrs. Culham. "Always bread."

To nobody, not even to her husband, had the erstwhile Miss Pratt confided that one flash of illumination that had come to her as—left-handed—she cut that loaf.

"I wonder if any of us, even the police, would ever have guessed," mused Mr. Culham, "if she hadn't cried out as she died, 'Left-handed!'"

"I wonder," said Mrs. Culham, meekly.

For—why tell? Why say anything about it—about that one moment of inspiration as, left-handed, she had sliced the loaf.

About that split-second decision as the whole plot unfolded itself to her.

Shall I cry out and stop her eating the crust and for death by the hangman's rope? But—if she should escape from that! She is a murderess nine times over. Is this not the moment to make sure she does not escape?

"She got more daring with each murder, I suppose," said John Culham. "And of course she preferred to see it happening.

"But for that and the fact that you're left-handed, the murders might still be continuing." Just a loaf of bread, he said, shaking his head at the ingenuity of it. And a breadknife...

An innocent loaf. Bought openly at the baker's unwrapped, untouched. Don't cut yourself—pass it to someone else, to anyone, it doesn't matter.

And, of course, the knife it's to be cut with.

All eyes on the loaf. Who looks at the knife?

For if you slice a loaf with a knife coated with poison—the poison will get on to *two* slices of bread.

But, of course, if you coat only one side of the knife with the poison—that's different.

You hold the knife in your right hand. You smear the side of the blade nearest to you with the poison. The loaf is held with the left hand, the knife cuts away the crust—which is innocent of poison.

But the next slice has been smeared with the poison on the near-side of the blade.

What's more the knife has been cleaned by the contact with the bread, and now shows no trace of poison.

All so splendidly foolproof. Except that Miss Pratt—as she then had been—was left-handed.

So Miss Pratt held the loaf with her right hand and the knife in her left, and the poisoned blade came next to the crust.

And Mrs. Camp claimed the crust—and opened her smiling pink mouth and sank her white teeth into white bread and golden butter and pale green lettuce and pale pink ham with its white fat glistening.

And all in one moment of horror, the long, grim saga of the Scampton Murders was ended.

THE FLY

John Bingham

John Michael Ward Bingham, 7th Earl of Clanmorris (1908–88) was a spy who became a crime writer. After working in journalism, he was recruited into MI5 by the spymaster and naturalist Maxwell Knight (who had himself published a couple of thrillers in the 1930s). A younger colleague called David Cornwell, who had previously made good use of his artistic gifts by illustrating two of Knight's books about birds and animals, was inspired by Bingham's literary success to become a novelist himself. He wrote under the name John le Carré, and has acknowledged that Bingham was a key inspiration for his series character George Smiley.

Bingham's first novel, *My Name is Michael Sibley* (1952), focuses on an uncompromising police investigation and both *Five Roundabouts to Heaven* (1953) and *A Fragment of Fear* (1965) were filmed. Thereafter Bingham's literary career faltered, and an attempt at the start of the 1980s to create a police detective (called Brock) in the mould of Inspector Morse yielded just two books that failed to achieve anything remotely comparable to Colin Dexter's success. Judging his career as a whole, however, Bingham remains a strangely undervalued crime novelist. This story was first published in the *Evening Standard* on 8 June 1953.

S UPERINTENDENT WILLS ALWAYS SAID THAT IF HE HAD NOT BEEN born British, he would like to have been born Norwegian.

From the moment when he landed with his fishing rods for his annual holiday, and made his way inland by lake steamer and by road, he felt at peace.

Moreover, at Sandsaeter, where he always stayed, the fishing was free, an important consideration for a modestly paid policeman with a passion for throwing flies over trout.

It began the second night of his arrival. As he had expected, Mr. Geoffrey Stoneham had already been at Sandsaeter a week. He was a retired architect who had been coming to Sandsaeter for the previous ten years, an elderly man whom Wills respected as a fisherman but did not care for personally.

Nobody was surprised, that evening, when Stoneham took his favourite rod after supper and said he was going to try a couple of hours' night fishing.

When he finally came back, or was brought back, he was dead, with a jagged wound in his forehead.

"A deplorable accident," said Red Lars, the hotel-keeper.

"Shocking," said Wills, staring at Stoneham's rod which had been found in the empty boat. "Where was he found?"

"In the river below the Elk Lakes. We began to search at dawn when we found his bed had not been slept in. But the body had drifted far with the wind that arose in the early hours, and it was many hours before we found him. The boat with his fishing tackle was lodged against a rock at the side of the lake."

Wills examined all that was left of Stoneham. The jacket had been half torn away by jagged rocks, there were slits in the trousers, and the body was shoeless. Wills felt in the soggy inside pocket of the jacket.

"His wallet?"

"Gone," sighed Red Lars. "Doubtless at the bottom of the lake, and with it all his money. He always carried it with him. I do not think he trusted us greatly."

Wills nodded and filled his pipe, and taking his own rod strolled along the route which Stoneham must have taken.

The summer was still young, and though the roads were clear of snow, and much of the ground, too, many of the lakes were still fringed with the remains of the winter's downfall.

Wills made his way to the place on the Elk Lakes where the little snub-nosed clumsy boat was habitually beached, and stared at Stoneham's footprints, thoughtfully, as he had stared at Stoneham's body.

The footprints led from the stony verge of the road down to the lake's edge, to where the boat had been beached; they were quite clear in the snow. Even the designs on the heavy rubber soles stood out distinctly; so distinctly that Wills looked at them for some time and felt puzzled.

Finally, he rowed himself across the lake, walked along the shore, then recrossed the lake, strolled slowly back to his hotel and put in a telephone call to Neilssen of the Bergen police.

"You'd better come out here, Nils," he said, when the call to Bergen came through. "An Englishman's been killed. I think the local police will report it as accidental death. I don't think it is. I think it's murder."

Neilssen looked down at Stoneham as Wills had looked. Neilssen was a tall, wiry man, with brown hair and grey eyes and a pale face.

"You've noticed it, of course?" said Wills.

"You mean—no shoes?"

"Exactly."

Neilssen nodded. "It is, I know, unusual for a victim to lose his shoes or boots in water."

Wills shook his head emphatically. He spoke with the authority of a Metropolitan police officer. "It's not unusual, Nils—it's almost impossible. In fact, I can't recall a single recorded case."

Neilssen looked at the tracks with his alert eyes and said: "Mr. Stoneham walked with his feet well turned out, I see. A townsman will often walk in such a way; or a man of leisure, without work accustomed to stroll along in his own time. Our hill people have no leisure. They learn to pass lightly over the uneven ground, with their feet fairly straight."

"Yes," said Wills, and added: "Stoneham normally turned his feet out slightly, but not as much as that."

Neilssen said quickly: "But if he was carrying a heavy weight he would turn his feet out considerably."

"He was carrying a light split-cane fishing rod when he left the hotel," said Wills, and turned to light his pipe in the wind.

Neilssen ticked off the points on his fingers. "Toes turned out more than normal. Yet no weight being carried by Mr. Stoneham. Imprints extra clear-cut. Yet Mr. Stoneham a light man."

"What's the only answer?" asked Wills.

Neilssen said slowly: "I do not think the impressions were made by Mr. Stoneham."

"Only indirectly," agreed Wills. "Only if he was being carried—dead or unconscious, by somebody wearing his shoes."

"Yes," said Neilssen, and looked across the lake.

Wills said: "Going to have a look in the snow across the lake?"

Neilssen nodded.

"I think I shall find the tracks of the same shoes, but this time the toes will not be turned out: they will be pointing ahead. They will be the tracks of a mountain man, who has rid himself of his burden, and is walking purposefully.

"I think they will lead to some snowless rock height from which the unfortunate Mr. Stoneham could be imagined, in the last resort, to have fallen into the lake. Then they will disappear."

Both men gazed into the valley where they could see a farm.

"When you search it," said Wills, "you'll probably find a man who has rowed for Mr. Stoneham in the past: a man who knows that Stoneham carried a great deal of money on him. A man about the same size as Stoneham, who met him in the darkness, and yielded to a sudden temptation, and hit Stoneham with a piece of rock.

"I think he tied his own boots round his neck and put on Stoneham's shoes. Don't forget to sift the ashes in the fires, Nils. You may find some eyelets and metal ends of shoe laces."

But Neilssen shook his head.

"They are frugal round here. They would rather risk a murder charge than burn a good pair of shoes."

Wills said nothing about the artificial fly which had first aroused his suspicions. The rod had been fitted up all right, to make it seem that Stoneham had been fishing when an accident occurred.

But the fly!

Not even a semi-skilled fisherman, let alone the experienced Stoneham, would have put on a Green Drake may-fly for night fishing at Sandsaeter, Norway. A Coachman, perhaps, or something else with light wings, but not that.

Wills would have liked to mention the point to Neilssen, but had decided against it. Neilssen wouldn't have appreciated the importance of the point.

Neilssen fished for trout with a worm. In Wills's view it was a blemish in an otherwise excellent character.

A HOLIDAY BY THE SEA

Will Scott

William Matthew Scott (1893–1964) was a Yorkshireman who enjoyed a lengthy literary career, writing as Will Scott. He married Lily Edmundson in 1915 and after the First World War he had a brief spell as art editor for *Pan* magazine before the couple and their two children moved to Herne Bay in Kent, where he began to combine journalism with writing fiction. He published several detective novels, three of them featuring a character called Disher, and also wrote children's fiction and for the stage. *The Limping Man* (1930) was one of three plays of his to be made into a film.

Will Scott achieved success in several fields, but he is perhaps best remembered as a prolific writer of short stories, often with a humorous touch. It is said that he wrote over two thousand, although I must admit I haven't tried to make my own count. Perhaps his most notable book is *Giglamps* (1924), which is now a fabulous rarity. The eminent American critic Douglas Greene said: "I have seldom enjoyed a book more than *Giglamps*, a collection of short stories about a tramp who sometimes acts as detective and sometimes runs afoul of the law himself—all told with rare warmth and humour". This story comes from that book and shows Giglamps—and Scott—at their best.

I

THAT YEAR THERE WAS AN INDIAN SUMMER, AND IN THE GLARE of it Giglamps found a friend. He found him in a hedge near Buckhurst Hill, near to tears because of everything; a short, fat man with disappointed, staring eyes and a new kind of sigh for each fresh minute. There was wonderful sarcasm in the name that had gathered about him on the roads. They called him Cheerful.

Together they walked across the ends of London, taking a number of days about it, Giglamps whistling, Cheerful groaning; and when they reached East Finchley on a broiling afternoon they came to rest in the pleasant shades of Cherry Tree Wood. Here Giglamps extracted a kernel of food from a shell of newspaper and passed a half to Cheerful. After which he settled down to eat and read the paper.

The papers, too, were under the spell of the unexpected scorch. Even that international sensation, the mysterious "Admiral," a new-time smuggler with new methods, who had puzzled the world and the world's police for a hectic fortnight, had now to give place to the weather, which came on ostentatiously and ousted him from his proud position in the first columns. It being too hot to think about the Admiral, he ceased to be thought about. Instead, the population turned its mind to a pleasanter if less sensational thing, the rolling sea. All round the coast the dying cinders of an ended season blazed up into flame again. Military bands and straw hats came back; the picture papers repeated the bathing photographs they had taken in June; pierrots were incredibly and incredulously delaying the long walk back to town; grandpapas were remembering something like it in '72; and everywhere suburban papas were planning, and even snatching, a second holiday beside the sea. It was phenomenal. And so glorious that even Giglamps began to feel there might be something to be said for Cheerful's blatant resentment.

"Some day," he said, taking a glance at his new-found friend, "some day *we'll* have a holiday by the sea."

"It can't be proved," sighed Cheerful.

Giglamps peered through his glasses at the thousand criss-crosses of the other's great flat face and wondered if anything could be proved to this pessimist's satisfaction.

"Tried laughin'?" he inquired, with a grin. "It don't hurt the face much, after the second day."

He smoothed out the newspaper and went on with his reading, leaving Cheerful to stare sadly at the tiny panorama of Cherry Tree Wood, to wonder why the sun was so hot, and why the shade was so cool, and why there was nothing to do, and why it would be so hard to do if there were. After which, having nothing left to wonder about, Cheerful sighed. And then he sighed again.

"*In re* the murmuring waves," said Giglamps at length, tapping the newspaper; "they ain't caught the Admiral yet."

"'Course they ain't," snapped Cheerful. "Nor will they, unless they stop wantin' to catch him, or unless 'e don't want 'em to catch him—or else they'll catch 'im an' not want 'im when they've got 'im. Or else something else. Lord! ain't it 'ot? It's a wonder it don't rain. Who's the chap you're talkin' about?"

"The Admiral?" said Giglamps. "Ah! there's a sight o' folks'd like to know that. There's a number-one-size reward out. But nobody knows. Some says he works from here, an' some says he works from the Continent; but they don't really know. They don't even know what he looks like. He's a mystery. He gets smugglerier an' smugglerier every day, but he manages to never have his tail where the salt is."

He rolled the paper into a ball and tossed it for a cat to play with. "No use showin' yer the bathin' pictures of Margate, eh?" he said.

"Waste o' time," Cheerful admitted.

Giglamps thrust his hands into his pockets and crossed his legs and sat back to enjoy the scene before his eyes, the sunlit suburban pastoral, errand-boyed and nurse-maided, playing to the music of rattling trams and rolling trains. Cherry Tree Wood is very far from the murmuring sea, but it is good enough to be going on with, if you have imagination. The little fountain and the melancholy shelter have the ugliness of a thousand fountains and a thousand shelters by the sea. The tripper is here, if only the tripper from the houses at your back, young, and due home for tea; and there are paper bags and crying babies. The trains, sleepily strolling along the embankment top, are not going down to the silvery sands; but you can't tell that by the look of them. The sad sea waves, indeed, are sixty miles from Cherry Tree Wood. But you can think that the tide is out.

"Lovely, ain't it?" said Giglamps, waving his hand.

"Putrid!" said Cheerful.

Restful streets peep over the railings of the little wood, and now on one of them came the roll of heavy wheels. A big pantechnicon drew up close to the rails and stopped: doors opened, chains rattled, and blasé men began to move furniture into a house.

"I'm thinkin'," said Cheerful, sourly, "that if we was to start for that 'oliday now, goin' at our speed we should just get there by Christmas. No, thank yer."

Giglamps smiled.

"Who said anythin' about walkin'?" he asked. "Not likely, my lad." And then he added with seeming irrelevance as he stooped to scratch the cat's ear: "My patron saint's a cat, Cheerful. I admire cats. The way they sleep an' rest an' think an' let big wise human bein's wear out their wrists pourin' milk into a saucer. I'm a bit like a cat myself, if you stand off an' look at me—'cept that I ain't got a tail to swish the flies off. But then, I don't need one. There ain't any flies on me."

He yawned and rose and walked through the stunted trees to the railing and stood in the shade, watching the van men work. The pantechnicon had a great inscription painted on its side, red and black letters on a flaming yellow ground, and it brought a grin to his face when he saw it. It said: *Mimms of Margate. May We Move You?*

"Cheerful!" he called; and when the pessimist had trundled to his side: "Further to my communication of five minutes ago, what d'yer think o' this? Very kind of ol' man Mimms of Margate, ain't it? Have we to let him?"

"Have we to let 'im *what?*"

"Move us."

"'Ow d'yer mean?"

But suddenly Cheerful saw that his friend's gaze had shifted from the van, and an answer to his question was not immediately forthcoming. A large box, carelessly dropped beside the railing, had burst open, and small furnishings were disclosed. One, a brass-framed photograph of a man, had fallen out on to the grass, and when the men took the box inside the house the photograph, unnoticed by them, remained. Something about it had arrested Giglamps' attention. Breaking a branch from the tree above, he poked it through the rails, drew the photograph towards him and picked it up.

"Very pretty, eh?" he said, showing the photograph to Cheerful. "Very sweet. Hardly the sort o' thing that fits in with East Finchley, but very ducky all the same. What do you think?"

It was the photograph of an exceedingly handsome man, with a small and dainty mouth and beautiful waving hair; a man in the uniform of a naval officer, with cap tilted jauntily over one eye. There was a touch of calm assurance in the man's smile, and almost a regal air in his bearing. As Cheerful looked at the photograph he felt creeping over him an overwhelming desire to hit it.

"Gaw!" he mumbled.

"Hallo!" said Giglamps suddenly, pulling Cheerful's sleeve. "Look here! What's this?"

Furtively from the house into which the furniture had been taken came a girl, agitated and a-flurry, who darted swiftly across the street to the van. The men were in the house; there appeared to be nobody to overlook her action; she began a rapid and thorough search at the van door and the foot of the railings and in the grass where the box had stood. Her brows were knit, her cheek was pale and her lip was bitten by her pretty teeth. At a sound from the house she started, but, nobody coming, she resumed her search with keener intensity, to end it with greater dismay.

"Gone!" she gasped.

Over in the little wood, unseen by the girl, the Sons of Dust kept watch, Cheerful with mouth agape, Giglamps with brows thoughtful and low. Then the latter leant over the railing and spoke.

"Arfternoon, missie. Mebbe—"

He observed a quick flush mount her pale cheek as she looked up and saw him and the photograph in his hand. Before he could continue she had stepped forward, reached through the railing and snatched the picture from him, had tossed her head haughtily and turned on her heel. As furtively as she had come from the house now she crept back to it and was gone. Giglamps looked at Cheerful and whistled.

"They say life's a book," he said, "but this is the first I've heard that the Brothers Melville wrote it. Mellerdrammer in East Finchley, son! What's it all about?"

"Somethin' wrong," said Cheerful. "There's alw'ys somethin' wrong."

"Somethin' strange, all right. An' I'd like to know what."

"It ain't safe, Gig," said Cheerful. "Nothin' ain't safe. No good'll come of it. No good never comes of nothin'. You leave it alone."

Giglamps laughed and snapped his fingers.

"Don't matter, anyway," he said, raising a leg and beginning to climb the rail. "We ain't got time to worry about the Mystery of Cherry Tree Wood. Come on, Cheerful, my lad. Take my hand, an' hop over."

"Where you goin'?" Cheerful asked.

"Margate," said Giglamps.

"'Ow?"

"Well, how d'yer think?"

He nodded towards the van. The last chair had been taken out and the men were gone on their last journey to the house. It was now or never. Nothing remained in the van but a pile of sacking in its darkest corner. To this Giglamps now led Cheerful.

"The easiest way, o' course," he whispered as they got under the sacking. "Leave it to someone else!"

Five minutes later, with doors closed and the men above on their seat, the great van was turning into the Great North Road, on its way to the sea.

II

Margate!

The van was stopped. Scraping feet told of men descending, and darkness, where cracks of light had shown for many hours in the van sides, hinted at fallen night. The keen smell of the sea mingled with the scents of a storage yard and the perfume of sacking and straw. Giglamps yawned silently, stretched, and listened to the talking van men, gathered in the yard.

"Back again termorrer," wailed one. "Back a-blinkin'-gain! Don't it give yer the doo-dahs?"

"Wot they orter do, William," said a second, "is chain an' muzzle us an' feed us on 'ay an' let's live in the blighted van. Eh? Gimme them keys."

"Who is it termorrer?" a third voice asked.

"Ol' girl up the 'ill," was the reply. "Name o'Tarrant, at Estuary Lodge. Fussy ol' bird. Comin' all the way from town on the five-thirty to see we start sharp at six. Thinks we're arfter 'er wallpaper, if you arsks me."

"It's a life. Well, we can only die. Where's them blighted keys?"

The clank of keys and big gates closing and men going grumbling away; and then with Cheerful's knife through one of the gaping chinks Giglamps raised the bar that held the van door, and a moment later they were across the yard, over the wall, and walking quietly along the side of the street.

"Talk about easy!" Giglamps laughed.

With Cheerful trotting morosely to heel, he led the way over the railway and through the silent streets to the hilly part of the town. Margate was laying its head upon the pillow and putting out a hand to snuff the candle. A late roisterer or two passed by, and here and there a shop remained futilely open, but for the most part the night had no interruption. Sniffing the air keenly, and with his shoulders squared back, Giglamps shuffled along, but even his trained and gentle crawl was too swift and strenuous for the flabby pessimist behind. Cheerful began to puff and wheeze indignantly, and he was tortuously thinking out an excuse for calling a halt, when suddenly Giglamps put out his hand and stopped.

"What is it?" Cheerful asked, seeing his friend's gaze riveted on a tall gate set back in an old brick wall. "It's only a gate."

"*The* gate!" said Giglamps.

"Which?"

"Look at the name on it." And Giglamps' long finger pointed to the sign, "Estuary Lodge." "You heard what the van johnnies said. Nobody home till six to-morrer mornin'. If there's food there, nobody wants it. If there's beds, we can sleep like business men. Not a soul to stop the doin's."

Cheerful hesitated.

"We'll get pinched."

"Tell 'em we saw it done on the movin' pitchers, an' they'll let us off. But what's it matter if they don't? They're makin' prison so nice an' homely now, with polite warders an' good cookin', that about the worst thing that can happen to a feller is to be sentenced to be slung out. That's how it is you hear about so many crooks walkin' the streets today, right under the cops' noses. You think they haven't been found out. But they've been found guilty, my lad. Come on."

He opened the gate and guided Cheerful up a tiled and moss-grown path to the back of an old brick mansion and a creaking window that long ago had looked down on the last of the "hoys" and the first of the bathing machines; a very "oldest inhabitant" of a house. Giglamps raised his hand to the window catch and nodded.

"The old knife again."

"All right," Cheerful whispered; "but don't say I never told you. Somethin' bad'll come of it."

Giglamps slipped back the catch and had both hands on the frame to raise the window, when suddenly Cheerful's hand gripped his wrist and Cheerful's shaking whisper said:

"Listen!"

"Eh?"

"Listen!"

Over the wall, a few yards away, somebody spoke in a low, soft voice. What was said could not be heard, but that their presence here was discovered was what the two men feared. Giglamps crept away into the shadows, and when he returned it was to whisper with his mouth close to Cheerful's ear:

"There's a mound of earth along the wall, under the trees. Foller me an' don't make a sound. We can see who it is."

They climbed to the top of the mound and peeped, with heads hidden in the thick foliage, over the wall. Under a gas-lamp in the street below stood a man and a girl, softly talking. Their heads were close together and great urgency seemed to be in their manner. The girl was well-dressed—expensively dressed. The man was attired in the uniform of a naval officer, and Giglamps' eyes narrowed behind his glasses as he looked at him.

"Midnight sharp, in the Square," the girl was saying.

"Midnate!" the officer echoed. "I'll have the car ready. Yuh'll—er—forget nothing?"

"Everything is packed." She squeezed his hand and murmured, "My hero!"

"My heart's delate!" he responded.

Their talk was lost in kisses and a tight embrace, and when at last they stood apart their hands met in a firm but furtive clasp.

"Midnate!"

"On the minute, darling!"

She left him and crossed the street and passed from sight through a low garden gate. For a moment he lingered, his gaze dwelling on the way she had taken; then daintily he made his way through the darkness down the hill.

"Well?" said Giglamps, looking at Cheerful.

"Awfully Percy Willy, ain't he?" said the pessimist. "Makes yer sick. Somebody orter 'ave trod on 'im when he was little."

"I mean, didn't yer see who it was?"

"Lor', no! Who?"

"That officer chappie. He's the johnny whose picture fell out o' that box at East Finchley!"

"Eh?"

"Fact!"

"Lumme!" said Cheerful. "Are you sure?"

"You bet!" said Giglamps. "There ain't two faces like that in all England—let's get down an' pray!"

"H'm! Lumme! My word!"

They climbed down from the mound and made their way cautiously back to the window. Giglamps was thoughtful and at first made no effort to enter the house. He stood strumming his finger-tips on the sill, his lips pursed in a low whistle.

"I'd like to know," he said, "what Mr. Venus de Milo was up to. He's one o' the reasons, remember, why the little lady at Cherry Tree Wood was so mysterious."

"P'raps we should 'ave watched him?" suggested Cheerful.

"P'raps," said Giglamps. "Couldn't have stuck that for long, though. He ain't no blighted cinema, as far as his face goes."

"I know," sighed Cheerful. "It's an elopement! No mystery about it, I'll bet. An elopement, you see? Percy Willy's too pretty to need any watchin'."

Giglamps' finger-tips ceased to strum.

"Don't be too unanimous about that," he said. "Appearances is deceptive. Handsome is ain't allus handsome does. You're in danger of comin' to the bad old conclusion that everythin' that's good to look at's good. It ain't, yer know. You can't judge a sting by its wasp!"

He turned and threw the window up.

"Anyway," he said across his shoulder, "Maud Evelyn can most likely get hisself into trouble without our help. What we want is supper. Up yer get, Misery!"

Half-past eleven was sighing desolately about the old grey tower of Margate church when the two pushed back their plates and rose from the table in the kitchen of Estuary Lodge, offering a grace to Luck for food and the opportunity for its theft. Then slowly they went upstairs to the best bedroom and took off their boots.

"When in Rome, yer know," said Giglamps with a smile, as he removed Cheerful's collar from the gas-bracket and his boots from the dressing-table.

They got into bed.

"Lumpy, a bit, ain't it?" said Giglamps, wriggling.

"Everythin's allus lumpy," Cheerful grumbled.

"Yes, but—"

Cheerful tried to lie still whilst his friend attempted to shuffle comfort into the bed, but after a moment they were both out again, rubbing their sides and groaning.

"Lumme!" exclaimed the pessimist.

Dragging at the mattress and pressing a doubled fist on the most offending lumps, Giglamps endeavoured to reduce the undulation; but when he ran the flat of his hand across he found them offending still.

"After the four miles east of Whitstable," he grinned, "this is the worst-laid surface I ever struck. They ran out o' wood blocks an' finished with granite, I think. Or p'raps it's one o' them beds Queen Elizabeth died in."

"Let's 'op down into the gardin an' sleep in peace," Cheerful suggested.

"I beg to remain," said Giglamps. "There's somethin' got into this here bed by mistake—or mebbe not. I want to see the doin's."

"Lumps, o' course."

"But lumps o' what?"

Throwing back the sheets and borrowing Cheerful's knife for the third time, Giglamps ripped open the binding of the mattress and inserted his hand.

"Wot's the wheeze?" Cheerful asked.

From out the mattress Giglamps drew a little red leather case, which, opened, disclosed a rope of shining pearls. Cheerful whistled and rubbed his hands and nervously touched the things.

"My!" he exclaimed.

"Wait a minute!" said Giglamps.

He slashed out the side of the mattress and tumbled its contents on the floor; the filling mixed with other little leather cases, shedding other and better jewels, legal-looking documents fluttering stiffly, like dead leaves falling, and last of all, small, square, hard, something upon which Giglamps seized at once and held to the light at the window.

"Lordy!" Cheerful gasped. "Wot 'ave we got?"

Giglamps displayed the small square object. Exquisitely silver-framed, it was another photograph of the naval officer whose beauty had twice already touched their lives, once across the railings of Cherry Tree Wood, and again, half an hour before, over the wall of this very house in Margate. Giglamps laughed.

"Mummy's little sweet again! Remarkable the way he keeps bumpin' into us, ain't it? What was it you said, Cheerful? What have we got? If you've a weak heart, don't listen. We've got the Admiral!" He sat on the ruined bed, excitedly twirling his glasses. "That's what we got, ol' son! His tail's near the salt at last! All the Customs gents an' all the cops have been lookin' for 'im all the year, but *we've* got him, Cheerful—little us! Warm an' ready to serve!"

"Lor'!" said Cheerful.

"Easiest thing out," Giglamps went on. "The cops is lookin' for a crew o' bold, bad pirates, an' all the time it's a crew o' bold, bad *women!* All except Percy Willy—to give him the benefit o' the doubt. That young girl at East Finchley an' this ol' girl here. Don't yer see? Ain't it sweet? It's his face does it. He's so pretty I bet he has his work cut out preventin' hisself from bein' overstaffed. It's wonderful what a face'll do, Cheerful. But p'raps you wouldn't understand that.

"The smartest thing about the old Admiral's wheeze is that all his lady friends is women with a little weakness for removin' from Margate to London. See? Once the stuff's landed they leave it to the innocent furniture shifters to get it to town. No suspicious parcels, in case the cops is watchin' the trains. Just stick it in the furniture! He can't be so silly. It looks as if the Admiral is good solid oak under his deal finish, eh? He's got a lemonade label, but there's a head on him when you come to open the bottle."

With respectful admiration Cheerful sat, rubbing his hands up and down his knees, at some distance from his friend.

"If you was to go into the detective business," he said, "you'd make a whackin' big name fer yerself, an' pots o' money, an' everybody talkin' about yer."

Giglamps grinned.

"No limelight for me, boy," he said. "Sometimes I've thought I would go into business an' make loud noises, but when it come to it I allus backed out an' went to sleep instead. No worse for that, eh? I don't think so. It ain't allus the best axle's got the biggest squeak, you know."

"Lots o' public—public—" Cheerful attempted.

"Publicerty," said Giglamps, "nine times out o' ten is insignifigunce with a temprechewer of 104." He slipped his glasses back on his nose and shook his head. "Besides, what a fag," he said. "'Avin' a brass plate on yer front door, an' everybody callin' yer ' sir,' an' baptisin' sweet peas an' roses after yer. Not fer me, thanks. It's easier to be a blade o' grass than a landscape."

Cheerful gave a deep sigh and rose from the bed.

"An' so, then," he said, "we let the Admiral drop?"

"His smugglin' I don't so much object to," Giglamps replied, "but his face is the blighted limit. His smugglin's a crime, but his face is a sin. I think we'll keep his appointment for him."

"No good'll come of it."

"We'll see. Slip into yer boots. That's a quarter to twelve strikin'."

They came out of the house and over the side wall as a policeman entered by the front gate. They did not see the policeman; he did not see them. He entered the house quietly by the open window as they crossed the street at a run towards a slight figure which slipped from the garden gate into which it had vanished an hour earlier and crept along the wall beneath the overhanging ivy. When she saw them a yard or two away she pulled up with a little cry of alarm.

"What do you want?" she demanded.

"You're rumbled, missie," Cheerful bawled authoritatively. "Like all the rest of us. Squodged!"

She half turned her head aside and upward. "Quiet!" she commanded. "What do you mean?"

Giglamps removed his hat and gave a little bow.

"Simply that you ain't goin' to keep your appointment tonight," he said. "You're hoppin' it straight back into the house."

And then, suddenly, somewhere a window was heard to open. A voice cried "Evelyn!" and the window closed. And a moment later pandemonium broke loose. Across at Estuary Lodge a police whistle cut into the air. A door crashed. The girl made as if to run, but Cheerful stood before her, blocking the way. An elderly man in a purple dressing-gown separated himself from the darkness and stood beside them, volcanic, his arms shaking and his great voice filling the night.

"Evelyn!" he thundered, snatching from her grasp a little travelling-case and bursting it open without an effort. "Ah! Yes! All the little trinkets! All the little presents! So! You are eloping! You are eloping with that dog of a man—that pussy-cat of a poodle-dog of a man! After what I said! Oh! are you?" He pitched the case and its contents over the wall and grasped the girl by the wrist, sweeping a contemptuous glance at Giglamps and Cheerful. "What dustbin do you pick over for your friends?" he bellowed. "And what's the police whistle for? And what's everything?"

Seeing here little more than erring innocence saved in time, Giglamps swiftly ushered the man and his daughter back through the gate, closed it and turned to Cheerful.

"You're a bad runner, Cheerful," he said. "You stop an' talk to the cops an' get some more of 'em in case they're needed. Tell 'em all about it. I'll get along an' see the Admiral before he grips the corks."

III

In the darkest corner of Cecil Square, in the deepest shadow, stood the naval officer. He wasted on the shabby stranger only the most casual of supercilious glances and then looked elegantly away. But when Giglamps stopped impudently and gave every intimation of remaining, he bestowed a second glance, supercilious as the first, but longer, travelling calmly from the tramp's tattered hat to his broken boots, and said:

"I have notheng to—ar—give yuh."

Giglamps rocked slowly to and fro upon his toes, and the corners of his mouth turned upwards.

"Did I request the pleasuar of your companay?" the officer asked.

Giglamps tilted his hat forward and laughed shortly.

"Dear sir—or madam," he replied. "Up to now I been tryin' to keep an open mind about you. I never care much which side it is pays. I don't mind a feller smugglin' or openin' a house or spoilin' a policeman once in a while. These things has to be done. But there's one thing I never was able to stick, an' that's a thing that was meant by Nature to be a traction-engine kiddin' it's a baby's scooter. You might make Gladys Cooper jealous, but you only make me wild. I'm chalked up against you."

"Haw, indeed? And what do yuh mean by thet?"

"I mean," said Giglamps, "that tonight's little affair's off. I mean that the girl ain't comin', though p'raps the cops is. I mean that you're rumbled."

The officer stared at Giglamps with a fallen jaw, then glanced behind in the direction from which the girl should come and hesitated. Suddenly he began to walk away.

"No, you don't!" said Giglamps, laying a hand on his shoulder.

A jab backwards with the heel to the stomach relaxed the tramp's grip. The officer jumped away and broke into a run. But the kick had done less—or more—than he had intended. With a savage spring

Giglamps leapt upon his shoulders and brought him to the ground. They crashed to the pavement together, spinning over and over, arms and legs and feet and hands mixed ludicrously in wild blows.

"Right-o, Evelina!" Giglamps shouted. "That's the stuff to give me, is it? Look after yerself, then. I'm goin' to take you seriously."

"I'd lake yuh to know—" gasped the officer, raising a bent arm and bringing the point of his elbow down on Giglamps' mouth.

The blow served to free him. He sprang to his feet and made off across the square, with Giglamps a few yards behind. Into the square at the opposite corner three policemen came running.

"This way!" Giglamps called.

The wild procession careered downhill and then uphill, and by a maze of dark old streets to the cliff top, the tramp gaining on the naval officer, the police gaining on the tramp. When Giglamps overtook his prey on the bridge at Newgate Gap the police were not a hundred yards behind.

He grabbed the officer by the throat and propped him against the coping and pounded his face. The officer screamed and retaliated with his feet. "The cops are comin' for you," Giglamps laughed, "but they'll not get you. They'll ask for you an' receive a worthless imitation. You won't add up to a total when I've finished with yer."

Into the chaos a policeman sprang, interrupting a blow of Giglamps' with his jaw. For a brief moment he tottered on the bridge, then over he went, clutching frantically at the thin grass and the crumbling chalk of the cutting, crashing to silence through the roof of a souvenir stall forty feet below. A second and a third sprang into his place, indiscriminately aiding victory and sharing defeat. The air was filled with fists and feet and curses.

"You're arrested!" shouted the second policeman, tugging viciously at the third policeman's ear.

"Hold him!" cried Giglamps, to nobody in particular.

They collapsed, a sprawling mass of blows. Undermost was the naval officer, feeling strangely large in arms and legs and dimly aware of a violent struggle happening upon his body. But his face, at least, was at peace. For the first time for many years he was not conscious of possessing a face at all.

IV

Six o'clock in the morning.

Margate was yawning and rubbing its eyes. Cocks had done crowing, pale-faced maids had done singing on area steps, milk-floats were beginning to rumble in the streets. In the dim light of the shrubbery behind the gates of Estuary Lodge Cheerful lay with face buried in the dead leaves of many dead autumns, trying to breathe silently, listening hard, not daring to look above.

Suddenly something fell upon his back and his nose was pressed deep in the mould. He rolled over and doubled a fist for a last hopeless fight, but the fist relaxed when he found himself looking up into the battered face of Giglamps.

"'Ello," he said sadly.

Giglamps picked up his glasses from where they had dropped in his leap over the wall, and through them peeped at Cheerful.

"Cheerful," he said, "d'you know what you are? You are Friday the thirteenth. A blinkin' fine mascot for a suicide society! I'm sorry I brought yer."

"Where you been?" sighed Cheerful.

"Me? All over Margate, all night long. First here and then there. Talk about hoppin'! I been dodgin' the vengeance o' the law. What about you?"

"Been 'idin' 'ere since midnight," said Cheerful, "waitin' fer the cops to get outer the street. D'yer know, Gig, we made the most awfullest mistake. Them things in the ol' mattress wasn't pinched at all. The ol' gal was afraid of burglars breakin' in an' banks breakin' down or somethin', so she just sewed 'em up there. She reckoned nobody'd ever know. She's just gorn inside wiv a cop. Better be quiet."

The sounds of wheels and whistling men, and the pantechnicon of Mimms drew up before the gates. Icy and tall, Miss Tarrant appeared with the policeman, and the work of moving the furniture out of the house was commenced. When for a brief moment the coast was clear Giglamps nudged his friend and inclined his head towards the van.

"Come on!"

They crept into the darkest corner and hid behind a wardrobe. In half an hour the gloom was darkness and rumbling wheels were carrying them back to town.

"I say," whispered Cheerful, when they dared to talk again, "what about the Admiral?"

"Eh? Don't talk to me about the Admiral!" said Giglamps.

"Why? Did you let 'im slip?"

"'Fraid I did."

"Well, wot is there to laugh at?"

"Eh? Oh," said Giglamps, "there's plenty to laugh at. You know you said last night that no good wouldn't come of all this? Well, let me tell yer. Some good's come of it fer the Admiral, who ain't caught yet. Some good's come of it fer that ol' girl, who'll have more sense now, p'raps. Some good's come of it for the old cove in the dressin'-gown, who ain't lost his daughter yet. An' some good's come of it for *her*, 'cos it turns out old De Milo was married all the time. An' some good's come of it for about fifty thousand other girls in Margate, too."

"'Ow d'yer mean?"

"Well, yer see, Cheerful, after the mess last night—it was the loveliest mess in history; me an' old De Milo an' three cops; the juiciest slaughter of loveliness you could imagine—after we got him down an'

I'd explained how we'd tracked him by his photographs, he gets quite perky an' proud, and he sits up an' says, 'My deah suh,' he says, 'there is a photograph of myself in every house in Margate, I sh'd hope. Over ten thousand of them have been saold, my deah suh!'

"An' it turns out that he ain't the Admiral at all, yer see? He's Handsome Harry, the tenor of the Merry Margate Middies, down on the beach, three times daily. An' that's what I mean—fifty thousand girls in Margate he'll never be a public danger to any more, which is what he has been. You orter see his face, Cheerful! Gaw! Absolutely ruined! It'll never be no good for anythin' but growin' ivy on now. An' so some good's come of it fer him too, if he only knew."

"H'm," sighed Cheerful.

"In fact," Giglamps went on, "it's really remarkable the amount o' good we done by comin' to Margate for eight hours, although there's all the cops in Kent lookin' for us, although the only chance we had to bathe was in trouble. We never got no nearer the sea than the smell, but we done a mighty lot o' good. Except to ourselves. We was the only ones what got properly bounced. Eh?"

"Ain't it a world!" sighed Cheerful.

"Never mind," said Giglamps. "Some day, as I was sayin' when I was interrupted by the last half a day, we'll have a holiday by the sea an' make up for all this. Move up, my lad. I ain't got room to have cramp in."

TWO ON A TOWER

Michael Innes

Michael Innes was the pen-name of Oxford don and mainstream novel-ist J. I. M. Stewart (1906–94). He was born in Edinburgh and retained a lifelong affection for his native Scotland, which features in books such as *The Secret Vanguard* (1940). Crime writing was something of a side-line as far as he was concerned and he does not appear to have been an enthu-siastic reader of fellow authors working in the Golden Age tradition. Nevertheless, his career in the genre lasted for half a century and even if some of his mystery novels may be described as "an acquired taste", his crime fiction still attracts a significant number of devotees—rather more, in fact, than the books he published under his own name.

Several of Innes' stories might be classed as holiday mysteries. These include one of his best-regarded books, *Lament for a Maker* (1938), which also benefits from a Scottish backdrop. In a much later work, John Appleby, Innes' series detective (and by this stage a veteran), is holiday-ing with his wife when he becomes embroiled in the events recounted in *Appleby's Answer* (1973).

I T WAS SOME YEARS SINCE THE BARBACKS HAD BEEN ABROAD, AND they decided to go to Italy. Or rather, Irene Barback decided this, and for once she carried her point. Charles whose responses to life were turning elderly far more quickly than they should, at first produced a surly opposition. He wasn't, he said, going to be pushed; and he continued for some time to collect and study illustrated brochures about a number of quite perversely dreary English seaside resorts. Then Irene had the bright idea of sending him to old Cheall, their family doctor.

Charles did, in fact, look rather badly run down, and anything about his health worried him tremendously. So the situation was hopeful, if only dear old Cheall could be persuaded to declare—whether with his tongue in his cheek or not—that Italy was quite definitely the tonic Charles required.

Irene remembered that all sorts of distinguished people had gone to Italy on medical advice—particularly poets, like Mrs. Browning and John Keats. Her husband wasn't a poet—but he was a publisher, which is roughly the same sort of thing: and she felt that medicine and literature between them might get Charles on the move.

And they did. Old Cheall rang up and said rather bleakly that Charles would benefit from plenty of sunlight and plenty of distraction; and when Irene mentioned Italy Cheall replied that Italy would be just right. Then there was another piece of luck. Gregory Fan, Charles's junior partner, announced that he was motoring to Naples, and that it would be most delightful if the Barbacks joined up with him at least as far as Rome. Irene thought this quite wonderful—she had never hoped for such good fortune—and Charles kindled to the idea when it became clear that he wouldn't be asked to share the expenses of running Fan's car.

These were the circumstances in which the Barbacks set out for a country which the English have always tended to associate with violent passions and dark crimes.

Sir John Appleby encountered them in Florence. He wasn't there on holiday himself; he had gone over to consult with the police about security problems attending an international conference soon to be held in that hospitable city. But he had a few days at his disposal when these duties were finished, and he ran into Fan and his friends during a leisurely afternoon in the Uffizi.

He knew Gregory Fan as a man of considerable drive in more directions than one, and he was interested in the contrast between this restless personality and his very conservative senior partner. Barback was senior in every sense, and certainly a good twenty years older than his wife. He didn't look a happy man. Nor, for that matter, did Irene Barback look a happy woman, although she was undoubtedly a strikingly beautiful one. Or *did* she look a happy woman, at least in some short-term way? The more settled lines on her face suggested boredom and frustration. But there was something else—something that you could get at only by noticing that she was making a very quiet and unobtrusive affair of her Italian holiday. She didn't have much to say to Fan. Indeed, she hardly looked at him. But there were some paintings in the Uffizi—not Florentine paintings, but glowing Venetian things, pulsing with sensuous life—that she seemed very well able to pass the time of day with.

"Did you hurry through to Italy?" Appleby asked. "I usually find myself doing that."

"Oh, no." Fan had shaken his head. "We've loitered along, and lingered in all sorts of pleasant places. Haven't we, Charles?"

Charles Barback agreed. But, Appleby thought, it was in an oddly bewildered way, as if much in this holiday were a puzzle to him.

"And we intend to potter about a good deal here, too," Fan said. "What about coming with us to Monterino tomorrow?"

And Charles Barback, who had been staring rather sightlessly at a Carpaccio, turned round.

"Yes, do," he said.

They made the trip in Fan's car, accompanied by Appleby's friend Cervoni, of the Ministry of Security. It was a wonderful day, and they stopped for a picnic lunch. Barback seemed depressed and reluctant to get on the road again. He fussed over the packing up; there was a wine-glass missing, and the cork wouldn't go back into the Chianti flask. He was almost certainly, Appleby thought, a tiresome man about the house. His wife, however, seemed scarcely to notice him. And at length they got on their way.

Monterino is an astonishing place; it stands on a hill, and in the Middle Ages its leading citizens vied with one another in building themselves tremendous towers. A sufficient number of these remain to suggest a sort of thirteenth-century first-cousin to Manhattan. You can climb some of these venerable skyscrapers and enjoy the most extensive views.

They climbed the tallest of the towers, and admired equally the tumble of picturesque roofs crowded immediately beneath them and the prospect of half Tuscany which lay beyond. Descending, they crossed the Piazza del Duomo towards a café where Irene Barback proposed they should explore the possibility of obtaining tea. But her husband and Fan became detached from the others, and when they looked back they saw the two men standing before another of the towers and waving to them.

"The Torre della Cisterna," Cervoni explained politely. "Our friends propose the ascent. But they signal, I think, that we should go forward and order our refreshment."

So they went on to the café and sat down. It was in a corner of the square from which the Torre della Cisterna was clearly visible.

And thus, five minutes later, they all three saw the thing happen. What drew their attention to the top of the tower was a scream—and an instant later they realised that it was Barback's voice. The scream came again—it was a high-pitched desperate call for help—and then they saw Barback himself appear from behind a turret and stagger backwards. He was clutching his face; suddenly he thrust out his arms as if to avoid a blow; and then he ran forward as if making a dash for safety. The movement took him once more out of sight. There was another scream; then silence; then a hubbub of many voices calling from the other side of the tower.

Appleby was already up and running; presently he was thrusting his way through a horrified little crowd: some of them tourists, most of them inhabitants of Monterino. They formed a ragged circle round what was all too clearly Charles Barback's dead body. It lay, dreadfully crushed and gashed, in the hot Italian dust—having fallen first to one roof and then to another, much as a ball might helplessly do on a pin-table.

Appleby turned away, rounded a corner, and arrived before the entrance of the tower just as Gregory Fan staggered out of it. Fan's hands were thrust deep in his pockets.

"I wasn't…" he stammered. "I didn't… I couldn't…"

Without speaking, Appleby pointed. And then—slowly, helplessly—Fan brought his hands from their concealment and held them out. They were covered with blood.

"Certainly Barback's blood." Appleby, sitting in the Palazzo Municipale and beginning explanations to Cervoni, was in a very dusty state. He had been clambering hazardously over the rooftops of Monterino; and now on the table before him were a pen-knife and some small fragments of thin, curved glass. "It was probably a good idea, declaring at our picnic that a wine-glass was missing; if he hadn't, and its disappearance had been noticed later, one of us might have begun wondering."

"He needed a receptacle?"

"Precisely. He slashed his wrist, collected the blood, and then put on that turn for the benefit of people on the ground below. At the first scream, Fan must have gone running up from the final chamber of the tower—a sort of museum—where he had been lingering. You can imagine him wondering what on earth had happened."

"My dear Sir John—indeed, yes."

"As he opened the door giving access to the roof, Barback tipped the blood on him, slashed himself again for good measure, gave another scream, hurled the wine-glass and pocketknife as far as he could across the rooftops of Monterino, and pitched himself over the parapet."

"Revenge?"

"Just that. He knew of the intrigue that was going on between his wife and Fan. And from what your doctor says, it is clear he must have known that he was mortally ill. He didn't mind dying a little sooner, if he could leave the suggestion that his wife's lover had attacked him with fatal consequences on the Torre della Cisterna." Appleby turned to Irene Barback, who was sitting immobile in a corner of the room. "I'm sorry. But it is best that you should understand the whole thing at once."

The wretched woman nodded. She appeared quite dazed.

"Charles wouldn't be pushed," she whispered strangely. "But he would jump."

THE SUMMER HOLIDAY

Celia Fremlin

Celia Margaret Fremlin (1914–2009) was born in Ryarsh, Kent, and worked on the Mass Observation project after leaving Somerville College, Oxford. Her deep interest in social issues and attitudes is evident in her first book, *The Seven Chars of Chelsea*, which had the misfortune (as she ruefully told her friend and fellow crime writer Eileen Dewhurst many years later) to be published at more or less the same time that the Second World War began. Her experience as a wife and mother informed her debut novel *The Hours Before Dawn* (1958), which won an Edgar award from the Mystery Writers of America. Her final novel, *King of the World*, appeared in 1994.

Fremlin's second novel, *Uncle Paul* (1959) was a suspense novel about a calamitous summer holiday. Events are viewed from the perspective of Meg, a young woman who is summoned by her sister Isabel to a seaside caravan because their older half-sister Mildred needs help. Fifteen years ago, Mildred's first husband, the mysterious "Uncle Paul", was arrested for attempted murder and now, it seems that Paul may have returned to the scene of the crime. Fremlin's crisp writing was well-suited to the short story form, and in her lifetime three collections of her short fiction were published. "The Summer Holiday"—which has an entirely different storyline from *Uncle Paul* but suggests that Fremlin had very mixed feelings about summer holidays—first appeared in *Ellery Queen's Mystery Magazine* in November 1983.

S HE WOULD NEVER HAVE BELIEVED THAT WIDOWHOOD WOULD suit her so well. She would have said, if you'd asked her, that she was one of those unassuming, dependent little women who would be lost without a man to lean on.

And now here she was not feeling lost at all, not the least bit. It was amazing—and, in a way, rather disturbing.

Oh, she had mourned for Harold at the time, of course she had. She had cried bitterly at the funeral, and for quite a while afterwards, too, recalling tearfully all the nice things about him, like the square set of his shoulders and the way he would call out, "Emmy, I'm back!" as he came in at the front door. Silly, really, because how could he not be back if he was calling out? But somehow cosy, all the same, and—yes—she'd missed it.

What had been rather awful, though—and it still made her feel guilty whenever she thought about it—was the number of things she *didn't* miss: the appalling number of small, everyday routines which were, quite simply, easier and pleasanter without him.

Lunch, for instance. She could have it on a tray now, just a cheese sandwich with perhaps a tomato, eaten in the sunshine under one of the windows, or with her feet up on the sofa, listening to *Woman's Hour*. Since his retirement, Harold had always expected a proper sit-down lunch at the dining-room table, rounded off by a proper pudding. Emmy herself didn't care for puddings, and though she'd never resented the extra trouble at the time it really was a relief, now, to know that she would never have to think about stewed apple—or suet, or custard, or hot jam sauce—ever again.

There were other unexpected little treats, too, incident on the solitary state. She hardly dared enumerate them, even in her own mind, so quickly had she found herself actually enjoying them, with Harold scarcely cold in his grave.

Reading in bed. Having the radio on while she dressed. Buying sliced bread. Leaving the crockery upside down on the draining-board all day instead of drying it and putting it away after every meal. All these things had irritated Harold, and so of course she'd mostly refrained from doing them—but, my goodness, what a relief it was now to relax her guard and do exactly as she liked! No "Emmy, dear, do you *have* to?" resounding in her ears ever again.

Ever again. Ever. Never. Words to wring the hearts of most widows, and bring tears to their eyes. It was awful how often, for Emmy, they brought instead a furtive little lift to her spirits, a tiny, guilt-ridden rejoicing at yet another small anxiety removed, another small burden laid to rest forever under the green grass and the faithfully tended flowers on Harold's grave.

Of all the small burdens—and indeed "small" was entirely the wrong word, because for Emmy it wasn't small at all—the burden of the Summer Holiday had been the most oppressive. The relief she'd felt—about two or three months after the funeral it must have been—when it had first dawned on her that there was now no reason at all why she should ever go on holiday again—ever!—was something she would remember, albeit guiltily, to the end of her days.

It had been April—Harold had died in February—and Emmy, drawn by the first real sunshine of the year, had dragged one of the deckchairs from its winter quarters and set it up on the lawn. And it was as she sat there, face upturned to the soft spring warmth, filled with a vague sense of newness, of dim, unexplored possibilities, that it occurred to her, quite suddenly and without warning, that *this* year she would be able to sit out on the lawn like this and enjoy the sunshine *every day*, all summer long! She didn't have to go on holiday at all!

The relief, the joy of it was breathtaking. Usually, by now—by mid-April—the shadow of the Holiday had already fallen. Already, Harold would be all of a fidget about visas, passports, hotel bookings, car-ferries, rolls of film, baggage regulations, Night Flights, Regular Flights, Cheap Flights, Tourist Flights, Standby Flights, Charter Flights—the lot. And naturally, as a good wife, it was her duty to fidget with him, not only about all these shared worries but also about those other, personal worries that were hers alone.

Her hair. To perm or not to perm—and if so, how soon? A couple of months ahead, to give it time to settle, or try to fit it somehow into that final frantic week so that there should be no risk that it might grow out?

And clothes. Holiday clothes were a nightmare all on their own at her age. Every year it was the same: every garment she possessed was too dressy, too dowdy, or made her look like mutton-dressed-as-lamb. And so, year after year, with gritted teeth and sinking heart, off she would drag herself to the West End, in and out of the lordly great shops, where under the withering eye of some flawlessly enamelled assistant everything she tried on was either too dressy, too dowdy, or made her look like mutton-dressed-as-lamb.

And so it went on, one dreadful problem after another, all through May and June—the loveliest months of the year spoiled and darkened by these mounting preparations, these ever-escalating anxieties from which there could be no escape, no reprieve, unstoppable save by one thing only—the arrival of the dreaded Day.

The terror lest the minicab they'd ordered wouldn't turn up. Or that it would take them to the wrong terminal. Suppose their luggage didn't get put on the plane. Suppose they arrived too late! That fear of arriving too late always haunted her dreams for days and weeks beforehand. Then there was the fear that the plane, once they were finally on it, would fail to take off—that there would be something wrong with it. Or that it *would* take off and that there would be an air-crash. Or sometimes, in her final desperation, that there wouldn't.

Had Harold himself really enjoyed it all? She'd never known, because she'd never asked him, any more than he'd ever asked her. A Summer Holiday was something you simply *had* every year, like Christmas or an attack of 'flu. You never thought of questioning it.

On the other hand, though, maybe Harold *had* actually enjoyed it. Certainly he'd enjoyed showing his slides the following winter.— But at the time? Mostly, he'd seemed bored: no doubt that was why he kept booking them onto those awful coach-trips to somewhere or other to look at something and to have a cup of tea which you couldn't enjoy for fear that there mightn't be a Ladies on the way back.

But this summer—for the first time ever—it didn't have to happen! She would be free! Free to sit in her beloved garden, among the birds and the wallflowers and the roses, day after golden day, planning nothing, worrying about nothing, with no grim deadline looming, no fearsome departure date casting its black, lengthening shadow across the bright days. For the first time in all her adult life she could spend the whole long summer as she had always yearned to spend it, tending her flowers, watering them, and sharing with each one its moment of glory as the season waxed and waned. This year, she would miss nothing, not the delphiniums, not the peonies, not the dahlias' scarlet and mauve and gold. She would be here to pick the strawberries as they ripened, and the blackcurrants; she would be here to harvest the lavender, to gather for wine the great white elder-flowers, big as dinner plates, at the very peak of their perfection.

*

It was barely three weeks later when the blow fell.

"You must have a holiday, Mother," her daughter-in-law Vivien announced one Sunday lunchtime. "Geoff and I have been talking about it, haven't we, Geoff, and we've decided that you must come with us this year. No, Mother, don't argue, Geoff can afford it easily, he feels it's the least he can do—after all, he *is* your only son. A holiday is just what you need after this dreadful winter you've had."

"But—but, Vivien dear, I don't really—!"

"Mother! I said, don't *argue!* We won't take no for an answer, will we, Geoff? You *must* have a holiday. Harold would have wished it—you know he would!"

Would he? Would he? And even if he would, did she have to go *on* doing the things that Harold wished now that he was dead and gone? She'd done the things he'd wished for the best part of thirty years— wasn't that enough?

Feebly, she tried to fight back.

"It's sweet of you, dears," she said, putting her knife and fork carefully together, "I really am very grateful—it's such a kind thought—but, you see, the thing is—"

Well, what was it? Rack her brain as she might, Emmy could think of absolutely nothing. Simply to say, "I hate holidays, I always have, and I've resolved never to go on another one as long as I live," was, of course, out of the question. People don't hate holidays. It's just not done.

"Mummy, why isn't Grandma finishing her chicken?" interposed seven-year-old Angie, whose sharp, beady eyes had been noting every nuance of her grandmother's discomfiture. "Grandma, why aren't you finishing your chicken?"

"Hush, dear," remonstrated Vivien, but there was no real reproof behind it. Vivien secretly relished, Emmy was sure, Angie's talent for spotting small flaws and inadequacies in her grandmother's menage and calling attention to them. It had become almost a family sport, at Emmy's expense.

"Why are Grandma's forks all yellowy instead of bright?" she'd asked earlier in the meal. And before that, wandering into the room where the three grownups were drinking sherry: "What are all those dead flies for, Grandma, on the window ledge in the spare room?"

It would be like that all through the holiday. "Mummy, why is Grandma wearing those funny shoes to the beach?" "Mummy, why is Grandma going to the toilet again? She's only just been."

Emmy forced herself to swallow another few mouthfuls of chicken— but the taste of defeat was everywhere. She was cornered, and she knew it. It was all *arranged*, you see, the hotel bookings, the air ticket, everything. They'd meant it as a *surprise*, a lovely surprise.

"Oh, *please*, Mother, stop being so difficult! What do you think people would *say* if we all went off on holiday without you at a time like this? Oh, Mother, don't be so *tiresome! Of course* you need a holiday!"

Of course—

Of course—

Of course—

By the end of the afternoon, everything was settled. At one point, looking out into her tranquil, sunlit garden, her joy in it already spoiled for weeks and months ahead, actual tears came into Emmy's eyes and she had to blink them away quickly before Angie could ask in her sharp, shrill little voice, "Mummy, why is Granny crying?"

Not that it would have mattered. They'd merely have thought she was crying for Harold, as a proper widow should, and that's what they'd have told Angie.

"She's crying for poor Grandpa," they'd have said, in suitably hushed tones, and would then have changed the subject quickly before Angie could pipe: "Why is she?"

*

She didn't cry for long. The idea came to her quite suddenly only a few days after the visit—but of course to start with she had to keep it to herself, hugging the relief and the joy of it close to her breast, secretly, while answering appropriately and with pretended enthusiasm the kindly remarks of friends and neighbours.

"Beginning to get excited about your holiday, I'll bet," said one. And another: "It'll do you a world of good! A real holiday is just what you need!"

And Emmy smiled to them all, and nodded, and went on watering her young tomato plants, almost bursting with the secret joy of knowing that, after all, on July eleventh she *wouldn't* be leaving them, just when the first thrilling green fruits were beginning to swell in the sunshine.

It was on July ninth that the plan had to be put into action. Geoff had brought over her air-ticket several days earlier, all tucked neatly into a crisp blue folder, together with lots of travellers' cheques and brochures and things, and she had put it all carefully away with her passports, in the top left-hand drawer of the bureau. Now, as the afternoon of the ninth waned towards evening, she took the documents out, passport and all, wrapped them in a plastic bag, and took them into the kitchen, the door of which opened straight into the garden. Already, earlier in the day, she'd dug the hole—on the far side of the lavender-bush where it wouldn't show—and presently, after sunset and before the moon rose, she slipped out into the sweet, scented garden and popped the package into its little grave, tamping the earth well down above it.

Then she returned to the kitchen, brushing loose soil from her hands, her heart thumping with such a mixture of excitement, trepidation, and triumph as she had never known...

*

"But Mother, how *can* you have lost them?" shrieked Vivien down the phone. "I don't understand—what did you take them to the Post Office *for*? Oh, God, I'd better ring them at once! Let's pray that someone responsible has found them and handed them in!"

But the Post Office hadn't got them, and nor had the bank or the supermarket or the Cosy Coffee House or any of the other places where it occurred to Vivien that her idiotic mother-in-law might have left them.

"Whatever did you take them out *for*?" she kept asking, distracted, in between the fruitless phone-calls—and she treated with the scorn it deserved her mother-in-law's wavering account of having transferred them to her handbag "so as not to forget them in the last-minute rush." How neurotic could the woman get?

"I suppose, if they're *not* found," Emmy ventured at last, making every effort to keep the jubilation out of her voice, "if they're *not* found, I won't be able to go, will I? Not without my passport or anything—"

"Oh, nonsense!" But Vivien was clearly rattled. She'd been around here all afternoon, with Angie at her heels, searching the house in every cranny without, of course, any success. Naturally, it never occurred to her to look in the garden, and so Emmy wasn't really worried.

All the same, there was one bad moment.

"Mummy, why hasn't Grandma packed any of her summer dresses? Why has she only—?"

Emmy's heart very nearly stopped. Naturally, knowing that she would be happily unpacking everything again tomorrow, she'd just shoved in any old thing, just to make the case look full.

"Mummy, come and look. Grandma's forgotten to put in her—"

Gasping for breath, Emmy raced upstairs faster than she'd done for years, slammed down the lids of the cases and locked them.

"And don't you dare touch them!" she cried to the attentive Angie. "Just you leave them alone!"

"Mummy, why is Grandma being so cross?"

But it was all right. It blew over. Vivien was far too busy, far too distraught, to follow it up.

"I'll just have to ring the police again," she said, pushing the hair back from her damp forehead. "Maybe someone's—no." She drew her hand back from the telephone. "No, I think I'd better go round and talk to them in person."

And off she went, leaving Emmy victorious—but somehow uneasy. The *police!* The documents wouldn't have been handed in, obviously—they couldn't have been—and surely no one would ever think of digging up the garden, but all the same—the police!

Her unease was justified. It was less than two hours later—barely nine o'clock—when Vivien rang up, and Emmy knew at once, from her ecstatic tone, that something terrible had happened.

"It's all right!" Vivien exulted. "No—they haven't found anything, but they've been *so* kind! People talk about 'faceless bureaucrats' and all that, but they're not like that at all—not when you talk to them personally. I told them all about your sad bereavement, and how you'd been looking forward so much to this special holiday, and they were so sympathetic, all of them—the police, the Airline, the passport people, everybody! They've rushed through an emergency passport for you—and a duplicate air ticket! All you've got to do is sign a few things. I'm coming to fetch you right away."

They had indeed been kind, all these officials. The thought of this poor lonely widow missing her longed-for holiday had really touched their hearts, and between them they'd fixed everything. Emmy felt awful, in a way, that all this kindness was going to be wasted; for she knew already what she was going to do.

★

Vivien drove her home, watched while she put the new documents into her handbag, and the handbag into the top left bureau drawer, watched while she locked it.

"And don't *touch* them, Mother, don't touch them *at all* until we come for you tomorrow morning," was her parting injunction; and Emmy nodded meekly, submissive as a little child.

This new lot she buried under the lilac, tamping down the soil well and thoroughly as before. And then, when it was midnight, she set to work to make the house ready.

She had always heard that burglars are in the habit of turning the place upside-down in their search for valuables, pulling books out of shelves, dragging furniture about, tipping drawers out all over the floor. She didn't want to make *too* much mess, of course, because who but she would have the job of clearing it up again? So she set about her task circumspectly, upending only those drawers which were in a mess anyway and could do with a good tidy, and pushing around only such articles of furniture as she could shift easily, such as the standard-lamps, the cane-bottomed chairs, and the spindly little telephone table on the upstairs landing, which she laid neatly on its side.

She took special care with the books—she had heard that burglars always go for these first, in case there are banknotes hidden between the pages. One by one, she took them off the shelves and set them gently, not to damage the bindings, all over the sitting-room floor, some open, some shut, to look as if they might have been thrown there. It was past two when she dragged herself, exhausted but triumphant, up to bed.

Tired though she was, she didn't fall asleep at once, but lay, tense and jubilant, savouring the triumph that awaited her tomorrow morning. They *couldn't* make her go now, not with this second lot of papers lost, and the house freshly burgled. A vast contentment and joy slowly filled her consciousness. But just as she was falling into a blissful sleep, a sudden thought struck her, jerking her wide awake.

Nothing had been stolen, except the papers! So preoccupied had she been with making the house *look* burgled that she'd quite forgotten that *real* burglars would take all the valuables they could lay their hands on. That's what they'd have come for.

Only small things, of course, that could be easily buried. The silver teaspoons? Money from her handbag? Jewellery from her inlaid sandal-wood box? Scrambling out of bed, and remembering just in time not to switch on the light lest a neighbour might notice, she hurried across the room and out onto the dark landing—where she tripped over the spindly little telephone table lying on its side in the middle of the floor and pitched headlong down the stairs.

It was the murder hunt of the century. Naturally, the police recognised within seconds that the burglary had been faked, and suspicion fell, briefly, on Vivien, who had spent the whole of the previous afternoon alone with her mother-in-law. But the times didn't fit, the motive was negligible (a few hundred pounds of insurance money), and so this theory was soon dropped.

It was when the first of the buried passports was found that the excitement began; and when the second, duplicate one also came to light, the excitement became a furore, making front-page headlines in all the newspapers and receiving star treatment on television. Clearly, this was no ordinary domestic fracas—there must be large-scale rami-fications. Russian spies? An international drug-ring? Some sinister ter-rorist organisation? Something, anyway, that demanded a false identity, a stolen passport, for someone crossing a frontier with some nefarious purpose. Some deceptively innocent-looking middle-aged woman, vaguely resembling Emmy, would have to be sought. No doubt it was this unlucky resemblance that had led to poor Emmy's death. Or maybe the poor lady had stumbled in all innocence on some piece of information that was a danger to the malefactors. Anyway, *some* kind of international criminal network it must be. Interpol was called in, and the C.I.D.—even M.I.5—but with all their combined expertise, they seemed quite unable to come up with any plausible theory as to what lay behind it all.

Angie, of course, could have told them. Indeed she did.

"Grandma lost her passport on purpose," she bossily announced. "She was only pretend-looking for it, I know she was. I watched her. And she'd only pretend-packed, too. I looked. You see, Grandma hated holidays. And—" she appended belligerently, just for the devilment of it—"*I* hate holidays, too. They're boring."

"Hush, dear, don't be rude," Vivien reproved absently, and returned to the serious matter of being interviewed by the C.I.D. Naturally, no one took any notice of this little bit of family bickering. Why should they? How could they be expected to guess that a cheeky little seven-year-old showoff might have come up with the correct solution to a mystery which for weeks now had been baffling the best brains of the best crime-detection squads in all the western world?

THE SUMMER HOLIDAY MURDERS

Julian Symons

Julian Symons (1912–94) was one of crime fiction's most influential writers and critics during the second half of the twentieth century, yet crime writing was not the only string to his bow. The diversity of his achievements, encompassing poetry, biography, military history, was reflected in a Festschrift published to celebrate his 80th birthday; it featured contributions by admirers as diverse as Patricia Highsmith, the poet Gavin Ewart, Thomas Narcejac (the co-author of the book filmed as *Vertigo*), Nicolas Freeling, and Donald E. Westlake. He wrote an important history of the genre, *Bloody Murder*, served as President of the Detection Club from 1976–85 and received the CWA Diamond Dagger, the highest honour in British crime writing. Three of his novels have so far been reissued as British Library Crime Classics.

Symons is sometimes perceived as a scourge of Golden Age detective fiction, but this is an over-simplification, as was his own contention that the detective story has evolved into the crime novel. The reality is that crime writing is a broad church, and there is room for ingenious puzzle-making as well as exploration of the darker recesses of the human psyche. Early in his own career, Symons himself showed that he was as adept at constructing a neat puzzle as he was at examining criminal psychology. This long story, also known as "The Crimson Coach Murders" is a good example; it was serialised in the *Evening Standard*, the first episode appearing on 25 July 1960, and was later included in the collection *How to Trap a Crook* (1977).

"IT'S RATHER STEEP, THIS PATH," SAID MISS PENNY. "AND A LITTLE bit slippery."

"You'll be all right," said her companion reassuringly. "Just hold on to the rail."

"Oh, don't worry about me. I haven't enjoyed myself so much for years. It was such a wonderful idea, the coach tour. Everybody seems so nice. And the weather." Miss Penny looked up, a little old birdlike woman wearing a mauve silk frock, a hat with a great deal of fruit on it, and dazzlingly ornamental dark glasses. The cliff rose up, as it seemed, a long way above her, overhanging so that the top was invisible. She saw sky and sea that, through her glasses, was not dazzling but muted blue. She saw the face of her companion, smiling. And below, quite near now, was a rocky cove hollowed out of the cliff, with little pools between the rocks.

"Rather a sharp turn," said her companion. A hand was laid upon her arm, upon the arm that held the handrail.

"This is really a great adventure," Miss Penny said gaily.

Quite gently the hand lifted her arm from the rail, a knee pushed her less gently in the back. Miss Penny fell helter-skelter down the last few steps, squawking like a duck. She caught her head nastily upon a rock, and before she could get up, before she really knew what was happening at all, hard hands gripped her shoulders and forced her resistlessly down so that her face touched the salt and slimy water in one of the pools. Miss Penny struggled then, and tried to speak, but when she opened her mouth water filled it. She did not struggle for long. It was the end of her great adventure.

Her hat floated on the pool, like a toy boat laden with cherries and strawberries. Her body lay face down in the water.

There was one more thing to do, and her companion did it. The time was just after six o'clock in the evening.

The Top-Grade Coaches Luxury Tour party sat in the lounge of the Barkbeck Hotel and waited for dinner. The Barkbeck was not the best hotel in Eastbourne, but it justified well enough, Gilbert Langham thought, the brochure's claim: *"The hotels specially selected by our experts offer* THE BEST OF EVERYTHING—*food prepared by Continental chefs, smiling service, and rooms with a view of the sea."* The room was comfortable, the service was quick, and there were pleasant smells coming from the dining-room.

But back to duty. This was really a piece of field research for Gil Langham, whose fifth detective novel was to be about a murder committed on a coach tour in Southern England. With a plot sketched out he found himself at a loss to imagine what sort of people actually went on such a tour. What could be simpler than to go on one himself, and find out?

He took a small black notebook from his pocket and studied what he had already written, after the trip down from London with its break for a "surprise" lunch (which proved to be a picnic), and a visit to Arundel Castle.

Wiliam and Mary Blake. Married couple. Husband much older than wife. Wandered off on their own this afternoon.

Gil Langham looked at them now, sitting on a window seat with hands touching, and wondered if they were honeymooners. At a table nearby sat the handsome grey-haired old man named Antrobus, and on a sofa Mrs. Williams, Elaine Williams, lay back studying her blood-red nails and looking bored. He read what he had written:

—*Antrobus*. Retired businessman? Made a fuss when we stopped for drinks, said he'd been charged twopence too much for tomato juice. But looks prosperous. Doesn't seem really to be enjoying himself.

Elaine Williams. Merry Widow spider? Looking for husband-fly to walk into her parlour?

A hand was placed upon his shoulder, and a voice boomed in his ear. "Hallo, hallo! This won't do. Settling down to work while you're on holiday isn't allowed. Have a drink, old man."

Tompkins was fortyish, almost bald, and obviously destined for the part of bore of the tour. But very likely his book would have a bore in it, Gilbert Langham thought with a mental sigh as he said that he would like a drink. As they passed the Merry Widow she looked up. Her eyes telegraphed an invitation which he ignored.

"Not a bad piece that," Tompkins said when they had their whiskies at the bar. "Did you notice her giving me the eye? But I always say, take it easy. You don't want to start anything you can't finish on a holiday like this."

"You've been on tours like this before?"

"I get around," Tompkins said vaguely. "Now, don't think I'm nosey, old man, but I always flatter myself I can spot a man's occupation. You're a schoolmaster, right?"

Gilbert had been prepared for this. "No, I'm a journalist, a freelance."

"Looking for copy, eh? Writing us up?"

"Of course not!" But he felt uncomfortable. The look in Tompkins's eye had been remarkably shrewd. He might be a bore, but he was far from a fool.

A young man came into the lounge, a young man with a brown face, dark hair carefully parted, and teeth that showed dazzlingly white when he smiled. This was Jerry Benton, the tour guide, who seemed to Gilbert Langham rather too much of a good thing. One couldn't make him a murderer in a story because it would be too obvious, but all the same—

"Don't like that chap," Tompkins said, cutting into and confirming his thoughts. "Don't trust him. 'Call me Jerry,' he says. I'll call him—" And he made a coarse joke.

Benton was going round from table to table, talking to all the members of the party, many of whom Gilbert Langham did not know. He chatted for a minute with Mr. Antrobus and then stopped beside the Merry Widow. They came over to the bar together. Benton performed introductions in a low voice.

"There is a dance this evening at the Winter Garden. For those on the tour there is no charge."

"Don't dance," Tompkins snapped.

"And a concert at the Pavilion. Again no charge. Tomorrow morning at ten-thirty there is a mystery tour that will last the morning."

"Same old South Downs mystery, I suppose," Tompkins said.

Benton was imperturbable. "Those who wish to stay here of course may do so. We leave the hotel after lunch."

The Merry Widow smiled at him. "Are you going to the dance?"

Benton smiled back. "Of course!"

The dinner gong sounded, and at the same moment the manager came into the lounge with a tall, hard-faced man wearing a blue serge suit. They came up to Benton together.

"Mr. Benton?" the man in the blue suit said. "My name is Lake. Detective-Superintendent Lake."

For a moment there seemed to be a break in Benton's perfect composure, then his smile was in place again. "Yes, Superintendent. What can I do for you?"

"You have a Miss Penny in your coach party?"

"That's right. But she's not here at the moment. She is a little late for dinner."

"Miss Penny won't want dinner. She's dead."

Mrs. Williams gave a little scream. Tompkins said, "An accident?"

"It seems that she fell down by some rocks, caught her head and drowned in a pool." The superintendent spoke with deliberate slowness. "But there's one odd thing. A book, with all the pages torn out, was by her side. The pages were scattered around."

"What was the book?" Gil Langham asked.

Superintendent Lake stared at him. *"The Adventures of Sherlock Holmes."*

Langham stared, and said with a gulp when asked his occupation: "I write detective stories."

A sergeant in the corner of the manager's office, where this interrogation was taking place, snorted slightly. Gilbert Langham gulped again, and decided that he might as well go on. "I'm here to get background material for a new book."

"You've been very successful." With the same grim sarcasm Lake said, "Using your no doubt exceptional faculties of observation, have you noticed anything odd on this coach tour so far?"

"I can't think of anything."

"Or about Miss Penny?"

Miss Penny, Miss Penny? They had hardly spoken. She was a face to him, no more than that, an old face inquisitive and perhaps vain, topped by a ridiculous hat. "I remember the fruit on her hat more than the face under it. Wasn't it an accident, then, Superintendent?"

"This is a queer business." Lake stared hard at him. "A crime writer might have thought it up." Langham flinched. "This little old woman goes off for a walk, climbs down some steps, slips—we can see the mark—falls, hits her head, and drowns in a pool of water. That's the way it looks. I think we might accept it as an accident. But then someone—someone, Mr. Langham—tears the pages out of a crime story, throws them all over the place, and leaves the gutted book by her body. If she was murdered, why should the murderer do that, after arranging things to look like a neat little accident? Or why should anybody else do it? This is the kind of thing that should appeal to a writer of crime stories."

The way in which these last words were spoken made Gilbert Langham gulp again. "Have you found out anything about Miss Penny? I mean, why should anybody want to kill her?"

The sergeant in the corner said: "Evelyn Penny. Spinster. Lived at 18 Cotes Avenue, Turnham Green, London. Told other members of party that she had retired from work in a drapery store, had small private income, went away somewhere every year. Did not appear to know anyone else in coach party."

"And her movements, Sergeant?"

"Coach arrived Barkbeck Hotel, Eastbourne, about three-thirty. Miss Penny had tea in lounge, then said she was going for a stroll. Was seen by Mr. Tompkins on front, later by Mr. and Mrs. Blake having photograph taken at the Nu-Stile-Picksher stall also on the front. This was about four-forty-five. Not seen afterwards until discovery of body just before seven o'clock. Purse appeared not to have been touched, no sign of bodily violence."

"There's nothing to connect this with the coach," the superintendent said. "But still, I'd like to keep what you might call an unofficial sort of an eye on your party. With your powers of observation, Mr. Langham, you could be a help to us in that way if you cared to." The superintendent smiled now. It made the request sound like an order.

"All right! But I don't really see what you want me to do."

"Just keep your eyes and ears open. We'll get in touch with you in a day or two."

Dinner was late, but it could not be said that Miss Penny's death cast a shadow over the coach party. Rather it provided a ready-made subject of conversation which could be added to weather and food. Gilbert Langham sat afterwards at a table with the Blakes and listened to them talking about it.

"Honestly, you know, Mr. Langham, I don't think the poor thing was quite all there," Mary Blake said, "I mean, we saw her having her photograph taken on the parade by those people who give away prizes every day—"

"Nu-Stile-Pickshers," her husband said. He was a hearty, tweed-jacketed, pipe-smoking man in his early thirties, perhaps ten years older than his birdlike wife. "Advertising stunt, you know. As a matter of fact we had our own pictures taken."

"But no luck with a prize," Mary Blake said. "Anyway, when the young man asked if she wanted her picture taken, she was primping and blushing like a girl of fifteen."

Mr. Blake puffed at his pipe, rustled the evening paper. "I reckon some man got hold of her, sex maniac."

"But Bill," his wife said with ghoulish eagerness, "there wasn't—I mean, she wasn't *interfered with*, was she?"

Bill Blake was having trouble with his pipe. He tapped out the dottle in an ashtray. "The superintendent didn't say so. If we're going to this dance, my girl, you ought to get ready."

Mary Blake excused herself. Her husband began to read the paper.

Gilbert Langham also went to the dance at the Winter Garden. The unattached women in the party, he saw, were beginning to pair with men. He found himself asking the Merry Widow to dance. They talked, as seemed inevitable about Miss Penny.

"I'm so glad it hasn't been allowed to spoil the tour," she said. "Jerry has been simply marvellous about it. You know how silly people are, they get worried, but Jerry's told them all it was just an accident."

"That was good of him."

"Yes, wasn't it? But he must have had a lot of experience in handling awkward situations. He was some sort of courier in the Middle East at one time. And then he was a smuggler."

"Really? What did he smuggle, Mrs. Williams?"

"My name's Elaine." She came close to him. The bloom of youth, he saw, had been replaced by the enamel of middle age, but she was still an attractive woman. She whispered in his ear: "Diamonds."

He wanted to ask why, if Jerry Benton was a diamond smuggler, he had this humble job of guide to a coach party, but after all it was none of his business if the guide liked to tell fairy stories to impressionable women. Instead he said, "Who was particularly worried about Miss Penny?"

"That's a funny thing. It was a man who keeps himself to himself. Mr. Antrobus."

Mr. Antrobus, grey-haired and really remarkably handsome, sat in the lounge drinking coffee when the party from the Winter Garden returned, gay and chattering. Tompkins also was in the lounge. He made a bee-line for Gilbert Langham.

"I've had a word with the super and told him my theory about the Penny murder—"

Jerry Benton interrupted him. "It was an accident. And anyway it's rather a gloomy subject, old man. I think it should be declared closed."

Tompkins glared at him. "It's a free country. This is my theory. That old girl, Miss Penny, had somehow got the wrong side of a chap who's a maniac about books, see. And this chap did for her, and then left the book by her side. What you might call symbolic."

There was a clatter from the other side of the lounge. Mr. Antrobus had knocked his coffee cup to the floor. He did not pick it up, but slowly rose and walked over to the lift.

"Good night," Tompkins said cheerfully.

Mr. Antrobus did not reply.

2

A man who is tired of Brighton is tired of life, Gilbert Langham said to himself, bringing Dr. Johnson up to date. He walked from the lawns of Hove to the Palace Pier in a trance of pleasure, leaving the promenade as he passed the Metropole to walk down beside the beach. Here children shrieked happily, their parents bought tea trays and sticky cakes, young men in vivid shirts left the sunlight to play earnestly on pin-tables in amusement arcades.

Behind this popular, vulgar Brighton lay the solid hotels full of money, behind them again the appropriately artificial glamour of the Prince Regent's onion domes. He stopped before a little hut that said Nu-Stile-Pickshers. Underneath was a sign in dashing scarlet calligraphy: *"Have Yore Foto Takn and Win Wun of Our Munny Prizes."* A curly-haired young man with an engaging smile was in charge.

"Step right up now, and take advantage of this stupendous offer. Three postcard size pictures for a bob, and a money prize if you get one of today's lucky numbers."

A chord was struck in Gilbert Langham's mind. "Haven't you got a place in Eastbourne?"

"Eastbourne, Littlehampton, Brighton, Worthing, Folkestone, a dozen places along the coast," the young man said. "But only one set of prizes each day, and each day at a different town. Today it's Brighton. Come along, you lucky people, we're offering you twenty-five quid to nothing."

"You were offering prizes in Eastbourne yesterday," Langham said. "Did you happen to see an old lady named Miss Penny?"

The young man looked at him sharply, shouted inside the hut, "Just going out for a cuppa," and led the way to a self-service café twenty yards away from the hut. He put three spoonfuls of sugar in his tea, stirred and said, "The name's Wilson, Charlie Wilson. What's yours?"

"Gilbert Langham."

"So now we know each other's monicker. I like to know who I'm talking to. Now, what's your interest?"

There was something a shade odd about the young man, Langham thought, as though he knew that working for Nu-Stile-Pickshers demanded a front of brass that was not natural to him. A university graduate seeing the other side of life?

"I'm one of the coach party she was with. I write crime stories and her death roused—you might call it my professional curiosity."

"Fair enough! She came along yesterday, had her picture taken. Funny old girl! I remember the way she mucked around with her hat, trying it this way and that for effect. Then she went off. I told the police." He hesitated.

"You've remembered something else." Gilbert Langham was careful not to sound too eager.

"Not exactly. It's just that they were only trying to fix a time, and I told them she came along at a quarter to five. They didn't want anything else, so I didn't tell them."

"Tell them what?"

"She seemed a bit excited, as if she was going to meet someone. And after she left the hut she did meet someone. I saw her."

"What did he look like?"

"I only caught a glimpse, mind. And side face. I'm not sure I could identify him. But he was a good-looking sort of a chap, about her own age I should say. And he had a fine crop of iron grey hair."

Mr. Antrobus.

"Superintendent Lake, please," he said into the receiver. "Tell him it's Gilbert Langham. About Miss Penny."

There was a click and he heard Lake's voice, with its faint undertone of sarcasm. "Yes, Mr. Langham?"

With attempted casualness he said, "I've been talking to a man named Wilson, who works for those Nu-Stile-Pickshers people. He saw Miss Penny walking with somebody after she had her photograph taken yesterday."

"Why didn't he tell us?"

"You were concentrating on the time," he said with a touch of complacency. "Wilson's not sure that he could identify the man, but says he had a fine crop of grey hair. From the description it might be a man on the tour named Antrobus."

There was silence. Then Lake said: "Miss Penny died between six and six-thirty. Antrobus was in the hotel lounge a minute or two after six o'clock. Three or four people saw him."

"Alibis have been broken before now," Gilbert Langham said. He put down the receiver.

The telephone box was opposite the Palace Pier. When he came out of it he hesitated. The coach party had split up, some of them going on a tour of the Royal Pavilion, and others preferring what was rather oddly called "Free Time". They were all to meet back at the Packham Hotel at half past six. With an hour to fill, Gilbert Langham went on to the Palace Pier.

He strolled idly, sniffing the salt air, until he saw ahead of him the grey hair and slightly shuffling walk of Mr. Antrobus. It was with a feeling that he was about to make a discovery of vital importance that he cautiously followed the grey head up the pier, and with some disappointment that he saw Mr. Antrobus turn into the Palace of Pleasure and settle down to play a game called Cup and Ball, at which he proved to be rather skilful.

He went up behind Antrobus and said, "Hallo!"

The grey-haired man turned round with what might have been a look of alarm but was certainly, when he recognised Langham, one of annoyance. "Good afternoon!"

"You didn't go to the Pavilion?"

"Evidently not."

"You're not forced to do anything on this sort of tour, that's what I like about it."

Mr. Antrobus did not reply. He shot up a small silver ball and dexterously caught it in the cup.

"Where did you go with Miss Penny, when you met her yesterday afternoon?"

Mr. Antrobus was about to catch another ball. His hand jerked, and he dropped it. He turned round and said very decidedly, "I did not meet Miss Penny. I did not even know her. You are being a nuisance. Will you please go away?"

Gilbert Langham went away.

When the tour of the Pavilion was over the Blakes and the tour guide, Jerry Benton, went down to the beach.

"Have you made up your minds?" Jerry Benton asked.

"Let me see it again." There was something greedy in Bill Blake's voice.

They sat down. Jerry drew from an inside pocket something wrapped in tissue. As he unwrapped it, the white stone sparkled in the sunlight.

"Oh Bill," Mary Blake breathed, "it's lovely, lovely!"

"You're asking a hundred," her husband said. "That's a lot of money."

"A quarter of what it's worth." Jerry Benton began to wrap the stone.

"Don't put it away. I told you, I don't know anything about diamonds. I'd need to have it examined by a jeweller."

"And have him asking where it came from? Not likely! I risked a five-year sentence to bring this in. I'm not having any jeweller poking his nose in."

"Bill," said Mary Blake in a small voice, "Mr. Tompkins said last night that he knew a lot about jewellery. Supposing he looked at it for us, would that—?" she left the sentence unfinished.

"That would suit me." Blake looked at Benton.

Benton hesitated, then shrugged. "Tompkins doesn't love me much. But all right. You can show it to him tonight."

He let the stone rest in his palm. Blake could not take his eyes off it.

3

"Another whisky?" Bill Blake said.

"I don't mind if I do." Tompkins was wearing a powerfully checked shirt, open to reveal his boiled red neck, and purplish linen trousers. He downed half the whisky at a gulp and sighed with pleasure. "This is the life."

"Mr. Tompkins." Mary Blake put her pretty arms on the bar counter and looked at him with her birdlike head on one side. "You said you used to be an agent for a firm of jewellers."

"Correct, my dear lady. Brant and Boulting, Hatton Garden, dealers in precious stones."

"Would you look at a stone for us?"

Tompkins frowned. "Mixing business and pleasure, don't like that. Why d'you want me to look at it?"

"We'd pay you—" Bill Blake began, but his wife interrupted.

"We're thinking of buying it, wondered how much we should pay. And we're awfully stupid about these things. We thought we'd come to an expert."

The frown changed to a leer. "Anything to oblige a charming lady," Tompkins said.

Upstairs in Tompkins's room, Bill Blake took out of his pocket the stone wrapped in tissue which Jerry Benton had given him, with the remark that nobody could say he didn't trust his fellow men. Tompkins glanced at it, raised his thick eyebrows, and then took from his suitcase a jeweller's glass which he put into his eye. He examined the stone carefully, turning it this way and that, for perhaps half a minute. When he spoke his tone was professional.

"It's a diamond, and quite a fine one. Not cut as well as it might be, but still a very nice stone."

"How much is it worth?"

Tompkins took the glass out of his eye, and grinned at them conspiratorially. "You notice I haven't asked where it came from, and I don't want to know. But if you were asking me to buy it, that's the first question I'd ask."

"I'm not asking you to buy it. What's it worth to me?"

"I'm telling you the difficulty about selling it is that any honest jeweller will ask the same question. He'll want to be sure it came into this country legally." Now Tompkins winked.

"We shouldn't want to sell it," Mary Blake said excitedly. "It's to make into a ring for me."

Tompkins rubbed his chin. "Hard to put a value on it. Wouldn't be dear at two hundred quid."

"Oh, you darling man," Mary Blake said. She kissed Tompkins on the cheek.

The Merry Widow was telling Gilbert Langham the story of her life, as they sat in deckchairs on the front. Her husband, a colonel in the Engineers, had gone through the war unscratched, and had then died in a yachting accident shortly after his retirement, three years ago. "No children," she said, turning upon him the full force of still-lustrous eyes. "And this rambling old house in Shropshire to look after. I'm a lonely woman, Gil."

Gilbert Langham was not much interested in her past. "You remember that yesterday evening we were sitting in the lounge of that hotel at Eastbourne. Did you happen to notice what time that man Antrobus came into the lounge?"

"I already told the police that as far as I could remember it was about six o'clock," Elaine Williams said coldly.

"You couldn't be more exact?"

"No. I must be going back to the hotel." As she got up she said, "I detest snoopers." Gilbert Langham sighed. The way of an amateur detective is hard.

That night there was a firework display at the end of the Palace Pier, and tickets were free for those who wanted them. "I must say," said Mr. Portingale, a self-important, pigeon-chested man who went about with a limp, long-nosed wife apparently permanently attached to his arm, "that young chap Benton knows how to manage things. As a business-man myself I respect efficiency."

"He's very good," Gilbert Langham agreed. He was watching Mr. Antrobus to see if he took one of the tickets. He did, after asking whether they were free.

"My husband had thirty men under him at his retirement," Mrs. Portingale said in a melancholy voice.

"A versatile young fellow, too," Portingale resumed. "Used to be in the diamond trade, I understand. Adventurous."

"It takes all sorts to make a world," Mrs. Portingale said sadly.

"Yes, indeed." Langham took one of the tickets. The Portingales took them, too.

The night was hot, the sea still. Rockets swished up skywards, burst into patterns of stars. A set piece slowly made the pattern WELCOME TO BRIGHTON. There was a burst of clapping.

"It's simply gorgeous," Mary Blake said. "Perfect. I want it to last for ever. Have you told Jerry about the ring, darling?"

"A hundred pounds is okay," her husband said. "I'll give you a cheque tomorrow." He produced the stone in its tissue and Benton took it.

"No cheques, old man. Strictly cash. If you can let me have the money at the end of the tour I'll hand over the stone then." His teeth gleamed in a smile. "You can ask Tompkins to vet it for you again then, if you like. See you later." He waved a graceful hand.

"I wonder why he insists on cash." Blake took out his pipe and tapped it thoughtfully on the rail.

"He's just being careful, silly. Ooh!" A cascade of coloured lights exploded just above their heads. The hand that she had placed over her husband's clutched at him, the nails dug gently into his palm.

"I want some cigarettes," Elaine Williams said, and opened her bag. "Oh, damn! I've forgotten my purse."

Portingale, who was sitting just behind her, took out his case. She murmured her thanks, lighted the cigarette, took a few puffs, then murmured something about going back to the hotel, and got up.

It was a few minutes afterwards that Langham, who had been temporarily enthralled by a set piece depicting the battle of Trafalgar, with the Victory's guns magnificently firing, noticed that Antrobus was not in his place. He got up and walked down the pier to look for him. But the man with grey hair had vanished.

Elaine Williams did not go back to the hotel. An hour later she was walking by the cliffs near Rottingdean, talking about her husband's death and the big house in Shropshire.

"Yes," her companion said. "Yes. Yes."

"The truth is I am a very lonely woman."

"We are all lonely." Her companion took her hand and led her nearer to the cliff top.

"Sometimes—you'll think it foolish—my heart really aches." She guided her hand to her aching heart.

"You're not foolish at all." Another hand encircled her shoulder.

She held up her face to be kissed. Then she felt herself being forced backwards, and opened her lips to scream, but the hand that had been on her heart quickly covered them. Her high heels scrabbled at the cliff edge before she went over.

4

It was no more than eleven o'clock in the morning, but already a fierce sun shone into the little room. The sandy sergeant he had seen before waved Gilbert Langham into a seat directly facing the window and the glare. Superintendent Lake sat in the shade.

"Now, Mr. Langham, I shall value your skilled observation. What have you got to tell me?"

"I still don't know exactly what's happened," Gilbert Langham said. "There are all sorts of rumours. Nobody knew that Mrs. Williams hadn't come back to the hotel until this morning. Your people haven't really told us much."

"She's dead," Lake said. "She fell, or was pushed, off the cliffs near Rottingdean some time yesterday evening. There's a drop of about eighty feet and she was probably killed at once. She'd been dead several hours when she was found, early this morning." Lake paused and then said, "There was a book found near the body, looked as if it had been thrown from the cliff top."

He held up a book on the desk before him, its cover spotted with damp. Gilbert Langham read the title on the back. It was *The Suicide's Grave* by James Hogg.

"That's not been gutted."

"Not this time. But the queer thing is that it should have been there at all. What sort of woman was Mrs. Williams?"

"I thought of her as the Merry Widow. She was flirtatious, particularly with young men."

"With you, for instance?"

"Yes. Though I lost favour because I didn't react properly when she said she was lonely. She seemed to like Jerry Benton, the guide. But it didn't mean anything. She'd have behaved in the same way with any other young man."

"Mr. Langham." Lake leaned forward. The outlines of his face were harsh. "It seems likely that Mrs. Williams died through what you call her flirtatiousness with a young man—or an old one. And since whoever killed her left a book, as he did with Miss Penny, it's a fair assumption that the murderer is linked with your coach party. I want you to tell me exactly what you saw and heard after going out to watch the fireworks."

"At about nine o'clock or a little after, Mrs. Williams left us, saying she was going to the hotel. She'd left her purse there, had no money to buy cigarettes—"

Lake interrupted. "She said she had no money, you're sure of that?"

"Yes. A man named Portingale was sitting just behind her, offered her a cigarette."

"Her handbag went over the cliff with her. There was a five-pound note in it, loose."

"No purse?"

"Her purse was in the hotel. But a five-pound note is money. Why didn't she use it?"

A bluebottle buzzed on the window pane. The glare of sunlight was hot on Gilbert Langham's body. He felt slightly damp. Lake went on:

"She didn't go back to the hotel, she went to meet somebody. It must all have been arranged in advance." He said sharply to Langham, "What happened after she left?"

Langham told him of Antrobus's disappearance, and his own movements.

"You say you got back to the hotel just after eleven. Nobody saw you?"

"No."

"You didn't go out again?"

"Of course not."

"I'm keeping the coach party here for the moment. Let me know if you have any intention of leaving Brighton, won't you?"

Gilbert Langham got up and said incredulously, "You mean you suspect *me*?"

"I suspect everybody." Lake smiled. "I'm still in need of suggestions, even from amateur criminologists."

"There ought to be some sort of clue in that book."

"There are no prints on it, if that's what you mean."

"No." Langham picked it up. "You see, this book is usually called *The Memoirs of a Justified Sinner*. This is a special edition, published in 1895, and it just might be possible to trace it."

"Nothing on the fly-leaf, sir," said the sergeant.

"No, but—" Langham leafed through the pages, and gave an exclamation.

"What is it?" Lake came round the table, and Langham pointed out what he had found. At the bottom of a page in the middle of the book, very small and faint, was a circular die-stamped mark. It said: *"Charles Antrobus. Dealer in Rare Books. Specialist in Crime and the Occult."*

Lake said to the sergeant, "Duff, I think we'll have a word with Mr. Antrobus. No, hang on a minute. Ask Benton to come in for a minute first. I'd like to know whether he's got any details of when and how Antrobus booked for this coach tour, whether his bookings were linked with Miss Penny's and Mrs. Williams's, for instance. That might help."

"Yes, sir."

"You're thinking we were stupid to have missed that," Lake said to Langham when the sergeant had left them.

"Why, no. This is a favourite book of mine. I happened to know it was an unusual edition—"

"It was careless. Two of us have looked through the book and we ought to have seen it. We've been doing fifty different things since the body was found this morning, but that's no excuse." He crossed to the window and stood looking out. The street was shimmering with heat. "I don't know why people go abroad when we have weather like this in England."

"Have you found out anything more about Miss Penny?"

"Yes. It confirms that she was just what she seemed to be, a nice old lady who hadn't got much money and lived a quiet life. There's no motive. Whoever did all this is slightly crazy. Duff's taking his time." He rattled money in his pocket.

The door opened, and the sergeant came in, breathing hard. "He's not there, sir."

"Antrobus?"

"No, Benton."

Lake's face went very red. "I thought I gave instructions that nobody in the party was to leave the hotel until I'd talked to them."

"Yes, sir." The sergeant said stolidly, "We had men at the front door. Reckon he skipped down the fire escape. There are some people called Portingale looking for him, say he was in the hotel ten minutes ago."

"Right," Lake said. "Let's get up to his room."

5

Mr. Portingale, wife connected to him like a broken-down car being towed by a van, was waiting for them in the passage. "Inspector, I have something I want to report to you—"

"Superintendent," Lake snapped. "It will have to wait." He turned to the sergeant. "Duff, he'll reckon on having at least half an hour's start. Chances are he'll take a train for London. Go to the station. Take someone with you who knows him by sight."

"I'll go along," Gilbert Langham said. In the car Sergeant Duff expressed himself rather scornfully about the likelihood of Benton catching a train.

"One of the super's not so bright ideas," he said. "There's more ways out of Brighton than out of a rabbit's burrow. If he tries the train he wants his brains tested."

"It's the quickest way of getting up to London," Langham said absently. He was astonished by the turn of events. If Benton was the murderer, what was the meaning of the books placed by the bodies? He was pondering this problem when the police car pulled up outside Brighton station with a screech of brakes. The station, clean and bright, was comparatively empty at this time of the morning and Duff, who had been so sceptical in the car, was full of energy in action. Within no time at all, as it seemed, he had learned that the last train for London had gone half an hour back, and that the next one left in ten minutes' time from platform three.

"Wouldn't have had time for the last one," Duff said as they walked along the train corridor. "Now, you look out for him. Brown face, medium height, good looking, bit film starish, you said. Might apply to me, eh?" He was in his forties and looked like a sandy-haired monkey.

Benton was not on the train. "Didn't suppose he would be," Duff said as they went back along the platform. "Knew it was a wild-goose chase. We'll just stay around until the train goes. You get over by the departure board there and make yourself inconspicuous. I'll stay by the entrance. Give me the office if you spot him."

Langham nodded. The train left at twelve-fifteen. At exactly thirteen minutes past twelve Jerry Benton walked briskly out of the station lavatory with an attaché case in his hand, looked once round the station, and began to walk over to platform three. Gilbert Langham raised his hand and Duff nodded.

Perhaps it was this gesture that made Benton look towards the departure board. He saw Langham, changed direction and began to run out of the station. Duff and Gilbert Langham ran after him. Benton had several yards start. He was almost out of the station when a family consisting of father, mother, babe-in-arms and a screaming small boy wearing a cowboy hat and carrying spade and bucket entered it. The small boy stuck the spade between Benton's legs and he went down with a crash. Before he could get up Duff and Langham were on him.

The small boy had stopped screaming, and looked slightly awestruck at the effect of his work. "Now, Bertie," said his mother, "you didn't ought to have done that."

"Oh yes, he did," said Duff, holding Benton's arm in a lock. "He's helped to make an important arrest. Are you Wyatt Earp?" he asked.

"Nah, I'm Matt Dillon."

"Well, buy yourself another gun, Matt, will you?" He gave the boy half a crown.

"Can't buy much of a gun for 'alf a crown," the boy said.

The last words they heard as they got into the police car were his mother's. "There you are, Bertie. I told you you should have left the gentleman alone."

"She's got the right idea," Benton said, and grinned.

He did not look like a murderer, Gilbert Langham thought. But then, had he any idea at all what this particular murderer looked like?

They went back to the hotel room where Lake had conducted his interrogations. There Mr. Portingale stood, indignation filling his pigeon chest. There also, Langham saw with surprise, were the Blakes.

"All right, Benton. What have you got to say?" Lake's tone was rough.

"I don't know what this is all about." Benton smiled. "I just got fed up with the job and decided to chuck it."

Lake sighed. "Mr. Portingale."

Mr. Portingale took from his pocket something wrapped in tissue. When he unwrapped the tissue a stone gleamed in the sunlight.

"You offered me this for a hundred pounds, said it was a diamond. Then this morning you asked me for twenty pounds cash deposit, which I gave you, and handed me the stone. Later on I happened to be speaking to Mr. Blake—"

"Just the same story," Blake said. He produced another stone. "We took them to a jeweller. They're not diamonds, they're quartz."

"How many more have you got in that case?" Lake asked.

"Six," Benton said calmly. "I don't know what they're moaning about. I never guaranteed the stones. They were sold to me as diamonds. I suggested they should contact somebody who would check on them."

"It's no good, Benton." Lake nodded to Duff.

The sergeant went outside. When the door reopened it revealed to Gilbert Langham's astonishment, the bald head, puce face and check shirt of Tompkins. The back-slapping geniality was gone, however. Tompkins had no eyes for anybody but Benton.

"You rat," he said, "skipping and leaving me to carry the baby. Did you think I'd wear that?"

"All right," Benton said. "It's a cop. But I had nothing to do with those two women getting done. That put the wind up me, I don't mind telling you."

"If I'm not much mistaken we shall find that both these boys have got records as long as my arm," Lake said. He addressed himself to the Portingales and the Blakes. "A nice little racket they ran together. You see how it worked. Benton spread a rumour about smuggling diamonds, then showed you the stone. He couldn't let you take it away and show it to a jeweller, so Tompkins meanwhile makes it known that he's an expert, and also that he dislikes Benton. He certifies the stone as genuine. If everything had gone as planned, you'd have handed over a hundred pounds each at the end of the tour and never seen either of them again.

You're lucky that Benton got the wind up, took part of the money from you, and tried to skip."

"We had nothing to do with the other business," Tompkins said. "You can see it queered our pitch, the police coming in."

"I believe you," Lake said, and sighed again. "Take them away."

"That leaves Mr. Antrobus," Gilbert Langham said. It was one o'clock, just two hours since he had made that momentous discovery about the book.

"Yes. We've delayed our talk with him long enough. What's his room number, Duff?"

"Second floor. Two fourteen. But he may have come down to the lounge."

The lounge was buzzing with excited members of the coach party who had seen Benton and Tompkins taken away by the police, but Antrobus was not among them. They took the lift up. Duff strode along the corridor.

"Here we are. Two-ten, two-twelve." He stopped abruptly, sniffing.

"Gas." Lake put a handkerchief round his mouth and nose, and turned the door-handle of room two-fourteen. The room was not locked, the blinds were drawn. The smell of gas rushed out at them.

6

Lake rushed across the room, pulled aside the curtains, opened the window wide, turned off the gas tap, and came out coughing. "Doctor," he said to Duff. The sergeant ran down the corridor.

Looking over Lake's shoulder Gilbert Langham could see the body of Mr. Antrobus lying on the floor, his head near to, but not quite resting on, a pillow. The hose connecting the gas tap to a fire set into the wall had been pulled away and lay just by the man's mouth. Lake drummed on the wall with his fingers while they waited for the gas to clear. "This looks like the end of the road."

"I suppose so." Langham felt queerly disappointed.

When they were able to enter the room they found further evidence. At a little writing-desk in one corner of the room was a scrap of paper pencilled in a fine, thin, clerkly hand: "I feel the bitterest regret for what has happened. I cannot go on."

Langham bent down to look at the note, and Lake said quickly: "Don't touch it."

"That paper has been torn off a larger sheet. I wonder why he was so parsimonious." The superintendent was kneeling by the body, extracting a wallet from the jacket. There was a pencil beside the note, a yellow Venus 3B. Langham opened his mouth to say something else, then closed it again. Lake was going through the wallet.

"Pound notes, a wad of them. Membership cards of various societies. Cheque book. Nothing personal. Ah, this is interesting. Membership of the Antiquarian Booksellers' Association in the name of Charles Antrobus. He simply told me he'd retired from business. Ah, hullo, Doctor."

The doctor examined the body briefly, then shook his head. "No hope, I'm afraid. He's had the gas tube very nearly in his mouth for hours."

"How many hours?"

"I wouldn't like to say. *Some time last night, certainly.*" The doctor said with a slight note of surprise, "He's had a knock on the head at some time. Not very long ago, either."

"Enough to stun him?" Gilbert Langham asked.

"Possibly."

"Supposing he'd turned on the gas tap and sat down to write his suicide note," Lake suggested. "He might have been overcome by the gas, fallen and struck his head on the gas fire. Could that have happened?"

"I suppose so," the doctor said, without much conviction.

"And that would explain why his head wasn't on the pillow but beside it. Suicides generally like to make themselves comfortable. But why didn't somebody find him earlier this morning? I think we might ask the reception desk. Then I suppose I should have a word with the rest of the tour party. Duff, will you get them together for me in one of the lounges?"

When they left the bedroom the photographers and fingerprint men were at work. Downstairs, Lake said to the young receptionist, "Did Mr. Antrobus in room two-fourteen leave any sort of message last night?"

"I'll find out for you, sir. Edward, the night porter, would have taken any message at that time."

Edward was old and gnarled as a tree trunk. "Mr. Antrobus? Yes, sir. He rang about eleven o'clock last night and said he had a migraine headache, didn't want to be disturbed until after lunchtime today."

"Do you know Mr. Antrobus?" Langham asked: "Would you recognise his voice?"

The porter shook his head. "Why, no, sir. He was one of those on the coach tour, that's all I know. Wouldn't know him to speak to at all."

"You're hard to satisfy, Langham," Lake said. "You put us on to Antrobus in the first place, Now when you're proved right you're still unhappy."

"Somebody else could have been in that room, hit Antrobus on the head, put the gas tube in his mouth, and rung down to the porter."

"In theory, yes. In practice the obvious explanation is the right one ninety-nine times in every hundred. Just wait till we dig into Antrobus's background. You'll find he's a psycho all right, and that he killed those two women for some reason that doesn't make sense to you or me then committed suicide. Now I'm going to break the news to the rest of them. If I'm not much mistaken, with three casualties and two arrests in the party, they'll want to go home. Are you coming?"

Langham shook his head. He walked moodily towards the potted palms at the hotel entrance. The name "Antrobus" spoken behind him, made him turn. A blonde girl wearing a dark blue frock stood by the reception desk.

"Were you asking for Mr. Antrobus?" Langham said.

"Why, yes. I'm Sheila Antrobus. He's my uncle."

"I'll handle this," he said to the receptionist. And then to the girl: "You must be prepared for a shock."

She was shocked, certainly, but she did not seem deeply surprised. "Uncle Charles had been getting odder and odder ever since his wife died two years ago. It made things a bit difficult for me, because he was my guardian."

"Odd in what way?"

"He was a dealer in rare books, crime books especially. Soon after Aunt Rose died he gave all that up, and in the last few months it's sometimes seemed to me that he really hated books."

"There's something else. You'll have to know about it soon. I may as well tell you." He told her about Miss Penny and Elaine Williams. "Do you think he might have done that?"

She said in a subdued voice, "I don't know. I'd like to see him, please."

They went up to the room. She looked at the figure on the floor, shivered and turned away.

"There's something I want you to see." He led her over to the desk and showed her the note. "Is that your uncle's writing?"

"His prints are on it," one of the fingerprint men said. "And on the pencil."

"Poor uncle," the girl said. Her face was very pale.

They walked out of the hotel, along the Marine Parade and into the Old Steine. "There's something I want to ask you," Gilbert Langham said. "Did your uncle draw?"

"Sometimes. He wasn't very good, but he liked to sketch." She looked surprised. "Why?"

"I know something about pencils. That note on the desk—the one that's supposed to be a suicide note—was written with a thin fine pencil, probably 2H. The pencil on the desk is a 3B, a drawing pencil."

She said nothing. They walked round into Church Street. The North Gate to the Royal Pavilion was in front of them. "Shall we go in?"

"All right." She stopped and faced him. "What does it mean, about the pencils?"

"I believe your uncle was murdered. And if he was, then everything that has happened has been planned, with him as the final victim. You said he made things difficult for you. How?"

"I want to get married. I'm only twenty. Uncle Charles didn't approve of Chris. In fact he very much disapproved. So we agreed to wait."

"Chris?"

"Chris Watling. The man I'm going to marry."

They stood in the Pavilion gardens, with the statue of George IV on one side and the cupola of the dome on the other, together with those fragments of the eccentric architectural past now transformed to respectable library and art gallery. She opened her bag and took out a photograph. He looked at it, and felt as though he had been struck between the eyes. The photograph told him almost the whole of the story.

7

"Tell me about Chris."

There was some unfathomable expression in her blue eyes. "You wanted to go into the Pavilion. Let's go, then."

He waved a hand at the onion domes. "Do you know Sydney Smith's joke about the Pavilion architecture? That the dome of St. Paul's must have come down to Brighton and pupped? But I like it."

She made no reply. They walked in silence through the Octagon Hall and the entrance hall. In the Chinese Corridor she said, staring intently at one of the bamboo plants on the wall, "What do you want to know?"

"About Chris."

"You've seen his photograph. He doesn't find it easy to settle in a job. That's what Uncle didn't like."

"He's been in trouble?"

"His father lost all his money when Chris was about thirteen. There was trouble about a couple of years ago over some cheques." She turned to face him, her face desperate. "But he's awfully nice—Chris—he's such fun to be with. He's always wanting to do something dashing, something that will get his photograph in the papers. He makes a joke of it, he's full of jokes. There's nothing bad about him really. You've got to believe that."

"It might be easier for you if I guessed some of the story and you filled in the details. Your uncle was quite rich, and most of the money comes to you."

"All of it. He's got no other close relations and he is—was—very fond of me."

"He disapproved of Chris, more strongly than you said. He blamed himself for letting you go about with Chris, told you to stop seeing him, threatened in a good Victorian way to cut you out of his will. Right?"

"I told you I'm not twenty-one yet and I didn't want to upset uncle. Do you think I cared about the money?"

"Chris cared about it, though. Didn't he?"

She turned and ran from him, ran back through the halls, while shocked respectable holiday-goers, wearing sleeveless shirts and with shorts above sun-reddened knees, looked after her. He found her in the garden. "If your uncle died the money would come to you, and there would be no obstacle to your marriage. Uncle Charles was eccentric, he did odd things like coming on this coach tour. Why did he do that, by the way?"

"He always went on tours. He was awfully mean in little ways, said they were wonderful value for money. And this one attracted him because of going to different places each day. All the places had piers. He loved playing on the slot machines." She smiled faintly.

"Yes. Uncle Charles was eccentric, but he wasn't crazy. If Chris murdered him and tried to make it look like suicide, questions would be asked. But supposing it could be shown that Uncle Charles had really gone round the bend—supposing he'd killed two people and left the books he hated beside his victims—then his suicide wouldn't be questioned. Superintendent Lake is prepared to accept it now."

"You mean that those two people, Miss Penny and Mrs. Williams, were murdered just to show—"

"To convince people that your Uncle Charles was a psychopathic killer? I'm afraid so." He paused, said abruptly: "You recognised that so-called suicide note, didn't you? It was part of a letter from your Uncle to Chris."

"I don't know. There *was* a letter in which uncle said something like that, about blaming himself for letting me go around with Chris, but I still can't believe it was the same. What makes you so sure?"

"Why, you see," Gilbert Langham said, "I know Chris."

When they got back to the hotel Mr. Portingale stood in the doorway beside the potted palms. "Have you heard the news?" he asked eagerly. "Do you know that we have been nursing a pair of scoundrelly tricksters in our midst?"

Langham had almost forgotten about Benton and Tompkins. "The superintendent has got them under lock and key, though, hasn't he?"

"Would you believe it, my dear sir, they tried to practise their arts on me. I'm afraid they picked the wrong person there, eh, Mrs. P.?" Mrs. Portingale, firmly attached to one arm, smiled and nodded. "But as a result our happy little party is broken up. The coach company is making a very handsome refund, and Mrs. P. and I are departing for fresh fields and pastures new."

To call the party a happy one seemed to Langham an overstatement. "Where are you going?"

Mr. Portingale beamed. "We are lucky enough to have been able to book with another coach tour. We are off to the New Forest. I believe that there are still one or two vacancies if you would care to—"

"No, thank you," he said hurriedly.

Sergeant Duff said cheerfully, "Where have you been? The super's been looking for you, wants to pin a medal on your chest, I shouldn't wonder."

He said a little pompously, "This is Mr. Antrobus's niece, Sheila. We've got to see the superintendent urgently. Some fresh information about the case."

Duff scratched his sandy head. "The trouble with you amateurs is you can never let well alone. The super's round at the station."

They went round to the station and saw Lake. He listened impatiently, until Sheila Antrobus produced the photograph.

"That's Chris Watling." Gilbert Langham said.

Lake gasped. Then he said, "This seems to be an occasion for a little telephoning." When he put down the receiver after a telephone call to London he said, "He's in Folkestone."

"What are we waiting for?" Langham asked.

From the promenade at Folkestone you can reach the beach either by way of the two lifts that go up and down together, working in series, or more circuitously, by the famous zig-zag with its right-angled paths separated by banks of shrubs. Or you can get to the beach by going through the Old Town, emerging near the harbour. The police car came round there and stopped.

They began to walk across the shingle, past the children's playground.

"You understand what to do, Miss Antrobus?" Lake said. "If you don't feel up to it, say so now."

"I'm up to it."

"Good." Lake was brisk. "We'll follow you slowly as you walk along the lower promenade. We shan't be more than a few yards away."

The lower promenade was full of people buying sweets, ice-cream and cups of tea. Children were crowded round a Punch and Judy show. Langham jumped down to the pebbled beach and watched. Sheila Antrobus threaded her way along through the people, putting one foot precisely before another, unhurried and cool-looking in her dark blue dress.

8

She stopped in front of a hut that stood beside an ice cream stall, and said: "Hullo, Chris."

The young man who had called himself Charlie Wilson was talking earnestly to a prospective customer for Nu-Stile-Pickshers. He stopped speaking, and the look on his face was for a moment that of one who wakes to find that some private nightmare, the death of a loved child or an ordeal by fire, has come true. Then his engagingly boyish smile was in place again, and he said: "Why, Sheila ducks, whatever are you doing in Folkestone?"

"You didn't tell me you were doing this sort of thing."

"I said I was doing a job for a few weeks that was great fun. Don't you call this fun?" He said to the customer, "Do go in, madam, you'll find the photographer inside. And don't forget, if you get a lucky number you win one of today's cash prizes."

"Chris, I want to talk to you."

"Of course, ducks." He shouted—and how well Gilbert Langham, who heard it, remembered his shouting the same words before—"Just going for a cuppa." He fell into step with her and said, "There's a little place along here with an old lady running it who just loves me."

"They all love you, don't they?" Sheila Antrobus said. "I mean the ladies."

He stared at her with what seemed unaffected surprise. "I just don't know what you mean. If you don't like my doing this job, all right, you're always saying I ought to work, and there aren't so many jobs that fit my peculiar talents."

Sheila Antrobus went on talking, slowly and without expression, as though some sort of machine had been wound up inside her. "Especially the ladies who got the prizes. That was the way it happened, wasn't it? You found out the people who were on the coach tour, got into conversation as they passed you, had their photographs taken or took them yourself, and then told the ones you picked, the unattached women, that their number had come up and they'd won a prize. After that, naturally they were delighted to meet such a charming young man a little later on to receive the prize. That was where the five-pound note came from that was in Mrs. Williams's handbag, wasn't it? Careless, Chris."

"Sheila." He jumped back as though she had jabbed him with a needle.

"And it wasn't really a clever idea to leave that note, out of the letter he wrote you. If I came down there was a good chance I'd recognise it. But I suppose you thought I'd marry you anyway." Very slowly now, the record dying down, she said: "After we'd married, Chris, what would have happened to me?"

He made an ineffectual gesture with his hand, still backing away. Langham began to move up the shingle and at the same time Lake and Duff, behind Sheila, quickened their steps. Chris Watling turned, bolted for the nearest entrance to the zig-zag and began to run up it.

Lake and Duff went after him. Langham paused beside the girl who stood, looking upwards, with no expression at all on her face.

"That must have been terrible for you."

Her voice was harsh. "I've done what you asked, haven't I? You said I could break him down, while the police might not be able to. Now he's running. That's what you all wanted."

"You talk as though you didn't want him to be caught. He's killed three people."

"I love him." She said it flatly. They watched the figures running up the paths between the shrubs. "He's gaining on them."

"Lake's got a man waiting at the top."

For a few moments Watling was out of sight, hidden by a turn in the path. Then he emerged, and they could see the man who stood solidly blocking the exit. Watling took something from his pocket, and ran towards the man at the top.

"He's got a gun," Langham said. They heard two small sharp cracks, and the man went down. They could see Watling now, far above, running along the front, firing backwards at Lake and Duff. He reached the entrance to the lift leading down to the beach, and paused.

"He's coming down." Langham began to run towards the red-brick Victorian lift house. The girl followed him.

When they reached it, Langham said to the attendant, "There's a man coming down in that lift who's wanted for murder. Can you stop him?"

"No, sir. He can't get out though. Door's bolted outside." They stared up and saw the great wooden cage on wheels descending. Above it was a sign: *"The Lift. Fare 3d. One Minute to Centre of Town."* The two lifts moving up and down worked together, and as the wooden cage from the top descended they could see some sort of confused activity inside it. There was a crash of glass, and they saw Watling climbing out of the window, still holding the revolver. He swung out and up on to the curved lift roof.

"He's going to jump over to the other one," Langham said. No doubt Lake and Duff were now running down the slope and Watling thought he might get away at the top. It was almost certainly hopeless—the crowd would never let him off the lift, revolver or no revolver—but he was going to try it. They watched him poised on the top of the sloping cage as it slowly descended and the other lift rose to meet it. When the two cages were almost level, he jumped easily from one to the other.

"He's done it," the attendant said.

But Watling had failed to get a proper purchase on the lift's curved top. They could see him desperately trying to get a grip with hands and feet. Like a figure in a slow motion film his body slipped away from the lift roof. Then suddenly he dropped, limp as a puppet.

Sheila Antrobus turned away her head and screamed.

The broken thing that had caught in the cable at the bottom was not quite dead when Gilbert Langham reached it. The lips moved, whispered, "Sheila."

"Yes?"

The smile was engaging as ever. "Tell her I shall have my picture in the papers."

ALSO AVAILABLE

'The red robe concealed the blood until it made my hand sticky. Father Christmas had been stabbed in the back, and he was certainly dead.'

The murder of Father Christmas in the grotto of London's busiest toy shop is just one of many Yuletide disasters in this new collection of short stories from the Golden Age of crime writing and beyond. Martin Edwards has curated a special collection with something for every reader of mystery and detective fiction, including classic offerings from masters of the genre such as John Dickson Carr, Michael Gilbert and Ellis Peters alongside gems from the 1980s and 1990s by Patricia Moyes and Catherine Aird.

Presenting fifteen stories of festive fraud, poisoned pies and cold comeuppances, this anthology parcels up a quintessentially perilous classic-crime Christmas—and offers the answer to the question burning like a fire in the hearth: *Who Killed Father Christmas?*

ALSO AVAILABLE
IN THE BRITISH LIBRARY
CRIME CLASSICS SERIES

Many of our titles are also available
in eBook, large print and audio editions